A Clandestine Mission

The dark cloister of Newton-Upon-Sea at night closed around them, and their hollow footsteps on the deserted streets echoed off the stillness. When they reached the Gibbs' home there was no lamp light shining through the windows. The house was as dark as death, and no one responded to the bell they rang. Nancy even tried pushing the door open, but found it locked.

"Perhaps we should try a window," Alexandra whispered.

"Good lord, miss! Are you suggesting we break into the house?"

"No, no, of course not," Alexandra said. But she knew there was no conviction in her statement. Examining the body again had become an obsession. If the answer to how the admiral died was available, she had to find it.

She sighed. "Nancy, I must be daft. How could I even think of . . ." She stopped speaking when she heard a noise coming from the alley behind them. There was a shuffling and then a low murmur. The words were not quite audible, and the voice was not quite human . . .

Dr. Alexandra Gladstone Mysteries
by Paula Paul

SYMPTOMS OF DEATH
AN IMPROPER DEATH

An Improper Death

Paula Paul

BERKLEY PRIME CRIME, NEW YORK

This is a work of fiction. Names, characters, places, and incidents either are the product of the author's imagination or are used fictitiously, and any resemblance to actual persons, living or dead, business establishments, events, or locales is entirely coincidental.

AN IMPROPER DEATH

A Berkley Prime Crime Book / published by arrangement with the author

PRINTING HISTORY
Berkley Prime Crime mass-market edition / November 2002

Copyright © 2002 by Paula Paul.
Cover art by Bryan Haynes.
Cover design by Judy Murello.
Text design by Julie Rogers.

Visit our website at
www.penguinputnam.com

ISBN: 0-425-18741-1

Berkley Prime Crime Books are published by The Berkley Publishing Group, a division of Penguin Putnam, Inc., 375 Hudson Street, New York, New York 10014. The name BERKLEY PRIME CRIME and the BERKLEY PRIME CRIME design are trademarks belonging to Penguin Putnam Inc.

PRINTED IN THE UNITED STATES OF AMERICA

10 9 8 7 6 5 4 3 2 1

*For Irene Kraas, the real Alexandra, and
in memory of the real Zack*

1

The sea, dark as the mouth of death, vomited up the body of retired Admiral George Edward Orkwright, dressed in nothing save his wife's underwear, and left him lying on the rocky shore near the town of Newton-Upon-Sea.

By morning a yellow fog had moved in from the water, encasing the village like impenetrable, tarnished armor. Nell Stillwell, the one-eyed wife of the butcher, was the only soul to venture out early in that oppressive mist, hoping foolishly that, in spite of the night's storm and the morning's fog, the fishing boats would still have come in from Great Yarmouth with their loads of cod and mackerel. She and her husband sorely needed the fish for their shop, since Lent was soon to be upon them. It was unusual, of course, for a butcher to sell fish in the modern world of 1881, but the town's fishmonger had recently died of a bilious fever, leaving a void into which the enterprising Mrs. Stillwell quickly moved.

The heavy mist kept Nell from seeing the body until she stumbled upon it, kicking it with the toe of her sturdy black boot. By the feel of it, she thought at first it might be the carcass of a large fish beached by the storm, but when she stooped to look more closely, she saw the unmistakable shape of a human. A female, she thought at first, when she saw the white, lace-trimmed drawers, and a scandalous one at that, since that seemed to be the only thing the poor unfortunate was wearing. Then when she moved closer and squinted her one eye for a better look at the seaweed-matted face and torso, she recognized the admiral and knew she had stumbled upon something even more deliciously scandalous than a scantily clad woman.

Dr. Alexandra Gladstone was out of bed and throwing on a dressing gown the moment she was awakened by the pounding on her surgery door. By the time she reached the landing at the top of the stairs, she was joined by Nancy, her maid-of-all-work, still fastening her own dressing gown. Zachariah, Alexandra's Newfoundland, who always slept at the foot of her bed, was close behind.

The two women glanced at each other only briefly before they hurried down the stairs, side by side, the soles of their soft slippers playing a muted syncopated staccato rhythm on the steps. Behind them, the large dog galumphed down the stairs in an offbeat counterpoint.

The two women, as well as the dog, were quite accustomed to late night or early morning visits from patients with medical emergencies. Nancy, who, besides her household duties, also served as nurse, did not go to the door. Instead, she followed her usual routine of checking to see that the mistress's medical bag was ready, should she need to go to the patient, before she started for the kitchen to set the water to boil should it be that the patient had come to her.

Alexandra opened the door and recognized the butcher's wife with the black patch on her left eye. "What is it, Nell?"

In the same instant, Nell spoke. "It's the admiral, Miss Alexandra, drowned, no doubt, and dressed in ladies' drawers." Her voice was not the high-pitched screech most people used when they came to the doctor's door seeking help. Instead it was low and hushed.

Alexandra was stunned for a moment. "Admiral? Do you mean Admiral Orkwright?" Of course that's who she meant. There was no other admiral living in Newton-Upon-Sea. But what was that about ladies' drawers? Staid and dignified Admiral Orkwright was a respected member of the community, proud of his long heroic career in the Queen's Navy. He carried the honorary title of churchwarden in Newton-Upon-Sea, granted to him solely because of his distinguished station, although he only occasionally attended services. He was married to a beautiful and respectable woman somewhat younger than he, and he was the father of two boys, one of whom showed promise. Sadly, the older of the two, who was the admiral's son only by virtue of his having married the boy's widowed mother, was a ne'er-do-well. He had drifted away, which grieved the admiral's wife deeply, and, it was assumed, the admiral as well, although, in the time-honored British fashion, he never spoke of it. Refined and taciturn, the admiral was not the kind of man to wear ladies' drawers. It must be, Alexandra thought, that Nell Stillwell was mistaken.

"Come in, Nell, please." She ushered the damp, shivering woman inside and called out to Nancy to bring tea. "I think the coals may still be hot in the parlor. Come along and let's get you warm and dry."

" 'Tis not a fire we're needing now, but a priest." In spite of her protest, Nell followed eagerly and just as eagerly accepted the afghan Alexandra draped over her shoulders.

"All right, tell me where you found him. I'll go immediately. You stay here by the fire. The tea will be out shortly." There was an urgency to Alexandra's voice.

"It's best there be two of us to face that scandalous evil." Nell's one good eye had grown bright, and she clutched the afghan tightly. "You mustn't go alone."

"You've gotten a chill, Nell. Just stay by the fire." Alexandra spoke as she tried to make her exit from the room to change her clothes and retrieve her medical bag.

"I'm going with you!" Nell's voice was firm as she strode across the room to join Alexandra.

" 'Tis the Prussian Evil that's brought this on. Have I not warned ye of its iniquity before? Ye mustn't subject yourself to it carelessly," Nell said.

Alexandra had indeed been warned. Nell always called the fog the "Prussian Evil" since, according to her, the thick, damp cloud swept across the North Sea to England from the dark environs of Germany and, so she said, brought the evil of those foreign lands with it.

Nell saw evil in most things foreign, but especially in anything Irish, German, or American. Alexandra, as always, tried to ignore her on that count.

She dressed quickly, and as she reached the bottom of the stairs called out to Nell. "Tell me where you found him."

"In the rocks along the shore." Nell had already reached the door, which she opened herself, and stepped out into the heavy cloud of night, still wearing the afghan over her shoulders. She turned around briefly, as if to make sure Alexandra was following.

Alexandra was fastening her cloak. "Never mind the tea," she called over her shoulder to Nancy. By the time Alexandra had fastened all the buttons on her cloak, Nancy appeared in the front hall fully dressed, including her own cloak. She was carrying an oil lamp.

"Where are we going?" Nancy was forced to pause on her way to the door because Zack, making his own way to the exit, had stepped in front of her.

"No need for you to come along, Nancy. Just go back to bed, and see that Zack does as well," Alexandra said.

Nancy handed her the medical bag. "Don't forget your scarf." She pulled the scarf from a peg by the door, set the lamp down long enough to wrap it around her mistress's neck, then followed the other two women out the door as if she hadn't heard Alexandra's order to stay. After Zack lumbered out to join them, she closed the door and locked it.

Alexandra thought of protesting again, but it would do no good, she knew. Instead, she gave a resigned sigh and spoke to Nell. "Lead the way, please. Give her the lamp, Nancy. We'll follow along behind."

"You've no business being out on a dark morning like this without the likes of Zack and me for protection." Nancy sounded defensive, as if she was expecting a scolding for ignoring Alexandra's command.

"And who will protect you and Zack?" Alexandra's voice had a cool edge.

"Why, we'll protect each other, of course," Nancy said with a distinct note of finality. It was difficult to argue with Nancy, and doubly difficult for Alexandra, because the two of them had been playmates since they were small when

Nancy's mother was the maid-of-all-work for Alexandra's father, the late Dr. Huntington Gladstone. Their relationship had been forged as friends long before they became mistress and servant, and neither of them fit into their respective roles very well as a result.

When Alexandra didn't respond to her last statement, Nancy apparently felt compelled to fill the silence.

"I say you're right, Nell Stillwell. 'Tis an evil wind that blows when something like this occurs. What do you suppose happened to the poor man?"

"I knows not what happened, lass," Nell called over her shoulder as she made her way through the waning darkness of early morning. "But by the looks of the gentleman, I'd say it could be the work of the devil, it could."

"How much farther, Nell?" Alexandra asked, picking her way along the rocky shoreline.

" 'Tis a ways yet." Nell plodded along in the sturdy boots she wore to protect her feet and legs from the blood of slaughter. Her stride was long and measured, making it difficult for Alexandra and Nancy to keep up with her. "I found him there, beyond the last pier," she said, pointing to an area where the land rose to a high cliff overlooking the sea. The admiral had built his house on top of the cliff to capture the view of the ocean.

"Just below his house?" Alexandra asked.

"Aye," Nell said. "At the bottom of the cliff. I walked out there to see if I could spy the fishing boats coming in from Great Yarmouth. But there was nary a fishing boat. There was nothing save the ungodly sight of a dead man."

It was several minutes more before Nell stopped and pointed at something ahead of her. " 'Tis there."

Alexandra could see nothing in spite of the sun that had risen a few inches on the horizon. The fog was still heavy, and the weak first light of sun did nothing more than darken the color of the unvented cloud. Zack, however, sounded an excited bark.

And then, suddenly, Alexandra heard Nancy's sharp intake of breath. Nancy had managed to wind her way in front of Alexandra during the treacherous walk on the beach. She was now bending over what was clearly a human body, eerily illuminated by the light from the lamp Nell held.

"Heaven help us! It *is* the admiral." She took another audible breath and put her hand to her mouth. "And he's wearing . . ." She glanced at Alexandra, wide-eyed. "He's wearing a pair of ladies' drawers!"

Nancy had been in the kitchen when Nell described the dead man's unorthodox attire, so she was now doubly shocked. Alexandra ignored her, however, and bent down to examine the body.

She knew even before she touched his wrist that he had no pulse, but a formal statement would require confirmation. She lifted the eyelids and motioned for Nell to hold the lamp closer. When she did, Alexandra saw that the cornea was clouded. Rigor mortis had set in but was not fully resolved. Both characteristics could mean either that his death had occurred in the last few hours or that the cold seawater had retarded the process of decay.

There was not yet any swelling of the body, however, and his skin and nails were still intact, which would indicate a relatively recent death, but, again, the cold sea could have slowed decomposition. There appeared to be no marks or wounds on the body, but she could not be certain until she had a chance to examine it properly. First indications, however, were that he had drowned at sea, and the seaweed wrapped around the body seemed to corroborate that assumption, as did a tangle of seaweed and other debris in his mouth.

If that was true, then it only raised more questions. Why would George Orkwright, a man who knew the foibles and treacherousness of the sea, venture out into a storm? Was it on purpose? If so, why would a man who seemed to have everything a man could want kill himself? And, of course, the most puzzling mystery of all, why would he wear ladies' undergarments either in life or death?

Alexandra stood and spoke to the two other women. "The two of you must fetch Constable Snow."

"The two of us?" Nancy's voice was high pitched with alarm. "And leave you here? I think not, Miss Alex, not when something like this has happened." She glanced down at the body.

"The lass is right," Nell said. " 'Tis no place for a decent woman."

"If that's the case, then perhaps I *am* the logical one to stay. You can leave Zack here with me if you think I need protection." Alexandra knew that Nell, like many others, not only in the lower classes but across all strata of society, considered it indecent that she, a woman, had followed in her father's footsteps and become a licensed doctor of medicine. She had not been allowed the full formal education afforded men, but she had attended what lectures she could at university, and her father had taught her the rest, then arranged for a hospital apprenticeship for her. It had been little more than four years ago that women were given the right to apply for a license to practice medicine. General acceptance, she knew, would be a long time coming, and in the meantime, because of her profession, she remained something less than a decent woman in the eyes of many.

Nancy, sharp-witted as ever, did not miss Alexandra's nuance, and she showed it with a small grimace that pretended to be disapproving and that almost succeeded in hiding a mischievous grin.

Nell, however, remained oblivious. " 'Tis a sad day,'tis, when a lady cannot walk along the sea without stumblin' on the likes o' this."

Nancy spoke at almost the same time. "All right then, we'll go if you keep Zack by your side. Mind you let no one approach you, hear?" It was difficult to tell whether the admonition was directed toward Alexandra or Zack.

Zack, who had spent the entire time alternating between pacing nervously and sniffing at the corpse, let out a sharp, agitated yelp when Nancy started to walk away, then glanced up uncertainly at Alexandra.

"It's all right, Zack," she said and tried to soothe him by rubbing his neck. She was able, finally, to calm him enough to get him to sit while she examined the body further. The admiral had been lying on his side when they approached the body, but the purplish color of his face indicated that the blood had pooled there, probably as he lay facedown in the water before he was washed to shore. There was no sign of a vessel, such as a punt or skiff he might have been in, however.

She scanned the area for anything unusual, but she could see very little in the dense fog. The heavy curtain of mist now hid even the cliff just ahead of her where the admiral's new house sat. The only significance she could see in the proximity of the cliff and the house, however, was that he did not stray far from home to die.

By the time Nell and Nancy returned with Constable Snow, Alexandra still had made no sense of the admiral's death. The constable was accompanied by Nell's husband, Dave, and Samuel, his apprentice. The men walked ahead of the two women, the constable leading the way and carrying his own lantern. Zack barked frantically at their approach. He seemed to be wanting to tell the constable what they had discovered, and it took both Alexandra and Nancy to quiet him.

Constable Snow wasted no time in taking charge of the moment. "Stand back, please," he said to Nancy and Nell and the two men. He glanced toward Alexandra, gave her a nod, and spoke his greeting. "Dr. Gladstone."

"Constable," she said in reply.

"You have examined the body?" His voice was tense, and it occurred to Alexandra that he was embarrassed that he had to be in the presence of women with the admiral dressed (or undressed) as he was.

"I have made only a cursory examination."

"And you have concluded . . ."

"I have not made a firm conclusion."

"Are there marks—wounds of any kind—on the body?" His expression grew more stern as he waited for her answer.

"I have not seen any, but I would prefer to examine the body further in better light." Alexandra felt as if she were a student trying to give the correct answer in an oral exam.

He continued to press the matter. "Have you found anything at all unusual?"

Alexandra hesitated only a moment. "There is seaweed in the mouth."

"That would suggest drowning."

His insistence puzzled her, but she stood her ground. "Perhaps, but I cannot eliminate other possibilities. Not until I have examined the victim further."

Snow was silent for a moment, and when he spoke, it was not to reply to Alexandra's request. Instead he turned to Nell and Nancy. "Thank you, ladies, for your bravery on this unpleasant morning. I suggest you both return to the comfort of your homes now. Dave and Samuel will transport the body to the undertaker's home, and Dr. Gladstone will accompany me to notify the admiral's wife." He turned to Alexandra. "We've already notified the vicar. He'll meet us there."

"May I ask, sir, why you are sending the body to the undertaker's home?" Alexandra was puzzled. The constable's order was unheard of. A body was always taken to the family home to be prepared for burial.

"I understand that the request is unusual," Snow said. "But in this case it is best. I'm afraid that having the body in the house will cause the widow undue stress."

The explanation was unsatisfactory, but Alexandra had no choice but to relinquish a reluctant Zack to Nancy and to accompany the constable to Gull House. It was a long trek up the hill to the admiral's home. By the time they reached the house, the sun had risen well above the horizon, but the light was still diffused by the shroud of fog. The house, constructed of heavy dark stone, lurked in the yellow vapor like a predatory beast. The admiral had named it Gull House, presumably because seagulls flew around it as if it were a ship. It was not an enormous house, yet it was grandiose in appearance with gables and turrets and pointed spires, rather overly elaborate and American-looking, Alexandra thought. In fact, the admiral's decision to build a house was an American affectation, since most of the middle class in England resorted to long-term leases of fine homes in town.

They were greeted at the door by a tall, big-boned maid with a grim face who told them in a hushed voice that Mrs. Orkwright would see them in the drawing room, where she was with the vicar. She led them through the dark front hall to a room brightly lit with flickering oil lamps. The vicar, Father Kingsborough, rose from his chair and moved rather hurriedly across the room to greet the two of them. Mrs. Orkwright sat poised and erect in a chair, a black shawl of a fine Persian weave over her shoulders. One of her arms rested gracefully on a table next to her chair. Her heavy, ginger-colored hair was swept back from her face, and that, along with high cheekbones and fine, wide eyes gave her a regal look. She stared straight ahead with an expression that was almost blank.

"I'm afraid she's in shock." Father Kingsborough spoke in a hushed voice. "I was certain she was going to faint when I first told her. It's a difficult thing to tell a wife of her husband's death."

Constable Snow ignored the vicar and approached Mrs. Orkwright. He spoke her name softly, and she glanced up at him.

Her eyes were still blank at first, but they slowly focused. "Are you quite sure it is the admiral?" Her voice was soft but clear.

"Yes, I am sure." Snow also spoke softly as he stood in front of her with his head down, his cap in his hands.

Mrs. Orkwright gave a little gasp and looked away.

"I'm sorry, madam." Snow kept his respectful and professional demeanor.

Mrs. Orkwright turned her gaze back to him without acknowledging his apology. "What time did you find him? And where?" Her hands trembled, and she clasped them in her lap, long alabaster fingers intertwining.

"It was Nell Stillwell, the butcher's wife, who found him on the beach while it was still dark, and she notified Dr. Gladstone."

Mrs. Orkwright turned her beautiful, tragic face toward Alexandra, as if waiting for her to speak.

"I believe he had been dead several hours when I examined him," Alexandra said. "It is difficult to know precisely how long."

"And the cause of death?" Her once dull eyes had now begun to burn brightly.

"It appears to be drowning, but I cannot be certain until I examine him further, and perhaps not even then."

Mrs. Orkwright dropped her eyes again. She seemed to be holding her breath, perhaps to keep from weeping, and her hands trembled again. When she looked up at her guests, she had regained her composure. "Please forgive me. I haven't invited you to sit. Perhaps you would like tea?"

"Tea won't be necessary, madam." Snow spoke as he settled himself on the edge of a sofa opposite Mrs. Orkwright. "But if you will forgive me, I must ask you some questions."

"Of course," she said and motioned for Alexandra to sit in a chair next to the sofa, also facing her. The vicar remained standing, but he moved protectively behind Mrs. Orkwright's chair.

"When did you last see your husband?" Snow was seated in a stiff pose, his long back straight but not leaning against the sofa, his knees rising at a sharp angle in front of him. His hands, as long and fine as Mrs. Orkwright's, moved and twitched self-consciously, like uninvited guests.

"I said good night to him at approximately nine-thirty, I think, when I retired to my room. He said he would have a bath and retire early as well. I assumed that was what he did." Mrs. Orkwright's voice trembled as she spoke, and her eyes remained overly bright. It was clear she was working hard at maintaining her composure.

Snow shifted uneasily on the sofa. "What was he wearing when you last saw him?"

"Wearing?" Mrs. Orkwright seemed puzzled by the question. "Why, his tweeds, I believe. He didn't dress for dinner, since he said he wasn't hungry. William and I had dinner alone."

"William. Your son, of course," Snow said. "If I recall, a boy of about six years."

Mrs. Orkwright spoke softly. "Yes."

"And where is young William now?" Snow asked.

Mrs. Orkwright stiffened. "He's still sleeping. I asked that he not be disturbed. I want to—to tell him myself that . . ."

"Yes, of course," Snow said. His long hands grasped both of his knees as if he thought they might jump away.

There was a brief, awkward pause before the constable stood and spoke again. "Thank you very much for your cooperation, Mrs. Orkwright. I won't trouble you again, and please, accept my condolences."

"You are very kind." Mrs. Orkwright's voice was weak,

and she had grown so pale, Alexandra thought she might faint.

"Excuse me." Alexandra's voice seemed to startle everyone. "I was wondering, Mrs. Orkwright, did your husband enjoy swimming?"

"Swimming?" Mrs. Orkwright seemed puzzled again as she glanced up at Alexandra.

The vicar spoke up for the first time. "Please, I'm afraid Mrs. Orkwright has had quite enough for this morning. I beg of you, let her rest."

Mrs. Orkwright ignored the vicar and looked Alexandra straight in the eye. "He detested that particular form of recreation. He always said the sea was meant for fish and naval vessels, and that human beings were poorly suited to direct congress with the sea, and that they should do their bathing in private."

Alexandra nodded slightly. "Yes, I do believe I've heard him use words to that effect myself on occasion, and that is precisely why I find it odd that he should drown in the sea."

"Dr. Gladstone, please, I believe we've taken quite enough of Mrs. Orkwright's time for now. I suggest—"

"No, please, Constable Snow." Mrs. Orkwright held up her hand as if to stop any further protest he might have. "I, too, find it odd that my husband should drown. He was a capable swimmer in spite of his dislike for it. I'm afraid I don't know what to make of it, except . . ."

"Except what?" Alexandra asked.

There was another pause before Mrs. Orkwright said, "Except that he had been drinking rather heavily last night." Once again her hands trembled, and once again she clasped them in her lap. The vicar placed a steadying hand on her shoulder.

"Then the drowning was most likely an accident," Snow said. "A gentleman in his cups who ventured too close to the water." He took a small step toward Mrs. Orkwright, who appeared to be on the verge of tears. At the same time he gave Alexandra a quick glance as if to warn her not to say anything more. "You said you retired at around nine-thirty last night, Mrs. Orkwright, and you're not certain when the admiral went to bed?"

"No, I'm not certain." Mrs. Orkwright's voice was little more than a whisper.

"The storm didn't begin until almost midnight," Snow continued. "So is it possible, maybe even likely, that the admiral went out for a walk along the shore and, once the storm blew in and since he was inebriated, fell into the sea?"

"I don't know," Mrs. Orkwright said. "I suppose it's possible." There was a moment of silence before she added, "And, yes, perhaps even likely."

"You must understand," Snow said, "that in spite of the obvious it is necessary to investigate these matters to make certain nothing untoward happened." He gave Alexandra another quick glance of warning.

Mrs. Orkwright's hands flew up to cover her face and a sob wracked her body. When she dropped her hands several seconds later, there were tears in her eyes and on her cheeks. "I understand, of course." Her voice trembled as she spoke. "You must do your duty."

"Thank you again for your help," Snow said. "We shan't trouble you longer." And then, as if to make sure they didn't, he took Alexandra's arm in a firm grip and led her toward the door.

Behind them, the vicar asked if Mrs. Orkwright would like his wife to come stay the day with her. Mrs. Orkwright refused graciously, saying she preferred to be alone.

Alexandra and Constable Snow walked together in the fog-weakened morning light, neither of them speaking until they reached the bottom of the hill. And then Alexandra could stand it no longer. "Excuse me, Constable, but why were you so intent upon my not asking questions that needed to be asked, and why did you not mention the admiral's unorthodox attire?"

"Well, I should think it would be quite obvious, Dr. Gladstone." There was a hint of exaggerated patience in Snow's voice. "Mrs. Orkwright was understandably distressed, and there is nothing to be served by upsetting her more, especially when it's obvious what happened."

"Obvious?" Alexandra stopped to look at him. "I'm afraid I saw nothing obvious."

"Did you not say that the admiral appears to have

drowned?" Snow did not stop, but walked on ahead of her.

Alexandra hurried to catch up. "I did say he *appears* to have drowned, but I also said I cannot be certain until—"

"He was drunk, Dr. Gladstone. Obviously quite drunk. So drunk that he didn't know what he was doing, and in his stupor, unknowingly put on an article of his wife's clothing after his bath, ventured out into the night, fell into the sea, and drowned. I saw no need to embarrass his widow by discussing those details. It will be enough that the butcher's wife will tell everyone who comes into their shop about the spectacle of finding the admiral in such a state. Mrs. Orkwright will have to live with the embarrassment of everyone knowing, and I don't see the necessity of compounding that embarrassment."

Alexandra was silent. The constable's explanation had tied everything nicely into a neat, if unlikely, bundle. It was not at all satisfying to her. Finally she spoke. "I should like to perform an autopsy, Constable."

This time it was the constable who stopped walking and stared at Alexandra. "An autopsy?" He spoke the word as if he had never heard of it. "Absolutely not, Dr. Gladstone. There will be no autopsy in this case."

2

"Said there was to be no autopsy, did he?" Nancy questioned Alexandra as she helped her spread a fresh linen over the examination table. The one she had removed was soaked with a compound tincture of camphor, which Alexandra had used to bathe the neck of the miller's twelve-year-old daughter. She was suffering from an inflammation of the larynx and had lost her voice. Her father had brought her in early, before Alexandra left the house for her morning rounds.

"Yes, and he seemed rather adamant." Alexandra smoothed the linen with her hands. "And I believe the reason he had the body taken to the undertaker's home was to make certain I had no access to it."

"Odd indeed." Nancy gave the cloth one final swipe and placed her hands on her hips. "And he has the events leading to the admiral's death all sorted out, does he? Says the admiral was drunk. So drunk, in fact, he mistakenly put on his wife's drawers and went for a swim in the cold sea?" She laughed. "A man would have to be pretty drunk for that, I would say."

Alexandra glanced at Nancy. "Indeed."

"Or it could be, wearing a woman's drawers is nothing unusual to the constable. Perhaps he has a pair just like them himself." Nancy giggled and turned away, pretending to be busy straightening a row of medicine bottles.

Alexandra scowled. "Nancy! For heaven's sake, such a

bawdy statement is unbecoming to . . ." She sputtered and turned away, unable to get the image of the skinny former schoolmaster in lacy drawers out of her mind. She had to give in, finally, to laughter that brought tears to her eyes.

Nancy laughed as well, and the raucous sound the two of them made brought Zack hurrying in from the parlor to see what was going on. He gave one sharp bark, a reprimand, perhaps, that he had not been let in on the fun.

The bark served to sober Alexandra, who wiped her eyes and managed to speak without choking. "Nancy, this is no laughing matter. A man is dead. His wife and son are grieving. And it all seems rather mysterious to me."

"Of course," Nancy said, "you are right. And you don't believe, any more than I do, that Constable Snow has everything resolved. The question is, how did he come up with such a story?"

Alexandra was trying to concentrate on stocking her medical bag with supplies she might need on her rounds. "First," she said, "consider that Admiral Orkwright was an upstanding and much-admired man and, I should think, a friend of the constable's. Obviously the admiral's drunkenness came as no surprise to the constable, although it seemed to embarrass Mrs. Orkwright to admit it. It is possible he's trying to protect Mrs. Orkwright from further embarrassment and to protect his friend's good name from any kind of scandal."

"And you think . . ." Nancy prodded.

Alexandra sighed and shook her head. "I don't know what to think. And my guess is, in truth, neither does the constable." She handed Nancy an empty vial to wash and refill.

"If that's true, then why does he object to an autopsy?" Nancy inspected the vial as if she half expected to find the answer inside.

Alexandra snapped the bag shut. "My father and I have influenced you beyond our culture, Nancy. Not everyone accepts autopsy so easily. Most people see it as a defilement of the body. Again, the constable is protecting the admiral's family from ridicule and scandal."

"But you expect to learn something, perhaps, that will clear the matter," Nancy said.

"I don't know what to expect. It is simply that I find it

curious that the admiral would have been out bathing in the
sea when a storm was due, even if he was drunk. Particularly
since he was known not to be fond of recreational bathing.
Yet, I did notice there were scrape marks on the body, perhaps from the rocks, and, as I said, his mouth was full of
seaweed."

Nancy's eyes widened. "Are you saying he was dead before he went into the sea? That someone killed him first?"

Alexandra shook her head. "I'm saying I don't know. I'm
saying it's a possibility. And I'm saying there's no way to
know without an autopsy, if then."

"And the drawers . . ." There was no hint of laughter in
Nancy's expression.

"Yes," Alexandra said, "the drawers remain a question."

Nancy shook her head, trying to remain serious. "Very
strange," she said, then turned away quickly and left the
room. Alexandra heard her giggling, the sound muffled by
her hand over her mouth, as she hurried away to the kitchen.

Alexandra picked up her medical bag and took her cloak
from the hook in the front hall, calling over her shoulder to
Nancy that she was leaving for her rounds. There was no
response from Nancy, but Zack bounded to her side. He always acted as if the morning rounds to visit homebound patients were as much his responsibility as Alexandra's.

The two stable boys Nancy had recently hired had Lucy,
Alexandra's mare, saddled and waiting for her. Rob, the
older of the two, stood ready to help her into the sidesaddle
while Artie, the younger, held Lucy's reigns.

"Is it true about the admiral?" Rob asked as she walked
to his side.

"You've already heard?" She gathered her skirt and
stepped onto the mounting stool. She wasn't surprised, really.
Artie and Rob, who she had rescued from a band of young
thieves several months ago, still had an uncanny way of
knowing everything of a darker nature that went on in
Newton-Upon-Sea.

"Heard 'e was dead, if that's what ye mean," Rob said.

Artie, who could not have been more than nine years old,
nodded his head. "Drownded, 'e was." He glanced at Rob.

"Bit odd for a old sea dog, what?" Rob took the reins

from Artie and handed them to Alexandra, who was now mounted on Lucy's back. Her knee was securely hooked over the horn, and her skirts discreetly covered every inch of leg.

Alexandra looked down at both of the boys. "And what else have you heard?"

They both sputtered with laughter, and Artie spoke first. "Wearin' 'is wife's knickers, was 'e?"

"Knickers? Where did you learn that word?" Alexandra did her best to keep her voice stern.

Artie gave her a frightened look, obviously afraid he'd spoken inappropriately. "I—well, I just . . ."

"Never mind. Just be sure you don't repeat gossip." She gave Lucy a nudge and turned her toward the gate. Obviously the constable's attempt at containing the gossip hadn't worked. She had to admit she wasn't surprised that the word had spread. Dave and Nell Stillwell's butcher shop carried more news than the *Times,* without the added burden of accuracy. What continued to puzzle her, however, was how the boys could have possibly heard it so early when, to the best of her knowledge, until a few hours ago, they'd been sleeping peacefully in their living quarters above the stables and had no contact with anyone other than herself.

She could not let their mysterious lines of communication concern her now, however. She had patients to see. Mary Prodder, an aging seamstress, forced to live now with her cantankerous daughter-in-law, had fallen and broken a hip the day before. The Blackburn baby had croup, and Hannibal Talbot, an oyster man, was enduring a great amount of pain from bladder stones.

The Prodder household had already heard the news of the admiral's death when Alexandra arrived. Mary's daughter-in-law, Edith, had gone early to the Stillwell's shop to purchase a shank of beef to boil.

Edith, almost giddy with excitement over the delicious news, leaned toward Alexandra and whispered. "Nell's the one what found 'im. Near naked 'e was, with all 'is privates showin'. And Nell seen 'em all. The full cluster!" She straightened and spoke in a louder voice. 'Twas only a pair of ladies' drawers 'e was wearin'. Some men is pure perverted, I say."

Alexandra adjusted the splint in which she had placed the elder Mrs. Prodder and didn't respond. She'd fallen late at night, taking a shortcut home after staying late with one of her customers. Constable Snow had found her and brought her home, then sent for Alexandra. It had caused the elderly woman a great deal of pain when Alexandra set the bone in her hip. She'd then applied a long splint. It extended from under her arm to her foot, and her legs were tied together in the hope of keeping the injured leg from shortening too much. Alexandra knew from experience that the bones would not be likely to unite properly, and her leg on the injured side would, in spite of her efforts, be shorter than the other. Broken bones that healed poorly were the curse of elderly women, and it seemed to worsen after the menses had ceased. The exact cause, however, remained a mystery.

"Is Mrs. Orkwright faring well enough? I'm concerned for her. She was always kind to me. Not like some people what treats their dressmakers like dogs." Mary seemed particularly agitated, and her face was pale and beaded with sweat, obviously from the pain in her hip. Current medical knowledge demanded that she be confined to her bed for two months. Of late, Alexandra had begun to wonder if it might not benefit the patient to shorten the time in bed, but she dared not harm her patient by experimenting.

"Mrs. Orkwright is in shock, of course, but I have reason to believe she will adjust. For now, though, I'm most concerned about your own pain." Alexandra suspected pain was something Mary Prodder knew too much of. An examination after her recent accident had revealed suspicious scars on her back and legs, most likely left by a rod long ago when she was a child. Mary, however, had insisted they were the result of a fall from a horse.

"My own pain is nothing," Mary said, "and I knows ye'll heal me."

"Pain?" Edith said. "She knows not what pain is until she's had to lift all the laundry I have to do, what with an extra person in the house. And the heavy cooking pots I must use with an extra mouth to feed. 'Tis my back what knows pain!"

Again Alexandra did her best to ignore the daughter-in-law. "Make sure you turn Mary several times a day, Edith, lest she develop bedsores."

Edith stiffened. "I does the best I can, but she's a demanding woman, she is, and there's no time for it all. I cannot take the responsibility for everything."

"Nor am I asking you to," Alexandra said. "I ask only for a little kindness and mercy for Mary. She is suffering greatly."

Edith took on a defensive look. "Kindness and mercy? I should be so fortunate as to get half the kindness and mercy I shows her. Just ask my husband. Fin will tell you I'm kind to his mother, 'e will."

Alexandra closed her medical bag and stood to take her leave. "Please see that the constant pressure on her backside is relieved by turning her frequently." She handed her a vial of laudanum. "If the pain is too great, see that she gets two drops of this no more than twice a day. If she requires more send for me."

Edith took the bottle absently. " 'Ave ye seen the admiral for yerself?"

"No," she said, hoping to end the conversation with that small lie. Edith, however, was so enthralled she refused to hear.

"Was he swimming half naked, as Nell said? What was he doing out in such dreadful weather, I'd like to know. And his wife, what did she have to say for herself, being married to a perverted man what dresses in women's drawers? Nell said you and the constable seen her and talked to her. All high-hatty, she is, livin' up there on top o' the world and lookin' down on everybody. I guess this will show 'er she's no better than the rest of us."

Mary spoke up in a trembling voice from her bed. "Poor woman. That's all I can say."

Edith glanced at her mother-in-law and scowled. "Doesn't know what she's saying half the time. Such a burden, she is! You can see that, can't you?

Once more Alexandra ignored her complaints and pointed to the vial. "Remember, two drops no more than twice a day."

With that last instruction, she left the house. Zack, who

was waiting outdoors in the sun, got up and followed her, watching over her carefully while she mounted Lucy, boosting herself up from a stump in front of the house.

She made her way to the Blackburn cottage a short distance from the village in the countryside. The cottage would have, under normal circumstances, been her last stop since it was outside of town, but Edith's gossip and attitude toward Mary had so distressed her, she felt she needed the ride to clear her mind.

Once there, she found little Saul, the Blackburn baby, was much improved. His stepmother, Darius, took as good care of him as she did her own infant, who was only a few weeks older. Darius had been hired as a wet nurse when Saul's mother and twin brother died at his birth. The arrangement as wet nurse had eventually resulted in a permanent position as Seth Blackburn's wife and mother to little Saul and two-year-old Phillip, something patently beneficial to each of them.

Feeling refreshed after the ride and after seeing the family thriving, she rode back to the village to look in on Hannibal Talbot. She found him in a restless, laudanum-induced sleep. His face was flushed and his body hot to the touch, suggesting that an infection of the bladder had set in. His wife was beside herself with worry.

When Hannibal first became ill, Alexandra had examined his urine under a microscope and diagnosed cystine deposits in the bladder. She had prescribed a preparation of iron, iodine, iodide of iron, and nitro-muriatic acid, and podophyllin for the liver, along with copious amounts of water. When he didn't respond to the medicine, she had recommended surgical removal of the stones, but he had, so far, steadfastly refused the operation, claiming a female could not possibly know a man's body well enough to accomplish such a procedure. He preferred, it appeared, to live in pain and beg for laudanum for occasional relief.

"Can't you do the surgery now, while he sleeps?" Mildryd Talbot's voice trembled and tears glistened in her eyes.

Alexandra shook her head. "I'm afraid not. See how fitfully he sleeps? He would feel the knife, and anyway it would be dangerous as long as the infection is present, not to mention unethical if he doesn't give me permission."

"Please," Mildryd said. "Can't you do something? I just wish your father was still around. He would have known what to do."

Alexandra had grown accustomed to a certain few of her patients continually comparing her to her father. Still, she bristled. "My father would have recommended surgery earlier, just as I did. It was your husband's decision not to trust me." While she spoke, she occupied herself by applying a glass suction cup over the area of his bladder in order to force more blood flow into the spot. The touch of the glass cup awakened him slightly. He thrust his arms about and swore, then groaned loudly as he felt the vacuum pressure of the cup.

"Is he still drinking the diuretic?" Alexandra spoke quietly to Mildryd as she worked.

"The what?"

"The infusion of wild carrot and hair moss I mixed for him. See that he drinks it six times a day. If we can get him to pass enough water to clear the infection out, perhaps he'll decide to trust me to operate."

Mildryd nodded in a distracted way, her eyes still on her husband. She remained distraught and preoccupied throughout the treatment and forgot, even, to see Alexandra to the door.

When Alexandra was outside on the narrow street, she once again mounted her mare, while Zack took his time rousing himself from his nap in the warm sun to follow. Once her morning rounds were completed, she would have, under ordinary circumstances, ridden home to a quick lunch before she opened her surgery to see patients. Today, however, she would not go home immediately, even if it meant opening her surgery late. Today she would stop by the offices of Constable Snow.

Robert Snow had been a schoolmaster before he took the job as constable in Newton-Upon-Sea. Since young females were not allowed to attend the village school, the late Dr. Huntington Gladstone had hired Snow as a private tutor for his daughter. He had allowed Nancy, the daughter of his housekeeper, to sit in on the tutoring sessions as well.

Alexandra secured Lucy's reins outside the constable's office and prepared to confront her former schoolmaster. Zack, having given up on finding another sunny spot, settled himself by the door as Alexandra stepped inside the office.

Seated at his desk, Snow glanced up when he heard the door open and rose from his seat. He spoke to her in his quiet, cultured, emotionless voice. "Good morning, Dr. Gladstone." The use of her formal title was the only hint she ever had that he respected her accomplishment and position. He had never expressed any pride that his former student had acquired the knowledge necessary to be named and licensed a medical doctor. Nor had he ever acknowledged that, because she was female and could not attend some of the necessary medical classes, her task had been doubly difficult. However, to his credit, he did not seem to resent the fact that she was a woman in what was considered to be a man's profession, nor did he even once compare her unfavorably to her late father.

Her reply to him as she removed her gloves and slipped the hood of her cloak from her head was equally formal and respectful. "Good morning, Constable Snow."

He motioned for her to be seated, and when she had been, seated himself. He wove his long, supple fingers together, then tested the warp and weave of it with the sharp point of his chin. He left his chin there, resting, while he looked at her. He didn't speak, but the electrical alertness of his being invited her to.

"I want to speak with you about Admiral Orkwright."

There was a slight tilt of his head while two forefingers unwound themselves to form an inverted V at the end of his chin.

Alexandra tried to force away old sensations of student and intimidating master. Yet she was tense, and she found she was holding her breath for a moment before she managed to speak. "It is my opinion that an autopsy is necessary, and I'm afraid I don't understand your insistence that I not perform one."

Snow's hands floated apart, and he rested one forearm on his desk as he leaned toward her. "You told me, did you not, that it is your opinion Admiral Orkwright died of drowning?"

"I did say that I believe it is possible, however—"

"Then I'm afraid I don't see the need for an autopsy if the cause of death is known."

Alexandra moved to the edge of her chair, her body even more tense. "The cause of death is not known, in the most technical sense. It is only assumed, since there is no other apparent cause at the moment."

"I believe you have just made my point, Dr. Gladstone." Snow spoke without the slightest hint of smugness.

"No, sir. The point is that while there is no other *apparent* cause, I have not ruled out all *possible* causes of death, and I shall not be able to without an autopsy."

Snow fixed his eyes on hers in exactly the same manner he had used as a schoolmaster when asking for the step-by-step explanation of an algebra problem. "What, exactly, would you be looking for?"

Alexandra met his gaze. "I don't know, sir. But that is precisely the point. I don't know."

Snow settled back in his chair. "Your scientific curiosity is admirable, Dr. Gladstone. However, under the circumstances, there is no need for an autopsy. As I have explained to you already, we have no reason to suspect foul play, and since drowning seems highly probable, and since Mrs. Orkwright does not want the body of her beloved husband subjected to the indignity of autopsy, there will be no autopsy."

"How do you know that, sir? That Mrs. Orkwright doesn't want an autopsy, I mean." Alexandra spoke as Snow riffled through some of the papers on his desk—a gesture that suggested he'd already dismissed her.

The look on his face when he glanced up at her was one of surprise. "I beg your pardon?"

"How do you know Mrs. Orkwright does not wish an autopsy?"

"Because she told me, of course," Snow said.

"She told you? When? Have you seen her again?"

Snow's icy glance said it all. She knew she had gone beyond propriety, yet she couldn't stop herself.

"Have you told her what he was wearing? That, alone, makes the case extraordinary, as I'm sure you agree. In fact, it makes it suspicious."

Snow stood and braced himself with the fingertips of his long hands pressed to the desk. "Dr. Gladstone, I can assure you I am aware of what makes a case suspicious. I am also well aware of my duties as a peace officer to inform the murder victim's family of anything unusual. Please rest assured that I have attended to all necessary details, and Mrs. Orkwright does not wish to have an autopsy."

Alexandra was momentarily stunned by his stern, schoolmaster scolding, but she recovered quickly. "Perhaps you should tell her that I have some suspicion as to—"

"Suspicion, Dr. Gladstone?" Snow's jaw tensed, and his lips whitened.

She knew he was angry, but she tried to ignore it. "Yes. Your explanation for his wearing a woman's undergarments was nothing more than conjecture and rather lame at that. I believe you should—"

"It is not necessary, Dr. Gladstone, for you to tell me how I should go about doing my job. I would not presume to tell you how to do yours. Perhaps you can afford me the same courtesy. If you will pardon me, Doctor, I have my duties to attend."

Alexandra started to explain, or perhaps to defend her position further, or perhaps to vent her frustration, but she said nothing. Instead she stood, secured her cloak tighter, and left the office. Outside on the street, she took several deep breaths trying to calm herself. Why was the constable so dead set against an autopsy? Had he really spoken to Mrs. Orkwright about it, or had he contrived that story for his own purposes? And if so, why? What was he hiding?

Alexandra rode down Griffon Street away from the constable's office and the jail, away from the local pub known as the Blue Ram, beyond the butcher shop, the cobbler, the blacksmith, and all the other shops until she reached the intersection of Straytham Lane. She should have turned there until the lane ran into Water Street, which would take her home. She didn't turn, however, but kept riding through a tangle of streets until she found herself riding up the hill that led to Gull House.

The housemaid she'd seen earlier opened the door to her knock. She appeared surprised. "Dr. Gladstone?"

"Is Mrs. Orkwright in? I would like to see her, please."
Alexandra glanced over the maid's shoulder, trying to peer
into the house.

"She is not well, as I'm sure you know."

"Of course, I thought I might be of some—"

The maid stiffened, her large frame filling almost all of
the doorway. "I'm afraid she's not receiving visitors."

"I'm not simply a visitor. I am a doctor, and I would
like—"

Before Alexandra could finish building her case, Jane Orkwright appeared in the hall. "Who is it, Annie?" she called.

"Dr. Gladstone, madam." The maid spoke without emotion.

"Please ask her to come in."

The maid moved aside begrudgingly and allowed Alexandra to enter.

"How kind of you to call again," Jane Orkwright said as
she led Alexandra into the parlor. She sat across from her
on one of the two burgundy-colored sofas in the room. She
had already donned widow's weeds. They made her pale skin
appear even more pale and accentuated the dark hollows
around her remarkably beautiful eyes. The dark shawl she'd
worn the day before was once again draped over her shoulders and only accentuated the heavy somberness of her attire.
Her voice was flat, and there was a sluggishness to her movements.

"I don't wish to trouble you, Mrs. Orkwright, but there is
something I feel compelled to discuss with . . ." Alexandra's
voice trailed off when she saw young William standing in
the doorway. She gave him a smile, but he dropped his eyes
and wouldn't look at her. She wasn't surprised. She had only
recently set a dislocated shoulder for him after he'd sustained
a particularly nasty fall. No doubt he remembered the pain
of that procedure. Very young children such as William often
associated her with just such unpleasant memories.

"William," Mrs. Orkwright said when she saw her son.
"Please come in and tell Dr. Gladstone hello, then you may
go with Annie to your room."

Young William's face clouded, and he seemed near tears.
"But, Mama, I want you to—"

"Please William, do as I ask. I'll be along in a moment."
Mrs. Orkwright spoke softly, and some of the flat, lifeless
quality was gone from her voice. Her son was obviously a
source of happiness for her.

William walked to her side and, with his mother's coach-
ing, gave Alexandra a timid, formal greeting, then left the
room reluctantly, glancing over his shoulder as if to make
sure his mother was still there.

Mrs. Orkwright smiled at her son, and her face softened
as she watched him leave. "Please forgive Will's lack of
manners, Dr. Gladstone. I'm afraid he's not quite himself."

"Of course," Alexandra said. "I'm sure he feels keenly the
loss of his father."

For a moment Mrs. Orkwright's eyes glazed over again.
"It . . . is difficult," she finally managed to say.

"Of course," Alexandra said again. She felt awkward, and
now she wasn't at all certain she could broach the subject of
the autopsy or the admiral's unusual attire.

Finally, it was Mrs. Orkwright who spoke. "You have
something you wish to say to me, no doubt, regarding the
admiral's death."

"Yes. I'm sorry, but you see . . ." Alexandra looked down
at her hands. Her agony was compounded by Mrs. Orkwright's silence. "I know Constable Snow has discussed this
with you, and you have voiced your opinion, but I felt I
should try to persuade you to change your mind."

There was another uncomfortable silence before Mrs. Orkwright spoke again. She wore a bewildered expression. "I'm
afraid I don't understand. I've had no discussions with Constable Snow."

"Regarding an autopsy," Alexandra managed to say, feeling more and more uncomfortable.

"Autopsy?" Mrs. Orkwright shook her head. Her face appeared even more pale and her eyes even more dark and
sunken. "I . . . I'm afraid not. Why would he want to discuss
that with me? Is it really necessary?"

Alexandra tried to choose her words carefully. "I thought
perhaps, given the circumstances, you would—"

"Circumstances?"

The woman's troubled expression gave Alexandra pause. It was clear Constable Snow had not discussed the autopsy with her. Why had he lied? Once again she couldn't help wondering what he had to hide.

3

Alexandra didn't know, at first, what she should say or how far she should push the issue with Jane Orkwright. However, the gossip about the admiral had spread all over town, and there was no way, ultimately, to protect either Mrs. Orkwright or her young son from it. It was better, she decided, to give her the truth, no matter how unpleasant the details, than to let her hear the distorted rumors.

"Mrs. Orkwright, I'm afraid—"

"Please, Alexandra, call me Jane. We were friends once, weren't we? At least I always meant to be your friend. Perhaps I was not very good at it. Perhaps I let my husband and my children occupy too much of my time. You see, I . . ." She was nattering uncharacteristically, but she stopped, looked away, and seemed to lose track of what she'd been saying. She was obviously not herself.

Alexandra watched her face, lined now with grief, but somehow, still beautiful. Her eyes stared unfocused. It was true, they had each meant to be friends. Alexandra had recognized in Jane an equal—another woman with whom she could converse on an intellectual level. She knew Jane had recognized the same in her. But their relationship had not gone beyond a handful of chance meetings. Each had been too busy with her own life—Jane with her husband and sons and Alexandra with her medical practice.

"Jane," Alexandra said, trying again. "There is something

you should know about your husband's death. Something unusual."

Jane's eyes refocused on hers, and Alexandra saw something there. Was it fear? Or dread? Or perhaps something else altogether different? "Unusual?" she said.

"Admiral Orkwright was . . . was not dressed in a traditional manner."

There was no response from Jane. Only the slightest rise of her eyebrows.

"He was wearing women's clothing. I'm afraid . . ." Alexandra felt as if her breath were trapped in her lungs, and her chest began to hurt. Jane's quiet, patient wait seemed only to make it harder for her. "I'm afraid he was wearing nothing save a woman's undergarment," she blurted.

There was another silence while Jane looked at her with the blank expression Alexandra had come to expect. "I don't understand," she said finally.

"Nor do I," Alexandra said. "I hoped perhaps there was some explanation, some light you could shed on—"

Jane shook her head. "I don't understand why you're telling me this. Isn't it enough that he's dead?" Her voice rose to a high, agitated timbre. She stood and walked to the window overlooking the sea. She spoke with her back to Alexandra. "Why is it important for me to know these details?" She seemed near tears, and she twisted the handkerchief she held until Alexandra heard a slight ripping sound.

Alexandra felt suddenly dirty, as if she had dragged both of them into some filthy quagmire. "I'm sorry, Jane. I know this must upset you, but—"

Jane whirled around suddenly, her face now livid with anger. "Upset me? You have no idea what you've . . ." Her lips quivered as she tried to go on, but she was unable to speak. She dropped her face into her hands and sobbed uncontrollably.

Alexandra went to her and tried to put an arm around her shoulders, but Jane winced and pulled away. She remained with her back to Alexandra for a moment before she turned around. "Forgive me." Her voice was steady, almost unnaturally so. "I know you're trying to help me. I suppose the village is full of gossip." She looked at Alexandra as if to find confirmation in her face, then she turned away again and sat on the edge of one of the sofas. "I appreciate your warning me."

"Jane, I—"

"I don't know why." Jane's voice was sharp and clipped as she interrupted. Her denial was too quick, Alexandra thought, as if she protested too much. As if she was lying. She had not meant to ask her "why." She had meant only to apologize again, then to drop the subject. Yet, Jane persisted. "I shall do all I can to keep this from Will. You understand that, don't you? You understand that I must protect him."

"Of course," Alexandra said. She was silent for another long moment, still standing near the window and looking at Jane, sitting in her rigid posture at the edge of the sofa. Alexandra spoke to her again, apologetically. "I must know if you think your husband's attire—the female undergarments—had anything to do with his death."

Jane glanced at her with a puzzled frown. "I don't understand."

"Is it possible he had done this before? Dressed this way, I mean."

Jane appeared even more puzzled. She shook her head. "I don't . . . I don't know what you're getting at."

Alexandra took a deep breath and let it out slowly, unsure about whether or not she should continue. "What I'm asking," she said, deciding to go ahead, "is if the admiral might have been associated with others—other men, that is—who may have dressed this way, or who enjoyed seeing him dress this way. . . ." She stopped when she saw the look on Jane's face. She was completely bewildered. It was clear she had no idea of such deviations in human behavior. It seemed cruel to confuse her more; it was best to get to the heart of the matter. "Jane, I just want to know if you believe anyone had any reason to murder your husband."

Jane's face grew white and she seemed to shudder. "I thought we were done with that," she said. "I thought that was what all of the questioning from Constable Snow was about." She glanced away for a moment, and then turned her gaze back to Jane. "Why would anyone want to kill my husband?"

"He had no enemies?"

"Of course he had enemies. He was an admiral in Her Majesty's Navy. Men do not rise to such a position without making a few enemies along the way. But certainly no one who would have wanted to kill him. Besides, he was retired. All of that was in the past for him." Her gaze, hot with a passion Alexandra didn't understand, burned into Alexandra's eyes. "Why do you think he was murdered?"

"I don't know, except . . ."

"Except what?" Jane said after a long pause.

"Except that, as I said, what he was wearing made the circumstances unusual, even suspect."

Jane grew pale again, and she shook her head as if to deny it all. "His unusual attire? That's your reason for wanting an autopsy?"

"That's only part of the reason. You see—"

"Is it not certain that he drowned?"

"It does look likely, but one can never be certain. Drowning can never be proven even with a postmortem examination."

"Then what would you be looking for?"

"Another means of death. Poisoning, perhaps, or evidence of apoplexy or heart disease."

Jane turned away again, considering it. She sat, still on the edge of the sofa, perfectly straight, with her hands folded in her lap. "I see," she said finally. Her voice was low, quiet. She turned back to Alexandra. "Then perhaps it is best that you proceed. But you must do it quickly and quietly. My husband has a brother in Suffolk, his only living relative, who, I am certain, would not consent to what I am sure he considers the indignity of the examination."

"Of course."

"And there is William. This must not be discussed in his presence."

"Certainly not," Alexandra said. "I shall notify the constable and proceed as quickly as possible. I assure you, nothing need be made public unless there is evidence of foul play."

"I'm sure you'll be discreet." Jane stood as she spoke, a signal, perhaps, that Alexandra should leave. Alexandra didn't hesitate to comply. Not only was she eager to begin the examination, but she was certain her presence was distressing to her hostess. She left, however, with something less than satisfaction. She had achieved her goal by getting permission for the examination but at great cost to Jane. Beyond that, she sensed that Jane, although she was naïve about certain aspects of deviant human behavior, still had not been truthful concerning what she knew about her husband's unconventional attire. But if she was hiding something, some shameful truth, was it simply to protect her son?

Nicholas Forsythe brushed at the dust that had accumulated on the cuff of his elegant black coat, then pulled at the velvet lapels. Finally, he used the tip of his cane to adjust his top hat, which was made of the finest, most luxurious beaver skin. He had just arrived by coach from London, along with a personal servant. He had been hired by a solicitor for the family of a young man accused of burglary to act as barrister in the young man's defense.

Nicholas got wind of the case by accident when he happened to overhear a conversation between colleagues who were discussing the fact that a solicitor for the mother of the accused was looking to hire a barrister for her son. The family, he had learned, lived in Essex at Newton-Upon-Sea. After that, he had maneuvered and manipulated and used the considerable influence of his family name to convince the solicitor, a Mr. Herbert Fitzjames, that he was the man for the job. He had never met the mother, whose name, he had been given to understand, was Mrs. Orkwright.

As it so happened, he would not have had to use any of his family's influence nor any of his manipulative strategies to acquire the case. No one else wanted it. His enthusiasm puzzled his colleagues, since it was a most remarkably ordinary case. The accused was simply some young ne'er-do-well arrested for burglary. He was the son, stepson to be exact, of a local dignitary in Newton-Upon-Sea. A retired Admiral Orkwright. Besides the ordinary character of the case, the mother's decision to hire a barrister had come rather late in the game, so there was little time to prepare, which made the case even more unattractive to his colleagues.

Newton-Upon-Sea was, as his colleagues reminded him, a singularly ordinary town, certainly not one for which most barristers would vie to visit either for pleasure or in the line of business. It was not the town, in fact, that interested Nicholas. It was a woman. A markedly peculiar woman in that she had chosen to educate herself as a doctor of medicine. One Dr. Alexandra Gladstone.

He had met Dr. Gladstone several months ago when he'd been a guest at a dinner party given by a former classmate, the late Lord Dunsford, whose country house was just outside Newton-Upon-Sea. Dr. Gladstone was also a guest at the party, and he had found her fascinating. Odd, yes, but fascinating. So much so that, when the opportunity arose, he had contrived to see her again. Then, as luck would have it, the young man escaped Newgate by some trickery as yet unknown. Nicholas saw it as his duty to travel to the young man's hometown to gather information. It did seem quite possible that the accused might return here to his family, and didn't that mean his barrister should investigate? As Nicholas saw it, Fate was working in his interest.

Now that he was in Newton, the first thing was to direct his manservant to attend to the practical matter of lodging. Until Lord Dunsford's recent unfortunate and scandalous death, he could have lodged at Montmarsh, the late earl of Dunsford's grand and gracious dwelling. Now, however, the house remained closed and unoccupied except for a caretaker, since there was still some dispute as to the rightful heir. Whoever the heir turned out to be, he would undoubtedly not even know of the existence of Nicholas Forsythe. And so, Nicholas thought, with regret, he would never again be likely to be a guest in the elegance of Montmarsh. Not that there weren't plenty of other country homes where he was welcome, including his own childhood home, Lockewood, to the north of London, near Oxford. His older brother was already quite prepared to inherit Lockewood by right of primogeniture.

Nicholas was far from homeless, however. His living quarters were an elegant house in Kensington, quite suitable for comfortable living and lavish entertaining. For the time being, however, he would have to content himself with a room in the inn above the Blue Ram, a true public house that was not only where local townsmen met to drink and socialize, but where the court of assizes met when it was in town, and where other meetings important to the populace were held.

Within a few minutes, Morton, his servant, had secured rooms at the inn above the tavern. When Nicholas entered his rented room, he noted that, although it was sparsely furnished, it was reasonably clean. He left Morton to see to his luggage while he walked the short distance down a street called Griffon to the office of the local constable, a Mr. Snow. It was best to give the man the courtesy of a visit and explain his business in Newton.

The constable was busy at his desk, but he looked up as Nicholas entered. "Good afternoon, sir," the constable said, laying his pen aside. He drew his long, slender frame to a standing position. "May I help you, please?"

"Forsythe. Nicholas Forsythe." Nicholas, with his hat under his left arm, offered him his right hand. "Perhaps you'll remember me as one of the guests at Montmarsh last year when the late Earl Dunsford met his tragic death."

"Ah, of course," Snow said, shaking Nicholas's hand. "Most unpleasant circumstances."

Unpleasant, indeed, Nicholas thought. The late Dunsford had been murdered in his sleep, and it was that peculiar, clever, and quite attractive Dr. Gladstone who solved the crime. Although, Nicholas could admit to himself with a certain measure of pride, he himself had been quite instrumental in helping her get to the bottom of it.

"You're a barrister, I believe." Snow resumed his seat, his long white hands folded on top of his desk.

"Quite so," Nicholas said. "I've been retained as the defender for a young man from Newton-Upon-Sea accused of burglary. John Killborn, his name. Stepson of a distinguished admiral. I believe the admiral's name is Orkwright."

Snow had been sitting with his head tilted back slightly so that he seemed to be pointing at Nicholas with the sharp tip of his chin. He dropped his chin and spoke. "Of course. John Killborn. I know of him."

"So I assumed." Nicholas shifted his cane from his left to his right hand, still with his hat under his arm. "I regret to

say he has escaped Newgate, and I thought to inquire if you
had news of his being in this area."

"I'm afraid not." Snow's face was expressionless as he
spoke.

"It was Killborn's mother, Mrs. Orkwright, who hired me.
You know his family, I assume."

Snow hesitated only slightly before he answered. "Of
course."

"I shall speak to the mother, certainly, but I wanted to
advise you of the details first."

Snow's eyes narrowed slightly. "Mrs. Orkwright is not
well, I'm afraid."

Nicholas' eyebrows rose in surprise. "Indeed! She seemed
in fine health when she met with me last month."

"A month can take a toll," Snow said. "I think it best that
I speak with her and determine what she knows of the in-
cident and then relay the information to you. An escape from
prison is, after all, law enforcement's responsibility."

Nicholas was momentarily stunned. Of course it was law
enforcement's responsibility, but Snow was making an effort
to keep him away from the woman who had hired him on
behalf of the client. Most unusual, he mused. Most puzzling.
His shock had caused him to delay too long. In the next
moment, Snow was dismissing him.

"I appreciate the courtesy, Mr. Forsythe. I shall contact
you in London as soon as possible."

Nicholas was even more puzzled. He had to think quickly
of a way to stall. "Perhaps Killborn has associates here to
whom I could speak, other than his ailing mother, I mean. I
was thinking of—"

"None that I know of," Snow said, interrupting him.

"I was thinking of some of the local criminals, perhaps.
Someone you may have imprisoned here." Nicholas was
grasping for ideas, anything that could keep him in Snow's
presence. He wanted to find out what Snow was trying to
keep him from knowing.

Snow rose from his seat and took a ring of keys attached
to a long metal rod from a hook on the wall and walked
toward a door. "This way, please."

He unlocked the door, and Nicholas, a bit stunned by the

constable's abruptness, followed him down a hall to a single room where a small opening with bars gave the prisoners a view of the hall. Compared to the goals in the London area with which Nicholas was familiar, this one was small; fewer than half a dozen occupied the room. Two of the men stood at the windows, and one of them whooped when he saw Nicholas.

"We got us a dandy comin' this way, boys," he said. That brought all of the prisoners crowding around the opening.

"You come to play, pretty boy?" the one who had called out said. "Or does we have to satisfy ourselves while we just looks at ye?" The lewd comment brought a chorus of laughter and more raucous shouting. Nicholas had expected no more than a few drunks to be incarcerated in a town as small as Newton-Upon-Sea. Perhaps it was the busy piers that brought a more hardened element here. Nevertheless, he felt the cold grasp of fear at his throat, but he didn't slow his pace, and when Snow unlocked the door, he was the first to enter.

"Quiet!" Snow's snarling command was only half heeded. There was still laughter and lewd gesturing. When Snow stepped in front of him, Nicholas saw that his usually pallid face was flushed with anger. "John Killborn!" he shouted. "Do any of you know John Killborn? If you do, step to the front!" The room grew unnaturally and unnervingly quiet. Snow shouted the name again, and once again there was no response.

He took a step toward the prisoners, and then another step, and another, until he was in their midst. He studied the face of each and occasionally even reached a hand to tilt a man's head back so he could have a better look at his face. Finally he walked away from the group and turned back toward them with his arms akimbo, his face hardened with what seemed to Nicholas, dangerous anger.

"Who knows John Killborn?"

There was still the long, highly charged silence.

Snow waited, then suddenly struck the wall with the metal rod to which the keys were attached. "Who knows John Killborn?" he shouted.

Some of the men were startled by the noise made by the

rod, and there was some uneasy movement and muttering for a few seconds, but there was no answer. Snow waited another long moment before he turned and walked toward the door, his demeanor unnaturally calm. He turned to face the prisoners before he unlocked the door.

"Rations will be restricted to water and a piece of bread for each prisoner per day. Perhaps next time you'll show more respect to a visitor." With that, he opened the door, gestured for Nicholas to leave first, then closed and locked the door behind him. He didn't speak until they had reached his office. "As you can see, I'm afraid you cannot expect any cooperation," he said as he replaced the keys and rod on the hook. He went to his desk and resumed reading the papers that lay there.

Nicholas could only stare at him, astonished for a few seconds before he turned away and left the building. He made his way across the street to the Blue Ram and found an empty slot at the bar where he ordered a glass of lager, wondering what to make of his conversation with Snow. He remembered him as a cold bastard from his last meeting several months ago. He seemed even more so now, along with being odd and uncooperative.

"Ye looks a bit grim and out of sorts, ye does. I hopes this'll help." The barmaid, a woman in her forties, set the glass in front of him and grinned at him, revealing several missing teeth.

"Thank you," he said.

She squinted, scrutinizing him. "I seen ye before, ain't I?"

"Not likely. I reside in London."

" 'Course ye does. A gentleman like you? Ye wouldn't be comin' from . . ." She stopped speaking and her eyes widened. "I seen ye before, I has. Ye was the barrister what helped that poor child accused o' murdin' Lord Dunsford. Right here in this tavern where the Queen's Court was held for the assizes!"

The woman was right. Although he had not been allowed to defend the accused girl when she was tried, he used as much of his legal skills as possible to help her. The trial was held at the biannual session of the assizes when judges from the Queen's Bench in London traveled to towns such as

Newton-Upon-Sea to hear cases. In Newton, as well as many other towns, court was held in a local tavern. He now recognized the woman as Sally Wheatstone, the wife of the tavern owner.

"Yes, of course," Nicholas said and gave her a pleasant smile.

She leaned closer to him and spoke in a coarse whisper. "Are ye here this time on that Orkwright business?"

Nicholas was startled. How could this woman know of Mrs. Orkwright's hiring him? "I beg your pardon?"

"Ye knows of what I speak, does ye not? The admiral. Dead. And under disgraceful circumstances, as they says. Drownded, they says." She leaned close once again and whispered. "Some says 'e was murdered. If ye ask me, I say 'twas that stepson o' his what done it. The boy never liked the old admiral, don't ye know."

"Indeed?" Nicholas did his best to appear merely curious. "I understood the boy is in Newgate. Couldn't possibly do the deed from there, could he?"

"Newgate?" Sally laughed. " 'Tain't likely. Seen 'im meself the day before the admiral died."

Nicholas's heart was pounding, but still he tried to appear disinterested. "Here in the tavern, I suppose."

Sally gave him an incredulous look. "In the tavern? Why, no. Never showed up once, and now I knows why. Been in Newgate, ye say? Can't say I'm surprised. I suppose 'e was shamed to show 'is face now." She sighed and shook her head. "His poor mother, ain't she had enough? No, 'e wasn't in the tavern. 'E was down by the sea when I seen 'im, and now that I thinks of it, 'e was actin' like 'e didn't want nobody to see 'im."

4

Alexandra had to hurry home to see patients during her regular surgery hours, and by the time the last one left, it was too late to contact Constable Snow about the autopsy. She was up early the next morning, however, and was waiting in front of his office before he arrived.

Snow removed his hat when he saw her and gave her a formal nod. "Good morning, Dr. Gladstone, I hope this early visit doesn't mean you've some trouble to report." In spite of his cordial words, his greeting lacked warmth.

"Not at all." She entered the door he held open for her. "I've come to you on behalf of Jane Orkwright."

Snow, who by this time had also entered the office and stepped to his desk, spun around suddenly to face her. His lips, drawn tight across his teeth, seemed to have lost all their color. He spoke one word. "Regarding . . ."

"She has given me permission to perform a postmortem examination of her husband. If you will be so kind as to help me arrange it, I shall see to it immediately." Alexandra had to struggle to keep her voice even. Snow's icy expression was more than a little intimidating to her. His eyes, though, were smoldering liquid.

"I'm afraid that will be impossible," he said.

"I beg your pardon?"

"The body is already being prepared."

Alexandra would not let her gaze falter as she looked at

him. "Preparation for burial does not preclude an autopsy."

Snow fired his retort back at her quickly. "There is no need for a postmortem examination. I have already told you that."

"But Mrs. Orkwright—"

"Dr. Gladstone!" The harsh sound of Snow's voice left Alexandra momentarily unable to continue. "Mrs. Orkwright is mourning her husband. She is in no condition to make decisions. Furthermore I find it shocking that you would stoop to persuade her to consent to the defilement of her husband's body merely to satisfy your own morbid curiosity."

Alexandra found, to her surprise, that she was trembling. "I can assure you I did nothing untoward."

"See that you don't in future," Snow said. He picked up a pen and began scribbling on a document, ignoring Alexandra completely. She left as quickly as possible.

Once she was on the street, she hurried as fast as her cumbersome skirts would allow, all the way to the home of Percy Gibbs, the undertaker, with Zack trotting along beside her. Since it was only a few blocks away, walking would be faster, she reasoned, than taking the time and effort to hoist herself up into her sidesaddle without the benefit of a groom, and she was now more determined than ever at least to have another look at the body. If the constable was hiding something, she was determined to know what it was.

Her heart was pounding more from agitation than exertion by the time she reached the undertaker's home. Zack lay down near the front door, as he had been trained to do. She pulled a handle and heard a bell ring inside, announcing her arrival. She waited for what seemed an eternity before the door opened. Mrs. Gibbs, the undertaker's wife, finally opened the door. When Alexandra asked to see Mr. Gibbs, the woman led her to a parlor and told her to wait.

The house was as gloomy as death itself. An old-fashioned painted cloth depicting the resurrection of Lazarus surrounded by a host of angels covered one entire wall. It was a style of decoration still popular with some and less costly than tapestry. Beneath the enormous cloth, several chairs in dark maroon and green velvet lined the wall. Alexandra tried to sit in one of the chairs and tried not to look at the hideous wall hanging. She was not successful at either for very long. She was pacing restlessly when Percy Gibbs appeared from an adjoining room. He was wearing a stained apron, which he quickly removed when he saw Alexandra.

"Good morning, Dr. Gladstone." He spoke in the hushed, grave tones peculiar to his profession.

"Mr. Gibbs, I've come about Admiral Orkwright." Alexandra regretted the way her words came out rushed and agitated. Her demeanor had no apparent effect on Mr. Gibbs, however.

"I see," he said in his dark, solemn voice, his hands folded piously across his sizable belly.

"Mrs. Orkwright, his widow, has given me permission to perform a postmortem examination." Alexandra had managed to effect a measure of calm to her words.

"I see." Gibbs changed neither his expression nor his stance.

"I should like to begin right away."

Gibbs half closed his eyes making him look oddly half dead. "She that is hasty of spirit exalteth folly. I shall have to see the customary documents."

Alexandra felt as if her heart had sunk to her stomach. Of course there were documents to be dealt with. She should have remembered, except that autopsies were rarely a necessity in Newton-Upon-Sea, so rare, in fact, she had momentarily forgotten that she would need signatures from both Jane and Constable Snow. Jane, of course, would provide her signature, and wouldn't Snow surely be compelled to do the same after he was assured of Jane's agreement?

"Very well," she said with a strong measure of impatience. "I shall have them for you by tomorrow afternoon."

"I'm afraid that will be too late. The funeral and burial will take place early on the morrow. That is the widow's request. 'A prudent wife is from the Lord.' "

"But, as I told you, she has given me verbal—"

"The documents are a requirement of the government. 'Render unto Caesar' as they say." He shook his head. "There is nothing I can do without the documents, I'm afraid. Now if you will excuse me, I must get back to work for 'the night cometh, when no man can work.' " Gibbs gave her a stilted smile and turned back to the door, leaving Alexandra alone with Lazarus and the angels, while frustration almost suffocated her.

She turned toward the door. There was but one thing to do, and that was to have the formal document signed by both Jane and the constable immediately. It took some time to retrieve Lucy, get herself mounted in the sidesaddle, ride to her residence, and secure Nancy's help to find a copy of the necessary document, then ride to Gull House.

When she reached the house, she hurried up the long walk and knocked at the door. After a long wait, there was no answer. She rapped repeatedly. Still there was no response. Behind her Zack paced nervously, growling low in his throat as if he were urging her to leave.

Alexandra ignored him and knocked again, louder, and called out Jane Orkwright's name. She tried again and again, each time with no response until, finally, she sighed and turned to Zack. "All right," she said, rubbing his head. "You're right, there's no need to stay."

When she arrived home, Artie and Rob were both in the stable yard.

"Dr. Gladstone!" Artie said in his childish nine-year-old voice. "Ye's home early from yer rounds."

"No, I'm afraid I haven't even started them yet," Alexandra said, allowing them to help her dismount. "I had some other business to attend to. I shall have to do my rounds tonight after I close the surgery."

"It's dangerous, ye bein' out at night," Rob said.

"I shall be perfectly safe. Zack will be with me."

"Small comfort that is," said Rob, who, at fifteen, was too worldly wise for his age. "There's plenty goes on a lady such as yerself never dreams of. Ye can take me word for that. Things yer better off not knowin'."

"He's right," young Artie said. "Ye best be home before dark."

Alexandra took their scolding with a smile and a promise that she would do her best not to be out too late, then she started for the house, preparing to face Nancy.

"Have you any idea how late it is?" Nancy's face was grim

and she all but snatched Alexandra's cloak from her.

"Close to noon, I'd say."

"Close to noon indeed." She hung the cloak on a hook and gave it an angry swat. " 'Tis past one and time to open the surgery and you've yet to do your rounds."

"I know, Nancy. How many waiting to see me?"

"Plenty, I should say. What took you so long?"

"I went to see the constable, just as I told you before. Then I spent several frustrating minutes talking to Percy Gibbs before I left to see Jane Orkwright to have her sign a document. She's given me permission for a postmortem examination."

"Does it take so long to sign a document?"

"It could have taken even longer, had I been able to rouse her. It appeared there was no one at home at Gull House, and I'm afraid I spent a bit of time waiting for an answer at the door or for some sign of a presence inside."

"You should be careful wondering all over the place. There's a murderer out there somewhere, you know."

Alexandra didn't bother to respond.

"And you've had nothing to eat all day."

She waved a hand at Nancy as if to brush away her concerns as she made her way to the surgery. "It doesn't matter, I can eat later."

"I'll get you something now." Nancy was still in a huff as she started for the kitchen.

"Nancy . . ."

She turned around and looked at Alexandra, the question in her eyes only partly assuaging her irritation.

"There's something I'd like to discuss with you," Alexandra said.

"Discuss with me?" Nancy took a step toward her. "Is it about the admiral?"

"It is, yes."

Nancy looked at her with eager anticipation.

"I'm afraid that an autopsy may not be possible. In fact, I may not even be able to examine the external body again."

"I don't understand. It's your duty, and you said Mrs. Orkwright has given permission."

"It's a complicated story, Nancy. But you're right, it is my duty, and the circumstances surrounding the admiral's death surely warrant it in my opinion."

She told Nancy how both the constable and Percy Gibbs had thrown stumbling blocks in her path and that she had not been able to arouse anyone at Gull House in order to have the necessary documents signed.

Nancy gave her a puzzled look. "Excuse me, miss, but it's still not clear to me how an autopsy will prove anything? You told me yourself that it's impossible to confirm drowning that way."

"That's true," Alexandra said, "but if I can eliminate anything such as poisoning or a blow to the head or some other mortal wound, then drowning will be assumed to be the cause of death by the process of elimination."

"Who could have poisoned him or given him a mortal wound?"

"Anyone could have done it, Nancy."

"Anyone?"

Alexandra nodded. "Yes, but how could anyone have gotten him in the sea in a storm without drowning themselves, since there was sure to be a struggle?"

Nancy frowned, contemplating it. "Unless he was poisoned or mortally wounded first!"

"Precisely."

"But the only way to prove or disprove that is by post-mortem examination, but that's not possible," Nancy said.

Alexandra was silent for a few seconds before she said, "Perhaps it is possible."

Nancy gave her a stern look. "You're not going back to Gull House now and leave the surgery full!"

"No, I'll take care of my patients first. Besides, there's no one home at Gull House, so I can't get Jane's signature yet, and neither the constable nor Percy will cooperate until I do."

"I suppose you have a solution," Nancy said.

"There is no solution except to do it without permission, since the funeral is tomorrow."

Nancy gasped and was unable to speak for a moment. "Oh lord," she said finally, "we're going to be body snatchers."

*   *   *

It was late before Alexandra finished seeing patients in the surgery and made her rounds to visit homebound patients. She had not come up with a plan to gain access to the admiral's body, with or without permission, and had decided the best approach was to confront the undertaker again.

Both she and Nancy bundled themselves in heavy cloaks with gloves and scarves to brave the cold February night, and Alexandra gathered the instruments she would need. Since she didn't own a carriage, and since Lucy was too small to carry two riders, they decided to walk.

"We must leave Zack at home this time as well," Alexandra said. "He's sure to be in the way if we're allowed access."

"What if Mr. Gibbs still won't allow you access? Will we become body snatchers after all?" Nancy, in spite of her eagerness to be in on the adventure, appeared uneasy.

Alexandra was not certain why she could not answer that question.

It was no easy task leaving the house without Zack. His protests were loud and dramatic. Alexandra could hear him even after she'd closed the heavy front door.

The dark cloister of Newton-Upon-Sea at night closed around them, and their hollow footsteps on the deserted streets echoed off the stillness. When they reached the Gibbs home there was no lamplight shining through the windows. The house was dark as death, and no one responded to the bell they rang. Nancy even tried pushing the door open, but found it locked.

With her hand still on the doorknob, she turned to Alexandra. "It's no use. No one is here."

"Perhaps we should try a window," Alexandra whispered.

"Good lord, miss! Are you suggesting we break into the house?"

"No, no, of course not," Alexandra said. But she knew there was no conviction in her statement. Examining the body again had become an obsession. If the answer to how the admiral died was available, she had to find it.

She left the front of the house and walked toward the back. Nancy followed her, demanding to know where she was going and why, but Alexandra didn't answer. The only window she found was at the back of the building, and it, like the back door, was locked.

She sighed. "Nancy, I must be daft. How could I even think of . . ." She stopped speaking when she heard a noise coming from the alley behind them. There was a shuffling and then a low murmur. The words were not quite audible, and the voice not quite human.

Nancy took in her breath and backed away while Alexandra's hand went to her mouth as if to stifle a scream. They grabbed each other, and Alexandra managed to warn Nancy with a soft "shhh."

They waited, clinging to each other and shivering in the darkness, both from fear and from the incipient damp cold. They waited for what seemed an eternity of silence so heavy they could feel it on their skin along with the cold. Then the murmur again, this time more human, but no less terrifying, and it was followed by an inhuman modulated groan. But the last was a welcome sound, and they each let go of their clinch and leaned toward the sound, both of them calling out at once, "Zack?"

He bounded out of the shadows, and pounced, placing his forepaws on Alexandra's shoulders. She would have fallen had Nancy not caught her. "Zack!" she said again, "what are you doing here?" She was barely able to speak the words for trying to dodge the dog's tongue, licking her face with uncontained exuberance. "For heaven's sake, Nancy, I thought I told you to leave Zack—"

"I did, Miss Alex! I left him locked in the house."

"Then how—"

"Shhh!" Nancy cautioned.

Alexandra had heard the sound at the same time. It was the low murmuring of a human voice. Zack, who had also heard it, dropped his forepaws to the ground and turned toward the sound, responding with one sharp, loud bark. Alexandra could feel the rhythmical swish, swish of his tail, playing a joyful beat against her skirts. He was by no means acting the part of the ferocious watchdog. The realization that he was no protection brought a paralyzing, icy fear to Alexandra until she heard the voice again, soft and as frightened as she herself felt.

"Are ye hurt, Doc? Are ye all right?"

"Rob?"

There was another shuffling sound and Rob emerged, recognizable not by his face, which was shrouded with the night, but by the size and shape of him and by the size and shape of the other, smaller figure that clung to his shirttail and then, unmistakably, by his voice again.

"What are ye doing here, Doc? Don't ye know creeping about in the night can be a danger to ye?"

"I might ask you the same thing," Alexandra said. "Just what *are* you doing here?"

"We had to follow ye, Doc." This from nine-year-old Artie. "We seen the two of ye leavin' in the dark o' night, and what with the two o' ye bein' ladies and not quite right in the 'ead, we knowed we had to watch out for ye."

"Hush, Artie!" Rob said.

At the same time, Nancy blurted, "What do you mean, not quite right in the head?"

"Well, ye don't 'ave a proper fear of things," little Artie said. "Not the dark, nor even strangers. I seen ye both goin' out in the night before, and I seen ye both welcome strangers into the 'ouse."

"Hush, Artie!" Rob said again.

Nancy spoke with a scolding tone. "They're not strangers, Artie, they're patients. And what kind of protection will the two of you be, anyway? One of you no more than a babe and the other scrawny as a scarecrow. And how did you get Zack out of a locked house?"

"Never mind," Alexandra said. "This was a dreadful idea anyway, to sneak around like common criminals. We must all go home. I don't know what possessed me to try this in the first place. Come along, all of you. We'll all have a cup of tea to warm our bones back at the house." She'd taken only a few steps before she realized that Zack was the only one who was following her. "Come along," she said again.

No one moved, and there was a lengthy silence until Rob spoke. "Ye was havin' trouble with the lock, was ye?"

"What?"

" 'Twas dark, but we could tell ye was at the door tryin' to get in, but ye don't know how."

"Oh my lord, Rob!" Alexandra was suddenly choked with guilt. "You mustn't think that I . . . Well, what I mean is, the example I've set is not—"

"We could show you how to get in," Rob said, interrupting before she could sputter more.

"Absolutely not!"

"It ain't no trouble, and ye don't 'ave to worry, we won't say a word."

"No! I most certainly won't—"

Before she could say more, she was interrupted by little Artie's voice as he emerged from the back door carrying a candle. He held the door open as an invitation. "Ye can come in now. I jimmied the front lock fer ye. But ye best be quiet less ye wakes 'im."

Nancy stepped forward and spoke with her scolding voice again. "You come out of there, Artie! Right away!"

"Shhh!" Artie cautioned. "Ye'll wake up that man what's sleepin' in here. And they's an awful stink."

"The man's not sleeping." Nancy sounded annoyed. "He's a corpse."

"Ye mean 'e's dead?" Artie glanced nervously over his shoulder.

"He's dead all right," Nancy said.

Artie let go of the door and scrambled out, hurrying to Rob's side.

Nancy gave him a scoffing laugh. "Now, why are you afraid of a dead man?"

"Why ain't you scared?" Artie asked. "Like I said, ye ain't right in the 'ead."

While Artie tried to deny his fear to Nancy, Alexandra took a cautious step into the building. "Where did you find the candle, Artie?" she called over her shoulder.

"I . . . I always 'ave it in me pocket, along with a match. Just like Rob taught me." He still sounded frightened.

"Hand it to me."

Artie complied, but reluctantly, as if it were his only defense against the evil around him. He backed away from Alexandra and the doorway as quickly as possible.

"Now go home, both of you, and take Zack with you."

Neither of the boys hesitated to obey her. Only Zack had

to be told twice, in Alexandra's harshest voice, to follow them.

Alexandra held the light in front of her as she walked into the back room, aware that Nancy was following. What she was doing was illegal, criminal even, but her curiosity demanded that she at least have a look at the body. The room was a narrow space, a shallow, dark cavern. There were a few shelves holding wrapping sheets and shrouds. In the center of the room was a crude wooden table that held the body of Admiral George Orkwright. A sheet had been draped across his body in a careless manner, leaving most of the face uncovered. Had the face been completely covered, young Artie might not have mistaken him for a sleeping man.

Several oil lamps were set about the room. As soon as Alexandra had closed the shutters and drawn the curtain on the room's one window, she used the candle to light each of the lamps. She handed one of them to Nancy. Neither of them spoke. When she lifted the sheet from the body, she saw that the face had deteriorated slightly, but somehow it now had a more peaceful appearance. The mouth was closed, and all traces of seaweed were gone. When she pried the mouth open, she saw that the seaweed had been removed from the inside as well.

She took a length of linen from her bag and wrapped it around her nose and mouth to alleviate some of the smell. Nancy did the same. Then Alexandra gave a signal to Nancy to hold the light closer while she examined the entire body, starting with the top of the head. There were no visible wounds, no sign of a blow to the skull or lacerations about the neck or the face. As she continued down to the shoulders, she noted an abrasion where the arm joined the torso, and when she lifted the heavy arm, she saw that the abrasion extended all the way under the armpit and around to the back. When she checked the other side, she saw the same abrasive pattern as if something, a rope perhaps, had been placed under each arm and pulled tight.

She glanced at Nancy, who met her gaze and frowned—a silent exchange that meant neither of them quite knew what to make of it.

Alexandra continued her perusal of the body all the way

down to the feet, finding nothing unusual. When she turned the body, Nancy had to put the lamp aside to help her, and even then it was a near impossible task, requiring all of the strength of each.

A careful examination of the back of the body revealed nothing except for the abrasion where the arm joined the torso and the pooling of the blood because the body was lying on its back.

"A rope burn?" she whispered to Nancy.

"That's my assumption," Nancy whispered. She opened Alexandra's medical bag and handed her a scalpel. "Are you going to need this?"

Alexandra didn't answer immediately, but she was about to grasp the scalpel when she saw the white rag lying in a discarded heap on the floor.

"Just a moment, Nancy." She spoke over her shoulder as she moved toward the rag. She picked it up and recognized it as the ladies' drawers the admiral had worn when she discovered him. In the bright light of the lamps, she saw dark stains on the garment that she had not noticed before. Was it dried blood? Perhaps, but there was a stickiness to the stains that puzzled her. There were a few blotchy stains on each leg of the drawers. If it was blood, then it was odd that there were no corresponding wounds on the admiral's body. She tore a strip of the fabric off and placed it in her bag to be examined later.

"Yes, Nancy," she said. "I shall need the scalpel." When Nancy handed it to her, she made a bloodless incision across the chest from shoulder to shoulder, crossing down to form a shallow V. Then, from the tip of the sternum she made another incision, which extended down the length of the abdomen to the pubis. There was virtually no blood since most of it had pooled in his back.

She had just cut through ribs and cartilage to expose the heart and lungs when a voice made her turn suddenly toward the door.

"Who's there?" the voice said. "What are you doing in here?"

5

Nicholas picked up his glass and moved to a table. He sat alone, trying to sort through what he had just learned. His client, John Killborn, who had escaped from prison, was here in Newton. Killborn's stepfather, whom the boy hated, was dead, and the gossip was that Killborn could have killed him.

Disturbing as all of that was, the most distressing thing was that Constable Snow had been so evasive. He must have known that Killborn didn't get on with his stepfather, yet he hadn't mentioned it. And wouldn't he have heard the gossip that Killborn killed the admiral?

"Come, now, sir, it can't be as bad as all that, can it?" Nicholas looked up to see that it was another barmaid who had interrupted his thoughts. She was younger and prettier than the bartender's wife who'd served him before. Her hair, pale honey reflecting light, fell to her shoulders in a careless manner, and she was fetchingly plump with generous mounds of breasts stretching the thin fabric of her dress. A smile lit her eyes and illuminated the rosy hue of her cheeks.

"I beg your pardon?" The smile was contagious. He felt one twitching at his mouth in spite of himself.

"Can I pour you another glass of lager, sir? Perhaps 'twould wash away that worried frown."

"Another glass? Yes, of course." He shoved the empty glass toward her, and she refilled it with the pitcher she'd balanced on her shapely hip.

"I heard you talking of the admiral and his stepson to Sally. Is that what's got you worried?" She kept her eyes on the amber liquid rising in the glass like mercury in a thermometer.

"I say, rather impolite, isn't it? Eavesdropping on conversations?" He was having trouble maintaining the scolding tone he knew he should with this cheeky lass. Not only had she been eavesdropping, but her manner was a bit too familiar with a person of his class.

She shrugged and giggled. "Couldn't help it, I guess." She balanced the pitcher on her hip again and looked at him.

Nicholas took a sip of the lager and set the glass on the table, looking up at her. "Did you know the admiral and his stepson?" he asked, deciding he may as well take advantage of her impertinence.

She shrugged. "Never knowed 'em well, if that's what you mean."

There was a loud guffaw from the table next to them. "Guess none of us knowed the old sea dog, did we? Considerin' 'is choice o' nappies." The speaker was a young man with a sparse, unkempt beard. His two companions at the table with him laughed and winked at each other.

The barmaid giggled again and gave them a dismissive wave of her hand as she walked away.

Newton-Upon-Sea was apparently full of eavesdroppers, Nicholas thought. He watched the barmaid's well-rounded bottom rippling under her skirt as she moved away from him. Before she disappeared completely, he called her back. "Leave the pitcher on the table, please."

She turned around and set the pitcher in front of him, then walked away once more with a knowing glance at the three men.

Nicholas glanced at them as well. Their remark about the admiral had piqued his curiosity. "Join me?" he asked, gesturing toward the pitcher.

The three looked at each other. The one with the scraggly beard nodded. "Sure, why not?" He pushed his chair back and picked up his glass. The other two picked up their drinks and followed him to Nicholas' table.

"My name is Forsythe. Nicholas Forsythe." Nicholas offered his hand to each. The scraggly bearded one shook it first and gave his name as Billy Chapman. The other two were Kevin Wingate and Sean Faron.

"So you know the admiral, do you? Orkwright, isn't it?" Nicholas filled the glasses of each of them.

"Admiral Orkwright? We seen 'im about is all. Down at the piers." Billy was apparently the most talkative. The other two merely nodded their heads in agreement, took a swallow of lager, and wiped their mouths with the backs of their hands. "Used to hang about down there," Billy continued. "Liked the ships, 'e did, but 'e was a snobbish bugger when it come to oyster rigs. We's all oyster men." Billy made a circular motion with his hand to include all three of them. "Called our rigs seagoin' trash, 'e did."

"Looks like 'e wasn't so high and mighty as 'e acted, though," the one called Kevin said with a laugh. That caused Sean to spew his lager out his mouth along with his laughter.

Nicholas glanced from one to the other. "He amused you?"

"Old bugger wasn't a bit amusin' when he was alive. But 'e made a laughin'stock o' hisself when 'e died," Billy said. He once again winked at the other two, which prompted even more laughter. Billy helped himself to more lager from the pitcher and glanced at Nicholas. "Old sea dog got hisself drowned wearin' a pair o' ladies' knickers."

Nicholas stopped his glass midway to his lips and set it down. "I beg your pardon?"

"Ladies' drawers. 'E was wearin' 'em when he died." It was Kevin who answered this time.

Nicholas was thoroughly shocked. "My word! But why?"

"Ah, even them like you what calls yerselves gentlemen knows the ways o' some men, I wager," Billy said. "They's them that's perverted toward wearin' a woman's duds and lettin' other men bugger 'em. Ye 'eard o' that, ain't ye?"

"Yes, of course." Nicholas sounded and felt shaken. "But . . . the admiral? Was he always . . . well, like that?"

Billy shrugged. "I ain't fer knowin' that, since I ain't one o' that sort meself. All I knows is that's what they found 'im in, them ladies' drawers."

Nicholas was still trying to sort it out. "Who found him?"

Billy took a swallow and wiped his mouth with his sleeve.

"The butcher's wife and Dr. Gladstone. She's a woman, if ye can believe it."

Nicholas almost strangled on his lager. "Good lord!"

Billy shook his head. "I knows what yer sayin'. A woman doctor and an admiral in Her Majesty's Navy wearin' knickers! These is awful times!"

Nicholas managed to collect himself to ask one more question. "He has a stepson, I understand. Do you know him?"

"Stepson?" Billy frowned. "Oh yes, I remembers. The little bastard was always gettin' hisself in trouble. Finally runned off to London, didn't he?" He looked to the other two for confirmation and got a nod from each.

Sean leaned back in his chair, taking on an air of importance. "I seen 'im 'tother day back here in Newton."

"Naw!" Billy said.

Sean nodded. "I seen 'im, Kinda sneakin' around, 'e was. Like 'e was up to no good."

"When?" Nicholas asked. "When did you see him?"

Sean frowned and seemed to think for a moment. "Come to think of it, 'twas just before the admiral died."

Nicholas poured himself another glass of lager and tried to appear casual. "The barmaid mentioned that he didn't get along with his stepfather."

"Did she now?" Billy sounded sarcastic. "Maddie tell ye that? She's a gossipin' whore."

They all laughed and turned the conversation to Maddie's whoring. When Nicholas saw that he was not going to gain any more information about his client, he pushed away from the table and tossed a crown and a few shillings on it.

"Help yourselves to another pitcher," he said as he walked away. He headed for the front door, thinking a walk in the cold air would help him make sense of things. He stepped out into an arabesque of shadows lying across the streets and stretching up the sides of buildings. The scene made him hesitate for the slightest part of a second. He was surprised to find himself reluctant to step into the web at first. But his other choice was to return to his small, badly furnished room upstairs in the inn.

With his cloak pulled tightly around him and his cane under his arm, he set out down Griffon Street, wondering where John Killborn was, wondering if he was lurking in the shadows or hiding behind the walls of one of the old buildings. He thought about Alexandra Gladstone. She would be home now, having finished her house calls as well as her surgery hours. Perhaps she was just sitting down to supper and cutting into a mutton chop. Or perhaps she had finished dinner and was now sitting beside the fire knitting. No, not knitting, reading. Some grisly medical text, perhaps.

Thoughts of her gave him purpose, and he turned off Griffon Street toward the edge of town where her house and surgery stood. He hoped it wasn't too late to call on her, hoped, too, that she wouldn't have forgotten who he was in these past several months.

He was only a few steps off Griffon when a movement in the alley caught his attention. There were three figures running from the back of a darkened building and disappearing into the shadow web. One of them appeared to be an enormous beast, a cow, perhaps. Or a bear. At least he hoped it was one or the other and not some form of demon, which was his first inclination.

"Who goes there?" His words made hollow sounds bouncing against the darkness. After a moment, he stepped cautiously into the ally. A light flickered and went out in the back of the building the figures had fled. In another second he saw a dimmer light, as if a curtain had been pulled before the lamp was lit, and he heard a murmur of voices.

He moved toward the building, then hesitated. Did he dare go further? Did he dare try to enter the building? Curiosity made him bold, and he walked to the door and placed a cautious hand on the knob. The door was not locked. He opened it slowly, cautiously, then took a hesitant step inside. He could make out three figures. One lying prone on a table and two more—females, it appeared—who were obviously performing some unholy deed on the prone figure. There was the stench of death in the room.

"Who's there?" he called. "What are you doing in here?"

There was a sudden intake of breath from both women, and a knife clattered to the floor.

Nicholas stopped his advance toward them when, in

spite of the mask she wore on her face, he recognized the woman. "Dr. Gladstone?"

"Oh my God! It's you!" a female voice said.

Nicholas wasn't certain which of the two had spoken, but he resumed walking toward them again, his eyes on Alexandra.

"Mr. Forsythe?" Dr. Gladstone's voice trembled slightly.

"Dr. Gladstone! I must say I'm surprised . . ." His voice trailed off when he saw the exposed entrails of the man lying on the table at the same time the stench almost overcame him. "Good God! I . . . I'm afraid I've come at an awkward time."

"Close the door, Nancy, and make sure it's locked this time." Dr. Gladstone's voice was no longer trembling. She turned to Nicholas with fire in her eyes and ice in her voice. "What are *you* doing here?"

Nicholas, with his hand over his mouth and nose, was working hard at trying to avert his eyes from the grotesque sight on the table. "I saw something in the alley. Two figures running away from something, so I came to investigate." The beast, he told himself with a measure of relief, must have been the doctor's Newfoundland, whose acquaintance he had reluctantly made on his last visit.

"Artie and Rob," Nancy said. "They ran out of here with Zack."

Ah yes, Zack. That was the name of the beast. And Nancy was the doctor's cheeky servant.

Dr. Gladstone spoke to him again, still with her hard, cold voice. "You're right, Mr. Forsythe. You *have* come at an awkward time. I was just performing an autopsy."

He was toying with the idea of asking her to call him Nicholas and wondering if that would be too forward when she said the word *autopsy*; and he found that his breath had left him for a moment.

"Are you all right, Mr. Forsythe?" Some of the coldness was gone from Dr. Gladstone's voice.

"Yes! Yes, of course. Why shouldn't I be?" He was trying desperately to keep down the lager he had just drunk.

"Perhaps you would like to sit down. Nancy, see if you can find a chair for Mr.—"

"No, no, that won't be necessary." He tried to sound convincing. "I'll just . . ." He allowed himself to look at the eviscerated man on the table, then swallowed hard. "I'll just . . . watch."

Dr. Gladstone continued to give him her cold stare for just a moment, then her look softened. "I'm sorry, Mr. Forsythe. I'm afraid you've unnerved me. You see, I'm performing this autopsy without—"

"Without enough light!" Nancy's interruption was quick and forceful. Nicholas glanced at her, wondering what lie Nancy was encouraging. "You see, this is the only time we had for the autopsy, and Dr. Gladstone is always so very careful, don't you know, that she becomes . . . well, edgy. Especially about interruptions, because the task is so exacting and . . ."

Nancy nattered on in her nervous manner, making it even more obvious that there was something unusual, and most likely improper, about what the two of them were doing. Nicholas had stopped listening to her, however, and was watching Dr. Gladstone's eyes. There was, he was almost certain, a small measure of fear there.

"Please," he said, "don't let me interfere with your work."

There was a nervous laugh from Nancy. "Well, it's for sure, the admiral won't mind whether or not there's an interruption."

"Admiral? Did you say admiral? Not, by any chance, Admiral George Orkwright?" He spoke through the fingers of his hand he still held over his nose and mouth.

Nancy clapped a hand over her masked mouth and slid a guilty glance toward Dr. Gladstone, who for the flicker of an instant appeared even more troubled.

"You were acquainted with the admiral?" Dr. Gladstone spoke with an amazing nonchalance, which made Nicholas admire her composure and self-control.

"No, only with his stepson, John Killborn."

"I see." Dr. Gladstone had gone back to her work and was now slicing into the heart. It was then that he noticed the other organs on a nearby table. They appeared to be the lungs, esophagus, and trachea. Beside her on a tray were samples of each organ, which appeared to have been carefully labeled. In time, Dr. Gladstone placed a sample of the heart on the tray, and Nancy labeled it in her fine script. When Dr. Gladstone had aspirated fluid from the lungs and placed the vial containing the fluid on the tray, she looked at the lungs, carefully examining the external surface before she sliced them and finally took a sample for the tray.

By now Nicholas was completely absorbed with the work Dr. Gladstone was doing. He forgot his nausea until she lifted a stomach, pancreas, and intestines from the open cavity. It was then he had to turn away and eventually step outside to rid himself of the contents of his stomach and to gulp in lungs full of cold, moist air. He stayed a long time, crouching on his haunches in the darkness until the muscles in his upper legs ached and he had to slouch into a sitting position with his back against the cold wooden slab of the building. He didn't know how long he stayed that way, didn't care. It was only when his face, his hands, his entire body grew numb from the cold and he realized he was shivering violently that he stood. Making a fruitless attempt to brush the damp earth from the seat of his trousers, he reentered the building.

The admiral's face was covered with an odd-looking cloth, and there now seemed to be organs everywhere on the table next to the body. Nancy was busy stuffing them back into the cavity. The expression in her eyes was as bland as it might have been had she been stuffing a Christmas goose.

Dr. Gladstone, in the meantime, was slicing off yet another sample from something. As he moved closer, he realized that what he thought was a cloth covering the admiral's face was actually his scalp. It had been pulled down over the front of his face and part of the skull had been cut away. It was only then that Nicholas realized Dr. Gladstone was slicing at the admiral's brain. He felt himself becoming sick again and hurried outside. He gulped the cold air again until he felt better, then walked into the dim light of the window to check his timepiece and noted that it was half past three. The doctor and her assistant were undoubtedly tired. He had seen it in the dull glint of their eyes, in the heavy movements of their limbs.

Nicholas stepped back inside, wanting to watch more of

the procedure, but he knew that if he did he would surely embarrass himself. There was naught to do but slump into a chair, as far away from the table as possible. And wait.

He had no idea he had slept until something startled him awake. Nancy was standing over him. It had to have been her steady gaze that had awakened him. He sat up straighter and moved his head in quick, nervous jerks, trying to get his bearings. He noticed the corpse, now covered with a sheet and, he assumed, stuffed and sewn together. Presumably he was dressed as well, since he could see a bit of a boot showing at the bottom of the sheet.

Dr. Gladstone stood apart from the table with its sheet-covered mound. She was holding something, a piece of white linen it seemed, and she was studying it intently. In the meantime, he became vaguely aware that Nancy was speaking to him.

"I say, sir, are you all right?"

"Yes, of course." He wished they would stop asking him that question so he could stop lying to them.

"It's been a long night," Dr. Gladstone said, walking toward him. She no longer held the white linen. It had been carefully folded and placed on a shelf. "I think it best we all go home."

Nicholas, now wide-awake, stood. "I'll see you to your house."

"That won't be necessary," Dr. Gladstone said, but there was an uneasiness in her eyes that belied her words.

"We'll be quite all right," Nancy said. She had already gathered all of the supplies and now she handed Dr. Gladstone her cloak. "It's only a short distance." With a protective arm around Dr. Gladstone's shoulders, she urged her toward the door.

They were almost outside when Dr. Gladstone turned around to face him. "On second thought, perhaps it would be a good idea for you to come along. There's something I must discuss with you."

He didn't miss the disapproving scowl Nancy gave her mistress.

He gave Dr. Gladstone his arm for the long walk through the darkness to her house. Nancy stayed close by on her other side the entire distance. Once they were in the house and coals were added to the fire and the enormous dog had completed his unnerving examination of Nicholas and settled himself by the fire, Dr. Gladstone sent Nancy off to the kitchen for tea. Nancy was more than a little reluctant to leave, and it was clear she was nervous about leaving the doctor alone with him. What was it she was afraid her mistress would reveal?

Dr. Gladstone spoke as soon as Nancy was out of sight. "Mr. Forsythe, there is something you must know about what I was doing tonight." Her voice was breathless, and her tone urgent.

"Of course," Nicholas said, trying not to appear too eager.

There was a long pause until, finally, Dr. Gladstone said, "You must not speak of what you saw tonight. Not to anyone."

She had his full attention now. "Indeed?"

"Yes. Please promise me you won't say anything."

"I'm afraid I don't understand."

Neither of them spoke for a moment, but Nicholas watched Dr. Gladstone's face carefully. There was more than weariness there now. She was clearly uneasy about something.

"Or perhaps I do understand," he said, finally. "You were doing something illegal."

The startled widening of her eyes told him he had hit upon the truth. Still, she denied it.

"Illegal?" She laughed a nervous, insincere laugh. "I should say that's a bit overstated."

Nicholas said nothing, a ploy he had learned from his father as a child, and one he had perfected as a barrister. When one is confronted with silence, one feels a need to fill that silence. Especially when one is guilty.

It didn't work. Dr. Gladstone shifted her gaze from his face toward the exit to the kitchen. "What's taking Nancy so long with that tea?"

Nicholas put a hand on her arm. "Dr. Gladstone, you said there is something I should know, and it seems to be troubling you. What is it?"

There was that hint of fear in her face again. "I . . . I

merely wanted to request that you not speak of this. A graphic description would be upsetting to the admiral's wife, and—"

"Dr. Gladstone! For God's sake, you must stop this equivocating and tell me what is wrong! Are you in some sort of trouble?" The hour was late, he was tired, and he had lost patience.

He had gotten her attention, and she leveled her gaze on him. "Yes," she said softly. "I'm afraid there is that possibility."

"What have you done?"

"I have performed an autopsy without permission. I did not have legal access to the body." Her voice was remarkably even, with no hint of fear this time.

For the first time he felt a measure of alarm. "You've become a body snatcher?"

"The very words Nancy used."

"Good lord! I'm afraid you are in rather a lot of trouble. Why on earth—"

"I believe there is something suspicious about the admiral's death."

"Other than what he was wearing when he died?"

Dr. Gladstone raised an eyebrow. "You know about that?"

"There's gossip at the pub."

Dr. Gladstone dropped her head into her hands. "Oh lord, just as I feared."

"What's going on, Dr. Gladstone? Start from the beginning." Nicholas spoke in his best barrister's voice, a combination of persuasiveness and command.

Dr. Gladstone told him the entire story, up to the point where she startled her by coming into the building. "You see, don't you? Why I felt I had to try to find out how he died?"

"Of course you would want to know," Nicholas said. "But why was an autopsy so important when you freely admit it is impossible to tell when a person drowns because fluid in the lungs could be caused by . . . what was it?

"Congestive heart failure. Dropsy, as it's sometimes called. It occurs when the heart is not strong enough to pump natural body fluids from the lungs."

"Was there fluid in the lungs?"

Dr. Gladstone shook her head. "Not an unusual amount. And there was no water in the stomach."

"Then he didn't drown," Nicholas said.

There was a troubled look on Dr. Gladstone's face. "I can't be sure of that. He could have died as a result of spasms of the larynx caused by water in the throat. That's a form of drowning. But there would be nothing physiological to show that in any autopsy."

"And for some reason you don't believe he drowned."

"I didn't say that." Dr. Gladstone's tone was more thoughtful than defensive.

"But you don't agree with Snow's theory about being so drunk he donned his wife's drawers and fell into the sea."

"It's ludicrous. Of course I don't believe it."

Nancy brought in the tea and poured a cup for each of them, but she didn't leave. Instead, she lingered by the doorway, eavesdropping, which didn't seem to bother Dr. Gladstone at all. Nicholas, however, was decidedly uncomfortable. The beast, lying in front of the fireplace, did nothing to calm him. He hadn't taken his suspicious eyes off of Nicholas since he arrived.

Nicholas shifted in his chair, then spoke in a voice that was so quiet it was almost a whisper. "It makes Snow look rather suspicious, I dare say. Furthermore, it appears he deliberately kept information from me related to this matter."

Dr. Gladstone's eyes widened. Nancy took a few steps closer to him. The beast rose from his reclining position and growled low in his throat, still not taking his eyes off Nicholas.

Nicholas rearranged himself in the chair again, nervously. "I'm defending the admiral's stepson in a criminal matter. The stepson escaped from Newgate, and it appears he may have come here. There've been reports of several citizens seeing him, yet the constable didn't mention that to me. Neither did he mention that the stepson apparently hated his stepfather. Possibly enough to kill him."

"John Killborn, you say? Here?" It was the impertinent maid who asked the question. Once again Dr. Gladstone didn't seem to notice her impertinence. The two of them exchanged a look that led Nicholas to believe they were keeping something from him.

6

"You heard what he said! He said you're in rather a lot of trouble." Nancy was emphatic as she gathered up the tea dishes. She had just seen Nicholas to the door.

Alexandra sighed and placed her own cup and saucer on the tray. "Yes, I heard, but I didn't think you did. Just how long were you eavesdropping?" Alexandra was surprised at how happy she had been to see Nicholas and how pleasant it was, in spite of the circumstances, to have him, at least for a few minutes, entirely to herself.

Nancy ignored the question. "I'm in this with you, you know. If you're in trouble, then I am as well. But I want you to understand, miss, that I'll stand beside you. All the way to the scaffold, if it comes to that."

"The scaffold? Good lord, Nancy."

"Surely you've thought of that. You knew you were breaking the law."

Alexandra suddenly felt overwhelmed. "I've obviously done a foolish thing, and I'm sorry I got you into this."

Nancy set the tray down, and her hands went to her hips in a decisive manner. "Now, don't be saying that. You needed me in this matter, foolish or not. And, by the way, it isn't foolish to do one's duty, now, is it? And isn't it your duty to examine a body, especially when the widow requests it? And especially when things look suspicious."

"I don't know, Nancy. I just don't know. This is all so

irregular. Everything from the way Constable Snow is acting to . . ."

"What do you make of that?" Nancy said. "Constable Snow not doing his duties properly, I mean?"

Alexandra picked up the tray for Nancy. "I don't suppose he actually has any obligation to tell Mr. Forsythe about the relationship between the late admiral and his stepson. Especially since Mr. Forsythe will be barrister for the defense of the stepson, yet . . ."

"Yet it doesn't seem right, does it?" Nancy reached for the tray and took it from Alexandra.

"Perhaps he's as distressed about the whole business as the rest of us." Alexandra's remark was without conviction. Forbidding her to examine the body was shocking.

"Distressed you say?" Nancy gave her an indignant "humph," before she turned away to take the tray to the kitchen. She stopped and looked over her shoulder when she saw Alexandra leaving the parlor as well. "You're not off to the surgery at this hour, are you?" Her tone was slightly scolding.

"I must look at those samples as soon as possible," Alexandra said.

Nancy gave her a displeased look, then turned off to the kitchen grumbling. Alexandra was not surprised, however, when, within a short time, she joined her in the surgery. She knew Nancy's curiosity would not allow her to stay away.

There was very little in what Alexandra found that would satisfy curiosity, however. She had been looking for some sign of poisoning or trauma, or perhaps disease. All of the samples she examined under her microscope appeared to be normal.

"Perhaps you can have another look after you've slept," Nancy said. "It's several hours past midnight, and we miss things when we're tired, you know." She was carefully placing each sample into jars of formaldehyde.

"Perhaps," Alexandra said, again without conviction. She was too stimulated to feel tired, and she was certain she would see nothing different at a later examination. "It's all so puzzling." She picked up the piece of stained linen she'd torn from the undergarment the admiral had been wearing.

"Wait!" she said when she saw that Nancy was about to cover the microscope with the cloth she kept over it to protect it from dust. "I want to examine this bit of cloth before I retire."

Nancy stepped back, and Alexandra slid the cloth into position, then looked into the eyepiece. "It's not blood, that's certainly clear." She spoke without looking up.

"Not blood? Of course it's not blood. I could have told you that. It's pitch."

This time Alexandra glanced up at her. "It's what?"

"Pitch. You know, the rather gooey substance that comes from trees."

"Of course." Alexandra realized Nancy was right, but she felt even more puzzled.

"It doesn't wash out of clothing well, I'll tell you that. My own mum, may she rest in peace, used to complain all the time when the two of us would come home with it on our frocks, and it was left to her to try to wash it out."

"Yes, I remember." Alexandra stood, paced a few steps. "There were no trees along the coast where the body was found."

Nancy brightened. "So does that mean he was killed somewhere else and dumped there?"

"Either that, or he encountered trees somewhere before he got there," Alexandra said.

"Perhaps," Nancy agreed, "There is a little wooded area near Gull House."

"Or the pitch could have already been there on the garment when he put it on," Alexandra said.

Nancy frowned and shook her head. "And how could that be? That pitch was rather fresh, I'll tell you that, so the only way it could have already been there is if Mrs. Orkwright had been . . ." Nancy suddenly clamped her hand over her mouth.

Alexandra gave her a hard look. "Go on."

Nancy shook her head. "That couldn't be. Mrs. Orkwright? Frolicking in the woods in her knickers?"

"Then she discarded them, and her husband found them," Alexandra said, finishing the forbidden thought for her.

Nancy was still aghast. "Are you saying he could have

learned she had a lover, then he did something foolish, such as put on the knickers to humiliate her, and she killed him? To keep from having him publicly embarrass her?"

"You've got quite an imagination, Nancy." Alexandra sank into her chair.

"Only it doesn't make sense, does it? It's all terribly out of character for Mrs. Orkwright. She doesn't strike me as the type who would want to risk her young son learning she was having an affair, even if she would do it in the first place. Which she would not."

"We can't be sure of that, Nancy. Unlikely as it seems, we simply can't be sure."

"But if that's true, how did she do it? Kill him, I mean?" Nancy's tone was almost pleading.

Alexandra shook her head. "I don't know. I just can't be certain how he died."

"Are you forgetting that it could be that no-count son of hers? John Killborn, I mean? The one who escaped from Newgate as Mr. Forsythe said?"

"No, I'm not forgetting." Alexandra rubbed her temples as if she could somehow massage an answer to the surface. "It's just that I don't know how the admiral died. We've assumed he drowned simply because we've eliminated virtually every other cause. We've come up with some wild speculation about a motive for Mrs. Orkwright, but there's nothing to substantiate it. Neither is there anything to suggest that John Killborn could have murdered him."

"Except that they didn't get on well."

Alexandra waved her hand in dismissal.

"Then perhaps no one killed him." Nancy's voice sounded very tired. "Perhaps he simply fell into the sea and drowned, as the constable said."

"Perhaps." Alexandra sounded tired. "If that's true, then I have broken the law and put us both in danger of arrest for nothing."

"Except . . . ?"

Alexandra raised her head to look at Nancy. "Except I still don't believe he drowned himself. And there is the oddity of the ladies' drawers."

"There is that," Nancy said. "So . . ."

"So I think I shall have to speak with Jane Orkwright again."

The sky was very bright when Alexandra awakened the next morning. She might not have awakened even then, had it not been for Zack nudging her and licking her face. She opened her eyes to see his black nose and equally black eyes very close to her. The sound he made was a squeaky growl, full of vowel sounds, as if he were trying to tell her in human words that he was hungry.

She glanced at the clock she kept on the mantel in her bedroom and saw that it was almost noon. Flinging the covers back, she sat up quickly. The house was unusually cold. Nancy must not have the fires going yet. She stood, reached for her robe, and hurried down the hall to Nancy's room. She knocked softly, but there was no answer, and when she carefully pushed the door open, she saw that Nancy was still sleeping soundly, lying on her back and snoring softly.

She waited there a moment, not wanting to wake her, yet needing to. Once again she had done a poor job of managing her time, so that now there was not enough time to make the usual morning rounds to see housebound patients before walk-in patients began arriving at the surgery door. There was barely enough time for breakfast and to get dressed.

Zack saved her the trouble of making a decision about waking Nancy with one loud, sharp bark. He was never one to equivocate. Nancy awoke with a startled look on her face, then sprang up to a sitting position like a stiff-bodied puppet pulled by ropes.

"Good lord!" she said. "What time is it?"

"Half past eleven."

There was a flurry of covers and Nancy moving about, her honey-colored hair flying about like wild grass in a storm. She brushed a strand away from her face and reached for her robe. "Why didn't you wake me?" Her voice was hoarse from sleep.

"I just awoke myself. If Zack hadn't—"

"I'll get the kettle on for porridge and tea." Nancy waved

a hand at Alexandra. "Hurry! Get dressed, miss."

Alexandra was used to obeying Nancy, who, since their childhood, had been more companion than servant. She rushed back to her room and hurried through her morning toilet, then went down to breakfast. She was only half finished with her bowl of porridge and Nancy was still scurrying about in her unbuttoned robe and ungoverned hair when the first patient arrived.

Alexandra touched a napkin to her mouth and hurried away to receive him, a task that Nancy usually considered her own. Zack, sensing the urgency, hurried along with her to offer what help he could.

The patient was a child with a quinsied throat. She gave him the same treatment she had given the miller's daughter by bathing the throat externally with a compound tincture of camphor. Then she prescribed a mixture of hops, wormwood, and mullein leaves to be boiled in a teapot with water and vinegar so the boy could inhale the vapors.

Alexandra was thankful that patients were few that day, but when a young mother came in and exhibited another case of quinsy, she began to fear an epidemic.

When it was four o'clock, and it had been an hour since she had seen the last patient, Alexandra decided to leave her surgery and to further delay her daily rounds for another errand. She left a few minutes after four, giving Nancy instructions to fetch her at Gull House, should she be needed.

*The housekeeper at Gull House opened the door for Alex-*andra, her face even more tight and grim than usual, as if her features had bunched up, bivouacking against something dreadful.

"Oh, it's you," she said and glanced over her shoulder, as if expecting her mistress to once again overrule her instinct to deny Alexandra's entrance.

"Please tell Mrs. Orkwright Dr. Gladstone is calling," Alexandra said in her firmest voice.

There was a moment of silence in which the housekeeper's features huddled even closer. "Wait here," she said, motioning for Alexandra to step inside. She disappeared briefly.

When she returned she informed Alexandra in a funereal voice that Mrs. Orkwright would receive her in the parlor.

When the housekeeper had shown her to the parlor and had even designated the chair in which she was to be seated, she left, leaving a measure of her gloom in her wake. Alexandra rose from her chair and went to the window, trying to allay the dismal mood as she watched the mottled sea stretching its stubby white fingers to eternity. Even that left her clammy with a sense of despair. She didn't turn away, though, until a small "hello" startled her.

She turned around quickly to see young Will standing behind her. "Hello, Will." She smiled at him, struck by his resemblance to his father. He had the same fair hair and stocky build of the admiral. His wide lapis lazuli eyes were his mother's, though.

"Are you here to see Mama, Dr. Gladstone? Is she ill?" His voice was young and frightened.

"No, I don't believe she's ill." Alexandra moved toward a chair and sat in it, bringing her eyes to a more even level with the boy's. "I've come to have a chat with her, that's all."

Will's wide eyes had never left her. "Is it about Papa?" he asked.

"Yes." Alexandra spoke softly, wondering at the confusion and grief the child must be feeling.

He sat on a chair next to her, his short legs stretched straight in front of him. "Annie says he's gone on a very long journey and won't be back until I'm all grown up."

"Annie? The housekeeper?"

He nodded. "But that's a fib, you know. My papa's dead."

Alexandra felt a moment of uneasiness. "Who told you that?"

Will gave her an incredulous look. "Why, Mama, of course. Mama would never fib to me."

"Of course not."

Will had now turned his attention to the toes of his shiny black shoes, which he was rhythmically bumping together. Alexandra hoped that his little boy thoughts had moved on to something more mundane. He glanced up at her, his expression grave. He had stopped flopping his toes together. "I must ask you something," he said, still looking at his shoes. Then, glancing up at her, said, "I'm afraid to ask Mama, and Annie wouldn't tell me the truth."

"Will, I'm not sure I should—"

"It's an easy question. You need only answer yes or no." He leaned closer to her. "Will I be sent to burn in hell when I die because I'm glad Papa is dead?"

A sudden flood of something—dread? surprise?—threatened Alexandra's breathing. And she was just as quickly distracted by the soft voice of Jane Orkwright.

"Will, I hope you're not annoying Dr. Gladstone." She walked toward them, bringing with her the scent and lightness of lavender.

"No, Mama, I'm not." Will scooted out of his chair, his pale face colored slightly with what Alexandra took to be a combination of embarrassment and guilt. He obviously did not want his mother to know about his confession, and Alexandra felt an almost ecclesiastical need not to divulge it. At the same time, she felt a burgeoning desire to explore what was behind the boy's remark by discussing it with his mother.

Jane held her arms out to her son and bent to embrace him and receive his kiss. "Let me have a little private chat with Dr. Gladstone, Willy, and afterward we'll have a game of draughts."

"Not draughts, Mama. Hide-and-seek."

"Very well." She gave him a gentle, playful swat. "Run along now."

He scurried out of the room, running directly into the taciturn housekeeper, who swept him up in her arms and carried him away.

As soon as he was out of sight, Jane sat down and spoke to Alexandra, a grave expression stealing the light Will had inspired from her eyes. "Why wasn't I told about Mary Prodder?"

The remark caught Alexandra off guard. "I suppose I didn't mention it because I thought you had quite enough on your platter."

"I counted Mary among my dearest friends. I should have been told!" Her voice was uncharacteristically angry, and there were tears in her eyes. Alexandra wasn't sure how to respond. Jane turned her face away then and whispered, "I'm sorry. I'm afraid I'm not quite myself."

"Of course. Mary is in a great deal of pain, which is to be expected, but she is more concerned for you since the loss of your husband than for herself."

"So like Mary." Jane dried her eyes with a delicate lace handkerchief that materialized from somewhere in her sleeve. "I want to see her as soon as possible."

"She will welcome your visit," Alexandra said, thinking how Mary must need a reprieve from her daughter-in-law's constant complaints.

Jane looked away again. When she spoke, her expression was grave. "You have news regarding the autopsy."

"Only that it revealed nothing. Your husband was apparently in a normal state of health."

Jane frowned, puzzled. "Nothing?"

"We come to the conclusion of drowning only by eliminating every other possible cause," Alexandra said.

"But how . . ."

"How did he drown? I can't answer that, except to say that, given the circumstances, it appears he might have drowned at sea. Perhaps he was drunk, just as Constable Snow suspected."

Alexandra watched Jane's face for some reaction, waiting for her to give her theory of what happened, but Jane didn't speak. She stared straight ahead while tears glistened in her eyes.

"I'm sorry." Alexandra spoke in a hushed tone.

Jane looked at her as if she had momentarily forgotten she was there. "I sometimes think I would like to move away. To London perhaps. Where there are no memories."

"I know it must be difficult for you," Alexandra said.

The brilliant blue of Jane's eyes had darkened somewhat with her unshed tears, but there was an intensity in her gaze that startled Alexandra. "You are still suspicious that my husband's death was the result of foul play?"

"There are so many unusual circumstances."

"Yes." The answer was quiet, almost disconnected.

Alexandra was silent a moment, trying to frame the questions she had come to ask. "I must ask you some questions," she said finally. There was another pause. "Was the . . . the garment the admiral was wearing when his body was discovered, was it—recognizable to you?

Jane stared at her blankly for a moment before she spoke. "I don't know. I haven't been allowed to see my husband's body."

Alexandra tried to choke back her embarrassment. "What I'm really trying to ask is if the garment belonged to you?"

The blank look returned to Jane's face. "I . . . I'm not sure." Her voice trembled, and she seemed to force herself to look at Alexandra.

"Do you know of any reason why he might have been in the woods?"

"The woods?"

"Around trees perhaps. Or perhaps, if he was wearing your garment, you had been there. Under particular circumstances." Alexandra knew she was handling the interview badly, but it was impossible for her to inquire about Jane having a romp in the woods, either with her husband or some other man.

"I don't understand." A perplexed frown creased Jane's forehead.

"Why would there be pitch or tree sap on the garment?" Alexandra forced herself to keep her voice steady, but she was perspiring, and something was pulling at her heart, making it leap and stutter.

There was that disconnected look from Jane again, and the tension was so high the room around them seemed to be holding its breath.

Jane tried to speak. "I . . . I don't . . ." She was silent again for a moment, then she stood and went to the window, staring out at the sea. When she turned around, she had regained her composure somewhat. "What does this mean? What does it mean to have pitch on one's clothes?"

Alexandra suddenly felt utterly weary. "I don't know," she said. "I hoped you would have some insight."

"I am not capable of having insight now," Jane said, sounding equally weary. "Besides the death of my husband, my son . . ."

"Your son?" Alexandra waited breathlessly, silently willing her to go on, to give her some clue as to why young Will would be happy that his father was dead. But it was not Will who was troubling Jane now.

"I have gotten word that my son has . . ." She stopped, took a breath, and continued. "Has escaped from Newgate. I am very much afraid he will come here."

"You fear for his life?"

"He . . . he could be blamed, you know. For my husband's death. They did not get on well together. But you must understand, John is not capable of killing anyone."

Alexandra said nothing, waiting for her to say more. Pain and grief were evident on Jane's face as she continued. "Alexandra, I must tell you something. I . . . You must not . . ." She tried to take a step toward Alexandra, but she swayed unsteadily before she collapsed to the floor.

7

"What have you done to her?" The housekeeper's cry shattered the fragile veneer of her self-imposed reserve and all her anger tumbled out in those few words. She hurried to her mistress's side, literally pushing Alexandra away.

Will, who had been with her, rushed toward his mother. "Mama?" he said in a small voice. His face had gone white with fear. He tried to reach for her, but the housekeeper kept him away, holding him gently yet firmly in her arms.

"Fetch my bag, please." Alexandra spoke in a firm voice, ignoring the housekeeper's insinuation that what had happened was her fault. "You took it with my cloak. I need it immediately!"

The housekeeper's eyes flashed with anger. She turned away without a word, Will clinging tightly to her hand.

Alexandra picked up Jane's limp arm and checked her pulse. Her hand, she noticed, was clammy and cold. The pulse was weak and erratic, but she was breathing regularly. When the housekeeper unceremoniously dropped the bag on the floor next to Alexandra, she opened it and pulled out the spirits of ammonia bottle, which she opened and passed under Jane's nose several times. She also sprinkled a few drops on her neck and at her temples.

Jane moaned slightly, and the housekeeper, still holding Will's hand, hurried away. She reappeared shortly, however, and wordlessly handed Alexandra a cool, damp cloth. Alexandra took it and bathed Jane's face until her eyes fluttered and then opened, wide and disoriented.

"Mama!" Will cried again and tried to pull free of the housekeeper's hand. Jane, in turn, tried to sit up and reach for her son.

"Shhh," the housekeeper said, holding on to Will.

"Help me get her to bed," Alexandra said.

The housekeeper let go of Will's hand with a whispered admonition to be quiet, then turned aside to help her mistress. Alexandra was prepared to work with her to get Jane to her bedroom, but the strapping housekeeper picked Jane up like a child and carried her to the bed. Alexandra gave her instructions to help Jane on with a nightgown.

"I'll go to the parlor for my medical bag," Alexandra said, thinking it prudent to give Jane her privacy as she undressed. "Call me as soon as she's in bed, and I'll give you both further instructions." She left the room, knowing that it would not be wise to question Jane further at the moment, a fact that she regretted. It would have been helpful to know more about the bad blood between the admiral and his stepson as well as his relationship with Will.

For now, though, she had Jane's welfare to concern her. She was going over in her mind the medicine she would prepare when she quite literally stumbled into little Will huddled at the top of the stairs. His wide, frightened eyes stared up at her.

"Will! Forgive me. I'm afraid I wasn't watching my step." She placed a protective hand on his arm.

"Is she all right?" His voice trembled.

Alexandra knelt down to him. "Yes, she's quite all right. She just needs to rest. It's understandable that she'd be a bit overwrought as a result of . . . of what happened."

"To Papa, you mean?"

"Yes," Alexandra said, unsure about how much she should encourage him to talk about it again.

Something came up behind the boy's eyes, something that made him appear far too old and knowing than he should have been, but the fear and hurt were still there as well. "He was mean to Annie. That's why I said I'm glad he's dead." His eyes welled with tears, and he gave them a fierce wipe with the back of each hand. "But I didn't mean it. I swear, I didn't mean it."

"Of course you didn't." Alexandra started to pull him to her, but she felt his resistance and dropped her hand from his shoulder. "When someone close to us dies, it's quite natural to feel angry and confused."

"Really?" His eyes widened again. "Then perhaps I won't burn in hell for saying I'm glad he . . . he is . . ."

"I'm quite sure you won't." Alexandra gave him a smile and once again restrained herself from exploiting him by questioning him further.

"I think Annie is glad, too." Will's words startled her, as did the fear that had returned to his eyes. "I think she would have run away long ago, except she had to take care of Mama and me."

"Run away?"

"Yes, but we mustn't talk about it."

"Really? Why not?" Alexandra was straining at her self-imposed rules of propriety now.

"Because Annie said—"

"Master Will! You mustn't bother Dr. Gladstone now." Annie's harsh voice startled both Will and Alexandra as she emerged from Jane's room, her large frame dominating the hallway. Alexandra stood suddenly and turned to face Annie. Will backed away as well, placing himself on the edge of the landing. Annie reached for him and pulled him roughly toward her. "Go to your room. Go on now!" She gave him a gentle shove when she saw his reluctance. "I'll be up with milk and biscuits later." She turned to Alexandra when she was certain Will was on his way. "Mrs. Orkwright is resting now. She'll be fine." Her voice was no less harsh, and there was an odd tautness to her speech that suggested fear and, without a doubt, dismissal.

"I'm going to leave a medicine for her." Alexandra saw Will pause in front of the door to his room, trying to hear all that was said. "I'm quite certain you're correct. She will be all right." Alexandra spoke the words for the benefit of the young eavesdropper. "The medicine will aid her recovery." She moved toward the stairs urging Annie to walk down them ahead of her. "Let's go to the kitchen. I'll give you instructions on how to administer it."

Annie hesitated a moment, then reluctantly started down with one furtive look over her shoulder, as if she was uncertain her mistress and young Will would be all right without her.

In the kitchen, Alexandra took a vial of compound spirits of lavender from her bag, along with another vial of aqua ammonia. She mixed a teaspoon of the first with ten drops of the latter in a cup, half filled with water. She then added a bit of sugar, which she'd asked Annie to find for her. When it was mixed, she handed the cup to Annie. "See that she drinks all of this right away. If she continues to improve, she need only rest in bed until I return tomorrow. But if she shows more signs of faintness, send for me immediately."

Annie gave her a solemn nod and turned away toward the hall that led to the stairs, taking great care to hold the cup with both hands. Alexandra was left to see herself out, which she did with reluctance, her mind buzzing with unanswered questions.

Nicholas saw her leave from his position behind an out-cropping of gorse in an open field next to the house. He had stationed himself there in the hope of finding John Killborn. He had reasoned that the young man would eventually show up at his mother's house if he was, in fact, in Newton-Upon-Sea.

His first instinct was to follow Dr. Gladstone and try to catch up with her. He would like to invite her for a carriage ride, perhaps. Or anything that would give him the opportunity to be alone with her. His reasons were not entirely dishonorable. Among other things, he'd like to know why she'd spent so much time in Gull House and what, if anything, she'd learned. But he wouldn't attempt to catch up with her just yet. There would be time for that later. For now, his mission was to catch up with young John Killborn and convince him to turn himself in to the authorities. That would improve, at least to a small extent, his client's worsening chances at trial.

It was only a matter of minutes before he saw a figure topping the steep hill that led up to Gull House. The quick, fluid movement of the body told Nicholas it was a young man, and although he had seen John Killborn only once when he was first assigned to defend him, he was certain it was Killborn.

Nicholas moved as quickly as he could through the gorse, his back hunched, trying to avoid being out in the open where Killborn could see him and be frightened away. Nicholas had to be quick enough to intercept him before he reached the house, however. Once inside, it could be difficult to flush him out. In spite of the fact that Dr. Gladstone had said Mrs. Orkwright was a reasonable woman, Nicholas would not discount a mother's instinct to protect her offspring. John was, after all, no more than sixteen.

By the time Nicholas reached the edge of the gardens of Gull House, one of his hands, as well as the side of his face, was bleeding from various encounters with the thorns on the gorse. The thorns had also badly snagged the trousers and coat sleeves of his fine hand-tailored suit. There was no time to worry about that, however. He sprinted across the lawn calling out John Killborn's name.

The young man paused for the briefest of moments, then ran down the hill again. Nicholas sprinted after him, shedding his coat as he ran. Ahead of him, the young man moved like a machine of expertly synchronized parts, churning at rapid speed down the hill. Nicholas was equally agile and close behind, and when he was near enough, jumped, turning his body parallel with the ground as he dove toward Killborn, and, upon landing, encircling the young man's legs with his arms while at the same time plowing several inches of gravelly soil with his own chin.

Killborn landed with a thud on the rocky road, burying his face in the dirt, too. He tried to struggle to his feet and out of Nicholas's grasp, but Nicholas held on to him. Killborn continued to struggle, but he was winded and losing vigor. Nicholas stood, pulling the gasping Killborn up with him. The boy's face was caked with blood and dirt.

"It's you!" It was impossible to tell whether that exclamation from Killborn was fear or relief, or perhaps only disgust.

"It is I, yes, and you bloody well better be glad it is," Nicholas said.

"How did you know . . ."

"How did I know you would come here?" Nicholas gave him a rough shove up the road toward the gardens where there was at least some cover so they could talk without being seen. "I'm a lawyer. It's my business to stay one step ahead of the lawless, as well as the law. Now you tell me what in bloody hell happened to your brain that made you decide to escape from prison." He gave him a shake. "Your crime was burglary of a few trinkets. I could have gotten you off perhaps with a few months. Now you've an escape charge to face, and you'll be damned lucky to get thirty bloody years. That is if you don't hang."

"It's none of your business what I do." He tried to wrench himself free of Nicholas's grasp.

"You idiot! It bloody well is my business. I'm your barrister, remember? I'm the only person who can save you." He gave Killborn another shove. Then, when they had reached a thin grove of trees, he spun him around to face him. "Now talk, damn you!"

"I have nothing to say." His words were a defiant snarl.

Nicholas let the words hang in the air for a moment before he spoke. "Very well." He loosened his grip on Killborn and brushed a bit of dirt from his damaged clothing, a futile gesture. "In that case, I apologize for the interruption, and I shall see you again when the police find you." He had taken only a few steps when he realized his ploy had worked.

"I . . . I had a score to settle." The defiance was gone from Killborn's voice, replaced with choking fear.

Nicholas turned around to face him. "Indeed."

"It's got nothing to do with that burglary. It's . . . a personal matter." His face, clouded with terror, now looked even younger than his sixteen years.

"A personal matter, is it? I dare say it would have been much wiser for you to have the prison authorities contact me to take care of it for you."

Young Killborn shook his head and some of the defiance

returned to his eyes. "No. It was something I had to do. No one else."

"Something regarding your stepfather perhaps?" Nicholas watched Killborn's face for some sign of fear or guilt or even anger. He saw all of it.

"I didn't kill the bastard."

"How did you know he was dead?"

Killborn's face went white, and his jaw tightened. Nicholas thought he might run again, and he grasped his arm to prevent it. "I didn't kill him!" he said again.

"Come with me, John. You're in quite enough trouble as it is. Don't make it worse," Nicholas said.

Killborn jerked free of Nicholas's grasp, but he didn't run. "I don't care how much worse it gets, I have to . . ."

"Have to what?"

Killborn looked down at the ground.

"John, listen to me. You may not care how much worse it gets for you, but what about your mother? Can't you imagine how she—"

Killborn raised his head suddenly to look at Nicholas. His eyes were hot with anger. "Keep my mother out of this, you bastard!"

"Listen to me, John." Nicholas tried to grasp his arm again, but he jerked it away. When he tried a second time to restrain him, Killborn swung at Nicholas's jaw, hitting it squarely with his fist. Nicholas staggered backward and felt blood trickle down his chin, but he quickly regained his balance and blocked another blow with his forearm before grabbing one of Killborn's arms and twisting it behind him. "Don't be a fool. Can't you see you're getting yourself deeper and deeper into trouble?"

Killborn made one more attempt to wrench himself free, but it was a halfhearted attempt. Nicholas felt him relax slightly, and he pressed his advantage. "Come with me to the local gaol. We'll get word to Newgate as quickly as possible that you've surrendered yourself. I'll make a plea for you that you'd heard of your stepfather's death and were upset. That may help you, especially since you're hardly more than a boy."

Killborn stiffened again. "I'm glad the bastard's dead. I wouldn't waste my grief on—"

Nicholas forced Killborn's arm to bend at an even more awkward angle behind his back, and he felt him wince. "Don't say any more, you fool. Just turn yourself in and keep your mouth shut." There was no response from Killborn, but Nicholas sensed a change. He relaxed his grip slightly. "Let's go!" he said.

By the time they reached the bottom of the hill, Nicholas was no longer restraining Killborn. Still, he walked close by and watched him carefully.

Snow was just locking the front door of his office, preparing to leave for the day when the two of them approached. He glanced up at them as they neared him. A sudden terrible light shone in his eyes, like shards of glass. He straightened his shoulders and seemed to will a dullness to his eyes. "Good evening, Mr. Forsythe." He refused to acknowledge Killborn with even a glance.

"I'm afraid I must disturb your plans to leave your work for the day." Nicholas's hand went cautiously to grasp Killborn's arm again.

"I see." For the first time Snow glanced at Killborn.

"Do you know who this is?"

There was no response from Snow.

"My client, Mr. John Killborn, wishes to turn himself in and requests that you notify Newgate Prison as soon as possible," Nicholas said, puzzled at Snow's lack of response.

Snow turned around and unlocked the door, then stood back for Nicholas and Killborn to enter. He went straight to his desk, and when he was seated, pulled out a form. Without looking up, he asked the routine questions of the prisoner while he wrote down his responses.

Name, age, city of residence, charges against him, next of kin. Snow must have known all of the answers without asking. Killborn gave his answers in a monotone. His face had turned as gray as lead and his lips were bloodless. Beads of sweat glistened on his forehead.

"Do you wish to make a statement at this time regarding your escape?" Snow still kept his eyes down and the pen poised over the line to be completed.

Nicholas was about to caution young Killborn not to say anything in that regard when the young man swayed slightly, clasped his hand to his mouth, and mumbled behind the hand, "I'm going to be sick!"

Snow looked up suddenly, then pointed with his pen to a side door. Killborn rushed toward it, flung it open, and stepped outside. Both Nicholas and Snow followed him. They both turned away when he began to retch, but Snow kept his hand firmly at the boy's back, his fingers grasping his belt.

Young Killborn continued to retch, bending from the waist. And then suddenly he was running, and Snow was left holding his belt. The boy had obviously unfastened the belt and slipped it off as he bent over. Both Nicholas and Snow ran to catch him, but he had disappeared into an alley. When they reached the alley, he was gone.

"He had to go either right or left at the end of the alley," Nicholas called to Snow. "You take the left, and I'll take the right." Nicholas ran, but he knew within seconds it was futile. Killborn was nowhere in sight. He continued to search, though, until the shadows grew too thick to see. He returned to the gaol, hoping Snow'd had better luck. He saw him standing at the back entrance, breathing heavily. There was no sign of Killborn, however, except for the stench and the puddle of his vomit.

8

Zack was not in a good mood. He made it clear he felt slighted because he had not been invited to accompany Alexandra on her last visit to Gull House. His first tactic was to sulk in a corner near the fireplace, emitting occasional whimpers of self-pity. His next was to follow Alexandra closer than a shadow everywhere she went in the house, as if to make certain she had no chance to leave again without him.

He leaned heavily against her leg as she sat at the kitchen table with Nancy, finishing her meat pie. Alexandra frequently took meals in the kitchen with Nancy, something her father, the late Dr. Huntington Gladstone, never did. He often scolded her for having a too familiar relationship with Nancy. "It's best for each of you to remember your station in life," he said. Yet, it had been he who had encouraged their friendship as children, and it had been he who had seen to it that Nancy received the same education and shared the same tutor as Alexandra when they were young.

"Poor Mrs. Orkwright. She seems to be taking it terribly hard," Nancy said. Alexandra had just told her everything that happened on her most recent visit to Gull House.

"I'm afraid so. She doesn't look at all well." As she spoke, Alexandra tried to free her foot from underneath Zack's heavy shoulder. He had been lying on it for so long, she had lost feeling in it.

"The little boy's comments make a person wonder . . ."

Alexandra raised her eyes from her plate to look at Nancy. "You're referring to his comment about being glad his father is dead."

"Well, yes. You'll have to admit that sounds—"

"I wouldn't read anything into that, Nancy. It's not at all uncommon for a child to feel anger over the death of a loved one. I should think it's merely part of his grieving."

Nancy gave her a frown fraught with skepticism. "Oh, come now, Miss Alex, didn't you tell me he said he was angry at his father for being mean to the housekeeper? Isn't it possible he mistreated her in some way? Perhaps he beat her, or—"

"Nancy . . ."

"Now, don't go shushing me, Miss Alex. I have no doubt the same thought crossed your mind."

When Alexandra didn't reply, Nancy pressed her advantage. "And isn't it true Mrs. Orkwright's older son detested his stepfather? The man must have been terribly unpleasant for one lad to fear him and the other hate him. One wonders why Mrs. Orkwright didn't detest him as well."

Alexandra gave her a stern look. "Are you suggesting that his stepson, or perhaps even his own young son, detested him enough to kill him?"

Nancy shrugged. "It's something to consider. One never knows what goes on behind closed doors."

Alexandra finished the last of her meat pie and touched her napkin to her lips. "I hardly think it worth considering that young Will could do such a thing, even if he did hate his father. And I'm not at all convinced he did hate him. I still say his anger could be just an expression of grief."

"And John Killborn? Can you explain that away as well?"

Again Alexandra did not immediately answer. The truth was, she couldn't explain John Killborn's dislike for his stepfather, and, in truth, she had no way of knowing whether or not he was capable of killing anyone. Except that he was Jane Orkwright's son, and irrational as it may be, she could not think of a person as gentle as Jane having an offspring who would commit murder. She'd mulled it over in her mind almost constantly, and now she suddenly felt very tired. She pushed herself away from the table.

"I don't know, Nancy. I suppose you're right. One never does know what goes on behind closed doors. But I'm too tired to speculate, so, if you'll excuse me, I'll retire to my bed. Our irregular schedule of late has left me rather exhausted." She started toward the door but turned back to look at Nancy. "I suspect it has you exhausted as well. Why don't we both—"

There was a sudden loud knock at the door that startled the two of them and Zack as well. His bark was sharp and loud. Alexandra and Nancy exchanged a glance, and Nancy started to the front of the house to open the door. Both of them, as well as Zack, were used to the occasional patient coming to the house late because of some medical emergency. Alexandra would have to forget that she was tired and minister to whomever it was who needed her.

Nancy opened the door, and Alexandra, standing several feet behind her, was surprised to see that it was Nicholas Forsythe who stood there. He was shivering without a coat, and the rest of his fancy clothes were torn. His handsome aristocratic face was bruised and bloody. Alexandra emitted a little cry and rushed toward him. Zack growled and followed her so closely she almost tripped.

"Mr. Forsythe! What happened to you?"

"I'm afraid I—"

"Let me have a look at those wounds," she said, not giving him a chance to answer. Nancy, in the meantime, had hurried away to the surgery to prepare the materials that Alexandra would need to stitch the cuts.

He tried to protest. "I'm sure it's nothing serious. You see, I—"

"Is there still hot water on the stove?" Alexandra asked just as she stepped into the surgery with her patient in tow.

"Of course. I'm on my way to get it now." Nancy spoke as she passed her on the way to the kitchen. Zack whined pitifully as Alexandra disappeared into the surgery. He knew it was forbidden territory for him, and he had to be content with waiting outside the door.

"I'm afraid I shall have to ask you to remove your shirt,"

Alexandra said over her shoulder as she washed her hands at the basin in her surgery, using water poured from a pitcher.

"My shirt?"

"That will be sufficient for the moment. Zack, for heaven's sake, be quiet!" Alexandra said, still with her back to Nicholas.

"For the moment?"

"I may have to examine your body for more wounds. Please don't allow that to concern you. I am a doctor. You must think of me that way. Don't think of me as a woman." She was quite accustomed to her male patients feeling uncomfortable when certain types of examination became necessary. She dried her hands and picked up a needle and needle holder Nancy had prepared for her, wanting to make sure it was the one she would most likely need.

"I'm afraid I would find that impossible. Not to think of you as a woman, I mean."

Alexandra turned around to face him. His eyes went immediately to the needle she held in her hand. His eyes widened, and his smile disappeared as the blood drained from his face. "You're going to . . . to use that? On my face?"

Alexandra put the needle back on the table, satisfied that it was the correct size, should she need it. "I'm not certain yet. I want to clean the cuts and examine them first."

Nancy entered the room with a basin of warm water and soap, and Alexandra went to work immediately, cleaning the wounds and examining his face and torso carefully. He was rather badly bruised, but the cuts, with the exception of one on his chin, would not need sutures after all. The chin cut, she thought, would probably need only three or four stitches.

"Just how did this happen?" She spoke as she dabbed at a cut on his jaw. "You look as if you've been in an accident."

"In a manner of speaking." He winced as she continued to clean the wound.

"What do you mean?" She was now examining his hands. The knuckles were covered with scrapes and blood.

"I've engaged in fisticuffs, as I'm certain you have surmised."

His answer surprised her. She dropped his hand and looked at him. "Fisticuffs? With whom?"

"John Killborn."

Alexandra heard Nancy's sudden intake of breath behind her, and she struggled to keep her own composure.

"Indeed?" Alexandra said.

"Yes. At his mother's house."

"You've been to see Jane?"

"In a manner of speaking."

"You keep using that expression. Just what do you mean?" Alexandra was not able to keep the frustration out of her voice.

"I've been trying to explain that ever since I got here, but you . . . Ouch! You won't give me the . . . Ouch! Can't you be a little more gentle?"

"I must get the dirt out of these cuts. Nancy, some alcohol please."

"Alcohol? Isn't that going to burn?"

"Perhaps a little. Now, go on with your story."

Nicholas eyed the bottle of alcohol suspiciously as he talked. "I thought young John might show up at his mother's house, so I waited for him, hiding in the gorse. When he arrived, we got into a bit of an altercation because, of course, he didn't want to surrender to me and have me take him to the gaol."

"Of course." Alexandra took the bottle of alcohol along with a bit of lamb's wool from Nancy. "Yes, you do have bruises and cuts that would suggest blows. Rather uncivilized of you, I should say. But this wound on your chin is quite full of dirt and small pebbles. How did you—"

"I performed what is called a tackle and plowed my chin into the ground in the process."

"A tackle, you say?"

"Yes. Rather like rugby players do. I played a bit at school, you see. Rather rough game, you know."

"Oh yes, of course."

"*Ouch!* Good God, woman, that burns like h . . . Rather badly, I mean." His voice had become weak, and his sudden loud cry had brought forth a single alarmed bark from Zack, who still waited outside the door.

"And did you have a chance to talk to young John? After the tackle and the fisticuffs, that is." Alexandra handed the alcohol and lamb's wool to Nancy, who took it and, in almost the same movement, handed Alexandra the needle threaded with catgut.

"We did talk a little, and he said something interesting about . . . What's that for? I thought you said you weren't going to sew anything."

"I said I didn't know. This won't take long, Mr. Forsythe. And I'm quite certain you'll live through it. Perhaps you've even encountered worse pain on the rugby field."

Nicholas didn't reply. He hadn't taken his eyes off the needle, even as it got closer and closer to his face.

"Go on, please. You were saying young John said something interesting." Nicholas was leaning back, trying to distance himself from her. "Nancy," she said over her shoulder. She needn't have bothered. Nancy was already at his side, one hand placed firmly on his back, pushing him forward. With her other hand, she picked up one of his to hold.

"Squeeze my hand if it starts to hurt." Nancy often invited patients to squeeze her hand if they felt pain. She claimed it would take their mind off of it.

"Perhaps a bit of brandy," Alexandra said, remembering, with some embarrassment, that she had once fainted when Nancy had to stitch a bad cut on her neck. The experience had at least made her more sympathetic with her patients.

"That won't be necessary." Nicholas spoke with a bravado that was perhaps a bit too exaggerated.

"Very well." Alexandra took her first stitch.

Nicholas' face went white again and grew whiter with each stitch until she was certain he would faint. He was still conscious when she finished, however, but when he spoke to her, his voice was no more than a croak.

"I'll take that brandy now."

Nancy gave Alexandra a knowing look as she wordlessly left the room to fetch the brandy.

Within a few minutes Nicholas was seated in an overstuffed chair with his feet on an ottoman and a snifter of brandy in his hand. Zack was curled in front of the fire, eyeing him with great suspicion. Alexandra was seated on the sofa. She had declined Nicholas's suggestion that she join him in a brandy, knowing that in her weary state it would have an immediate effect like that of sleeping draughts.

Nancy had left the room, but Alexandra was certain she hadn't gone so far away that she couldn't hear everything that was said. She was, no doubt, dallying in the hall, just outside the parlor.

"Now, Mr. Forsythe." Alexandra leaned forward, ready to listen. "What were you saying about young John telling you something interesting?" She was not so weary that she couldn't give up the hope that she could learn something that might help clear up the baffling mystery of the admiral's death.

"My concern is that he may have implicated himself in something more serious than burglary or even prison escape. As his lawyer I want to make certain whether or not that's the case." Nicholas stared into the fire and seemed to be talking more to himself than to Alexandra.

"What did he say?"

He turned his gaze to her. "He could have meant anything by the remark, of course, but, given the circumstances, this is not something I would like to come out in court. Of course the judge could use his prerogative to question him, but if the matter hasn't been introduced then, by the law of the court—"

"For heaven's sake, Mr. Forsythe, stop musing over all that legal gibberish and tell me what the boy said!" Alexandra's lack of proper sleep had left her short-tempered. Tomorrow, perhaps, she would regret her outburst.

For the briefest of moments, surprise shown on Nicholas' face. He collected himself quickly, however. "He seemed rather protective of his mother. Said I was to leave her out of things when I mentioned how upset she was sure to be at the news of his escape."

"Mr. Forsythe. . . ."

"One shouldn't be surprised at a boy being protective of his mother, but—"

"Mr. Forsythe . . ."

". . . but, it struck me that he was truly a good boy, who under normal circumstances would never turn to lawlessness, but who somehow—"

"Stop evading the issue!" Impatience and weariness once

again got the best of her. "Your clever barrister's tricks of evasion won't work with me! What-did-the-boy-say?" The last said in measured tones, as if she was speaking to a dullard.

Nicholas paused, cleared his throat, looked down at his hands, and then raised his eyes again to Alexandra. "I'm afraid I may have spoken out of turn. I'm afraid I would be betraying my client's confidence to relay what he said. It's just that, after the altercation and then his second escape, I felt rather unnerved and—"

"His second escape?"

"I'm afraid so." Nicholas gave her the entire story of the boy's surrender and escape.

"Constable Snow must have been chagrined."

Nicholas looked at her with a wry expression. "One never knows with that fellow, does one? Rather taciturn and odd, what?"

"More brandy, sir?" Nancy had somehow materialized and already had more brandy poured in the bottom of Nicholas' snifter before he had a chance to answer.

Nicholas, who had looked as if he wanted to protest, stared at the second helping of brandy with a resigned expression, swirled it a few times, and took a sip. "One could almost say Snow looks like a suspect, given the odd way he's been acting."

"Not the only one acting oddly, I'd say." It was Nancy, being impertinent and forgetting her place again, or ignoring it. Nicholas was too intrigued to let it show whether he noticed or not.

"Oh? Who else?" he looked up at Nancy.

"That housekeeper of Mrs. Orkwright. An odd bird if I ever saw one." Nancy stole a quick glance at Alexandra as she spoke. "Seems she might have even had a reason to do the old sea dog in."

"What?" Nicholas glanced at Alexandra. Nancy took the opportunity of his distraction to splash more brandy in his snifter.

Alexandra, who had been glaring at Nancy as a signal to say no more, now saw the futility in resisting. "Perhaps that's a bit of an exaggeration," she said, "but it does appear the

admiral may have shown some cruelty toward the housekeeper."

"Indeed?" Nicholas was now thoroughly captivated. He
took another sip of his brandy and held up his hand as a
signal to Nancy that he wanted no more. Nancy, however,
ignored the signal.

Alexandra told him the story of young Will's odd behavior
and what he had said about his father being cruel to Annie.
"Nancy has pointed out that since both boys seemed to dislike the admiral, it's possible he had a cruel streak that
showed itself against John and the housekeeper."

"Um-hum," Nicholas said, "perhapsh she's right." He held
his hand up again to stop Nancy from adding more brandy
to his glass.

"And it could be," Nancy added, pouring the brandy nevertheless, "that either the housekeeper or the stepson felt they
had a score to settle with the admiral and did him in. Or they
could have even done it together."

Nicholas glanced up at Nancy, who still stood by his chair.
He had to grasp the arms of the chair for support. "A score
to shettle? That's 'zacly what John said. I have a shore to
scettle. Dangerous thing to say if there's been a murder,
what?" He chuckled softly at his own witticism. "But!" He
held up one cautionary finger and tried to focus his eyes on
Alexandra. "You don't know for sure the bastard was murdered. Could have jusht drowned, you know." He hiccuped.
" 'Cept for those drawers. Now there's a mystery for you.
And how did John know the bashtard, 'scuse me, the admiral
was dead?"

Nancy and Alexandra exchanged a quick glance. "Indeed?" Alexandra said.

Nicholas shook his head. "No, I can't talk 'bout that.
Young fool knew he was dead before I tol' him, but you
know I can't talk 'bout that, so don't ask me to tell you he
said that."

"Of course not," Alexandra said.

"Shall I prepare the bed in the guest room, Miss Alex?"
Nancy asked.

Alexandra nodded. "I think that would be wise."

"No need! I have rooms at the inn." Nicholas was having a difficult time standing up from the chair.

Nancy gave him a gentle lift. "Come this way. Careful now." She led him to the stairs. "Now, one foot after the other. That's it. One foot up. Next foot up." She gave Alexandra a reassuring look.

"So kind of you," Nicholas mumbled as they disappeared up the stairs.

Robert Snow could admit to himself that the remorse he felt about John Killborn literally slipping through his fingers was born more of embarrassment than concern over the need for justice. But it wasn't embarrassment that had pushed him into his current state of depression. It was distress that the entire Orkwright affair had gotten so out of hand. There was so much a man in his position should have foreseen, yet he had not.

One thing he could never have foreseen, however, was the undertaker rushing into his office and telling him someone had desecrated the admiral's body. It had taken him a good half hour to calm the man.

"I say it was the work of the devil if I was a religious man! Or witches!" There'd been more anger than fear in the poor man's voice. "Came in the middle of the night to work their evil! While the wife and I supped with our son, it was! I tell you, nothing is safe in this world anymore, not even a dead man. 'Thou shalt not suffer a witch to live.' And if I could ever get my hands on the one who—"

"Calm yourself, Gibbs, and start from the beginning," Snow had said.

"The beginning? 'In the beginning was the word,' and 'the word was made flesh, and dwelt among us,' and if that is so, then the word is is evil. All is evil, I tell you—"

"Gibbs!" It was often necessary to keep the man on track, since he was a man of confusion—a self-confessed atheist whose profession kept him forever in the presence of depressing circumstances. Namely preachers and dead men.

"Defiled my work, they did, and I would never have discovered it had I not noticed the dead man's shirt was a bit

soiled. Had to change it, didn't I? Is not the body more than
raiment? they say, but verily I say unto you, there's not a
one of 'em but would have my hide if the raiment be not
perfect. So I changed the shirt, I did, and that's when I saw
it!"

"Saw what?" Snow asked.

"Why, the scar. Y-shaped, it was. Like is done when a
dead man's guts is looked at by a doctor. But there was no
doctor there, I tell you. 'Twas done in the middle of the
night, and no self-respecting doctor, not even Gladstone herself, would perform such a sacrilege in the middle of the
night."

"You're sure of that?" Snow asked.

"You told her yourself she was not to do it. Ah yes, I
know what you will say. She is a strange one, and not a
Christian, either. For no Christian woman would make herself acquainted with the ways of the world and the bodies of
men as she does. With that I will agree. But still, she knows
the book of Ecclesiastes where it says that the giving heed
unto law is the assurance of incorruption."

"Perhaps she does not fear corruption," Snow offered.

Gibbs gave him a surprised look. "All women fear corruption. They have not the boldness and stamina of men. Not
even Gladstone. She is bold and vulgar, but she is not a man.
And wise enough not stray into dangerous territory."

"Wise as the serpent, perhaps," Snow said.

Gibbs fell silent for a long moment, thinking on Snow's
words. Finally, he spoke, low and self-accusing. " 'Believe
a woman or an epitaph, or any other thing that's false.' "

"You quote Byron as well as the Bible," Snow said.

"I am a fool!"

"Don't concern yourself. I'll investigate the matter," Snow
had assured him. "Perhaps the good doctor simply misunderstood my instructions."

"Ha! She is descended from the cunning creature who
would damn the world for an apple, is she not? Be wary of
her, my good man!"

Snow had finally gotten him out of his office. He had not
gone to confront Dr. Gladstone, however. Instead, he had
spent the day dreading it. She had blatantly disobeyed his

orders, because she knew he was wrong to forbid the autopsy. He should have expected it. Being Alexandra Gladstone's teacher had been an enlightening experience for him. He'd never taught a female until then, and he found both Miss Alexandra and her young maid bright. Nancy had a quick, eager mind and an earthy common sense about her. Miss Alexandra, as he knew her then, was precocious and impatient to learn, ever questioning and challenging, and in some ways defiant. At once a source of delight and a thorn in his side.

Even he had been surprised when she carried her defiance so far as to follow in her father's footsteps and become a doctor of medicine. He thought old Huntington, who had been his friend, had been a bit shocked and puzzled by it as well. By that time, however, the old doctor had long since stopped trying to get his daughter to conform to the rules of society and resigned to teach her the skills of his profession himself, since she was allowed to attend only part of the lectures in medical school. Those that were deemed improper for a woman were not open to her. Of course, the late Dr. Huntington Gladstone would never admit he had started the whole thing himself by allowing her to get an education as a young girl.

Now she had created a dangerous sea of trouble by what she had done. Now he had no other choice but to confront her, in spite of the fact that he dreaded her revealing what she might have learned.

9

Alexandra, dressed in a suit of soft black wool, was in the kitchen taking her morning tea while Zack lay curled at her feet. It was rare that she had the opportunity to have a leisurely morning, but, because of Admiral Orkwright's funeral, she wouldn't be making her morning rounds. The funeral was scheduled for nine o'clock. Most of the town would be there.

In truth, she was unable to take advantage of the release from duty and enjoy the morning. Her thoughts were full of what Mr. Forsythe had said the night before. That John Killborn claimed he had a score to settle, and that he seemed to know his stepfather was dead before anyone could have told him. If he killed the admiral, did Jane know about it? If she did, she would most certainly try to protect him. That could only be an added burden to her, along with the grief of her husband's death.

Should she go to Jane and try to comfort her? Or would Jane see that as an intrusion? After all, Alexandra thought, it was only speculation at this point that John might have killed the admiral. Still, if it was true, or even if Jane heard only the gossip, the grief and stress she would experience had the potential of making her ill. Alexandra could at least be prepared for that.

Nancy, who'd eaten her breakfast earlier, was just placing a rack of toast on the table, along with jam and butter, when

Zack sprang to his feet and shattered the morning calm with a single loud bark followed by a menacing growl.

Alexandra turned her head in the direction Zack was aiming his attention and saw what was left of Nicholas Forsythe standing in the doorway. His coat was missing, and his soiled and dirty shirt was buttoned irregularly so that it was skewed over his chest with the collar protruding on one side at an odd angle. His face was the color of yesterday's whey, and he had to use both hands to brace himself in the doorway.

"Good morning, Mr. Forsythe," Alexandra said. "You don't look well."

He said something incomprehensible, then made his way with uncertain steps to a cupboard, which he used as support as he took a few more steps until he was close enough to the table to risk taking two unaided steps to reach it. Once there, he sat down heavily across from Alexandra. Nancy set a steaming cup of tea in front of him.

Nicholas immediately jerked his head toward her and demanded, "What's in this cup?" He then seemed to regret his sudden movement as he pressed his fingertips into his temples and closed his eyes and groaned again.

"It's tea, sir." Nancy's answer sounded uncharacteristically prim.

Nicholas managed to open one eye. "Are you certain? I have reason to believe you are trying to kill me."

"Kill you, sir?" Nancy's eyes were wide with feigned innocence. Alexandra had seldom seen such a fine performance.

Nicholas turned to Alexandra. "I have never felt so dreadful in all of my . . . Excuse me!" He stood and rushed to the back door and out into the cold February morning. He came back shortly, wiping his mouth. Nancy handed him a cool, damp cloth. He pressed it to his face, then sat down again across from Alexandra. This time he picked up the cup and swallowed some of the tea.

"So you've decided to trust me," Nancy said, watching him take another sip.

"No." Nicholas returned the cup to the saucer. "I've simply decided that if you've poisoned my tea, I'd rather drink it and die than to go on feeling as I do this morning. How in hell did you get me to drink so much?"

" 'Twasn't any trouble at all, sir."

Nicholas glared at her and seemed about to say something but took some more tea instead.

Alexandra signaled Nancy with a slight movement of her head that she was to leave them. Nancy scowled and turned away reluctantly. Zack started to follow her but changed his mind and turned back to Alexandra. Rather than lying down at her feet, though, he stood like a soldier at attention next to her side and kept his eyes trained on Nicholas.

Nicholas ignored the dog and spoke to Alexandra. "Did I do anything I should apologize for?"

Alexandra smiled. "You were a perfect gentleman. Would you like a piece of toast?"

"No."

"If you eat it unbuttered, it will help settle your stomach." Alexandra pushed the toast rack toward him. He reluctantly took a slice, broke it in half, and took a small nibble. "Did I say anything regrettable?"

"As I said, you were a perfect gentleman."

"I was referring to my own professional demeanor. That evil woman plied me with liquor to get me to divulge the information you wanted."

Alexandra laughed. "Nancy isn't evil. Impertinent, yes, but not evil. And you said nothing of any particular importance."

"I don't know whether to be relieved or insulted."

"You have nothing to worry about, Mr. Forsythe. You have no cause to be concerned that your client's confidence has been betrayed." Alexandra took a sip of her tea, as if to prevent herself from speaking another lie.

"Then the evil one got me drunk for nothing."

Alexandra took yet another sip of tea. Her silence saturated the room until Nicholas was overcome with its possibilities.

"You've just lied to me! I did say something." He glared at her.

Alexandra, who was never very good at lying, couldn't think of a single word to say to him that wouldn't make matters worse for both of them. She was relieved when Nancy disobediently stepped into the room. She was wearing her funeral dress of black crepe and a small black bonnet.

"It's half past eight, Miss Alex. Shouldn't we be on our way?"

"Of course." She stood and spoke to her guest. "Please excuse me, Mr. Forsythe. Nancy's right, we must leave lest we arrive late."

Nicholas looked puzzled. "Late? Late for what?"

"Why Admiral Orkwright's funeral," Alexandra said. "I'll just get my bonnet, Nancy, and we'll be on our way." She turned to Nicholas again. "Please do forgive me for rushing off, but I must attend the funeral."

Nicholas stood, awkwardly. "Of course, and so must I." He appeared confused. "How did I get here? Do I have a carriage waiting?"

"I believe you hired our town's only carriage," Nancy said. "But since it is the only carriage for hire, it waits for no one."

"Quite so," Nicholas said without looking at Nancy. He addressed Alexandra. "And will you be walking to the church?"

"Yes, it's not far." Alexandra spoke to him over her shoulder on her way to retrieve her bonnet. "I'm sorry I can't offer you a ride to the inn, since it's a bit more of a walk, but as you know, I don't own a carriage."

"Don't trouble yourself. As you can see, I'm in fine shape this morning." He made his way unsteadily to the door.

"Careful you don't catch a chill," Nancy said. "It's rather cold this morning, you know."

Nicholas paused and turned toward Nancy. "How kind of you to be concerned about my welfare. And, may I add, how surprising." He opened the door and disappeared into the fog.

It was only a few seconds later, just as Alexandra reached the bottom of the stairs with her bonnet in place that there was a knock at the door. When Nancy opened it, Constable Snow was standing in front of her. Nicholas stood some distance behind him, looking as if he had met the constable on his way out and had turned around to follow him back, perhaps unbeknownst to the constable. He wore a troubled look.

"I must speak to Dr. Gladstone." The constable's voice was as cold as the morning.

"I'm sorry, sir," Nancy said. "Dr. Gladstone is just about to leave for—"

"What is it?" Alexandra was afraid he had come to take her to someone who was ill.

Snow's eyes moved first to Nancy, and then back to Alexandra. "I must speak to you alone," he said.

Alexandra felt a sudden emptiness in her chest. She feared she knew why he had come. "Of course," she said. "Nancy, please go on without me. I'll be along in a moment." She saw the uneasiness on Nancy's face before she turned away and walked out the door. Nicholas had advanced to the door by now. He stepped aside to allow Nancy to leave.

Snow, who had finally noticed him, spoke to him. "If you will excuse us, please." His voice was as grim as his expression.

Nicholas straightened with as much dignity as his disheveled appearance would allow. "I am Dr. Gladstone's solicitor. She has a right to have me present." Alexandra knew then he must have guessed the reason for Snow's visit, just as she had.

"You are a barrister, Forsythe," Snow said in his icy voice.

"I am both."

Snow glared at him a few seconds before he spoke again. "Perhaps it is best that you stay, after all."

"Please come into the parlor," Alexandra said, leading the way. "I'm sorry I can't offer you tea, but as you know, I was just about to leave." Her heart was beating rapidly. It wasn't to take her to a patient that the constable had come. It must be about the autopsy.

Snow seated himself on one of the sofas and leaned forward. "I had a most disturbing visit from Mr. Percy Gibbs recently."

When neither Alexandra nor Nicholas responded, Snow spoke again. His eyes were focused directly on Alexandra. "I suppose you know what he said and why it was so disturbing."

Alexandra could see that Nicholas was about to say something, but she outmaneuvered him. "Perhaps you should tell me what he said, Constable, and then perhaps I can diagnose why you are disturbed." She saw a look of relief as well as a slight smile flash across Nicholas' face.

"Did you perform an autopsy on Admiral George Ork-wright after I denied you permission?"

Alexandra took a deep breath. "Ye—"

"Don't answer that!" Nicholas said.

"But I—"

"Don't answer!" Nicholas said again.

"I understand," Snow said, "that you were not convinced the admiral's death was an accident. Given that, I can see that you felt it was important to learn as much as you could about his death."

Alexandra remained silent, and Nicholas looked relieved, temporarily at least.

"Why did you do it?"

"Because Jane Orkwright asked me to," Alexandra said, this time before Nicholas had a chance to stop her. There was only the slightest change in Snow's expression—a minute rise of the eyebrows.

"You must know she is not herself at a time like this," he said at length. "And that is beside the point anyway. You acted without authority."

"My authority was the widow's wishes." Alexandra noted that Nicholas had gone quite pale. Was it the liquor or what she was telling Snow? She hoped he wasn't going to be sick again.

"Did she truly request it, or did you simply plant the idea in her mind?" Snow did not for one minute take his eyes from hers.

Nicholas, who had never been seated, took a step toward Alexandra. "Dr. Gladstone, could I have a word with you, please? In private."

Alexandra ignored him and addressed her comments to Snow. "It would not be likely for her to have the idea on her own, sir, but after I explained certain things to her, she readily agreed that an examination should be done, and she requested that I do it. I told you that earlier when I came to you for permission."

"Which I refused." Snow's face flushed with emotion. "You broke into a private building in the dark of night. You acted without authority. You cannot deny that you have broken the law."

"I didn't have to break in the building, sir. I simply walked in."

Nicholas edged closer. "Dr. Gladstone, I implore you. Don't—"

"And as for my acting without authority—"

"Alexandra!" Nicholas sounded almost feverish and didn't seem to notice he had used her first name.

"I felt time was of the essence," Alexandra continued, still addressing Snow. "I knew that the admiral's body would be removed for burial this morning."

"You've gotten yourself into this situation because you still foolishly insist that his death came at the hand of another." Snow looked as if he might explode with his anger.

"I did at the time, sir."

His eyes widened. "At the time? Am I to assume you found nothing from the autopsy to support that theory?"

"Dr. Gladstone!" Nicholas seemed about to explode himself. "I must warn you, don't say—"

"Your assumption would be correct," she said.

Something changed in Snow's eyes. It was impossible to say what it was. He was silent for what seemed an eternity but could have been only a few seconds before he said, "May I see your notes, please?"

Alexandra was puzzled. "I beg your pardon. I see no reason why I—"

"I am an officer of the law. If there is even a suspicion of foul play, then I have a right, and I insist that I see your notes."

There was another pause, then, "Of course," Alexandra said at length.

"I implore you, Dr. Gladstone . . . !" Nicholas said, but she was already on her way to her surgery.

Snow had risen from his seat when she stood, and he started to follow her. Zack was directly behind her, however, and Snow stopped when the animal turned his head and emitted a sharp bark. Alexandra returned shortly and handed him several sheets of paper. Snow examined them carefully and handed them back to Alexandra. There was another long pause before he spoke again. "We must all hurry, lest we be late for the funeral."

In her peripheral vision Alexandra caught Nicholas' sudden look of surprise. "Certainly," she said to Snow.

"Perhaps you're right. Perhaps Mrs. Orkwright's request places the situation in a new light," Snow said. It was unlike him to give up his argument so easily. "And the fact that you went into the dwelling late at night to perform the autopsy is, perhaps understandable, although certainly in bad form, if not illegal. We can discuss this later. For the moment, however, you are fortunate that Mr. Gibbs's concern was that you had desecrated the body and not the fact that you entered his property, locked or unlocked, without his invitation. Perhaps I will be able to make him understand the circumstances." He had already started for the door.

Alexandra and Nicholas exchanged a quick glance. "Of course," she said to Snow's back. She watched him leave before she turned to Nicholas. "He seemed relieved, didn't he? That I didn't find anything, I mean."

"Uncommonly relieved," Nicholas said, "and, oddly, not anxious to arrest you for your decidedly illegal act of entering a house not your own without permission. What do you make of that?"

"As I said, he was quite obviously relieved that I didn't find anything, and he was willing to let my indiscretion pass in the hope that I will be grateful enough not to stir things up more."

"Precisely. You were quite lucky, Dr. Gladstone, but you were foolish to speak so openly. You could have incriminated yourself."

"The important thing is that I didn't." Alexandra took her cloak from the rack near the door.

"We can't be sure of that," Nicholas said, helping her with her cloak. "And you must never contemplate discussing your actions without consulting me first."

"I'm afraid that would be rather inconvenient." She opened the door. "I must hurry, Mr. Forsythe. You are quite welcome to stay here with Zack if you like."

Zack growled.

"I shall see you at the funeral." He followed her out and

walked toward the inn while she took another direction toward the church.

A large gathering of carriages was waiting outside the church when Alexandra arrived. The funeral coach, draped in black velvet, was among them. Six black plumes ruffled in the breeze atop the heads of the horses. They were attended by a groom, also dressed in black and with an old-fashioned weeper tied around his top hat, the length of the black cloth flowing down his back. Inside the church was more black, row after row of it, like a field of blighted wheat. Neither Jane Orkwright nor young Will were among the mourners, since it was not customary for ladies of her class nor their children to attend the funeral.

Alexandra slid into her pew next to Nancy, who gave her a worried look, then leaned toward her and whispered, "What did the constable want?" Alexandra responded only by a reassuring pat on her hand and turning her attention to the eulogy the vicar was reading, extolling the admiral's admirable career and faithful service to the queen, her Royal Navy, and to England.

Admiral Orkwright was known to have family in the area. He had, in fact, grown up as the second son of some minor landed gentry in a neighboring parish, which accounted for his coming back to the general area to retire. It also accounted for what must have been a few male acquaintances occupying the front pews. The ladies in the family, if there were any, did not attend. They would be at Gull House comforting Jane.

It was not until the service ended and the sealed casket had been removed from the church that Alexandra saw Nicholas. He had obviously slipped in late, and he had transformed himself into a properly dressed, if somewhat bruised and sallow-faced gentleman. He saw her as well and signaled to her. Alexandra tried to acknowledge his signal and move toward him, but Nancy distracted her.

"You've got to tell me, Miss Alex, what did the constable want?" She spoke in an animated and nervous whisper.

"To inform me that he knew about the autopsy I performed on the admiral." Alexandra whispered her answer as she kept her eye on Nicholas.

Nancy grabbed her arm and kept her from advancing toward him. The expression on her face was one of pure fear. "I knew he'd find out! And now it's the gallows for us!" she said aloud.

"Not yet, Nancy. That's one adventure we'll have to postpone for a while." Alexandra spoke in a low voice, nodding to others who greeted her.

"I beg you, don't toy with me, Miss Alex, not when I'm about to succumb to apoplexy."

"What is it about funerals that brings out the theatrics in you? Apoplexy would be a waste of your time, since I think the constable has lost interest in us. He seemed quite relieved when he realized that I'd learned nothing as a result of the autopsy."

It took Nancy no time at all to digest the meaning of that. "Relieved, was he? What was he afraid we'd find?"

Alexandra didn't have a chance to tell Nancy that she was wondering the same thing before Nicholas approached.

"There are some advantages to arriving late and sitting in the back," he said, taking her arm and leading her toward the crowd that had followed the casket to the grave site in the churchyard. "One hears all the gossip on the back pew."

"Gossip?" Alexandra said.

"It seems you and the boys at the tavern aren't the only ones who thinks the admiral's death was no accident," he said. "The back pew people are convinced they know who killed him."

"Back pew people, sir?" Nancy tempered her impertinence with that last *sir.* "You mean the likes of Nell Stillwell and her husband, Dave don't you? And of course there's Lil Sommer, the cobbler's wife, and Edith Prodder, a gossip if ever I've seen one. My own mother always told me not to take stock in gossip from the likes of them, but Miss Alex here says it bears considering."

"Indeed?" There was a look of surprise on Nicholas's face. He seemed to have forgotten, for the moment at least, his earlier assessment of Nancy's evil nature.

Nancy nodded, and Alexandra felt her face grow hot. "Nancy, that's not exactly the way I—"

"She says whether 'tis true or not, it holds a key that will help one come to the truth."

"I say, rather interesting theory. An aficionado of gossip . . . hummm." Nicholas was enjoying himself.

"More like a student of gossip, sir. So what was the gossip, sir? Something about the old salt, I suppose." Nancy was trying but failing to be on her best behavior.

Nicholas shook his head. "Oh no, the admiral was a much-admired man, it seems."

"Yes," Alexandra said, hoping that if she spoke Nancy would not. "He had a good name in this community."

Nicholas glanced at her, and his expression became more serious. "They're blaming John Killborn. They say he's ungrateful for all the admiral did for him. They say he's simply a bad seed."

Nancy glanced at Alexandra and spoke the words Alexandra would not allow herself to say. "And I think Constable Snow thinks he did it, as well. So why is he protecting him?"

10

Mary Prodder's condition was worsening rapidly. She had developed an unusually high fever. Edith, her daughter-in-law, was, as usual, oblivious to it. She could talk of nothing else except the admiral's funeral, the growing rumor that John Killborn had murdered him, and, of course, her own real or imagined ailments.

Alexandra had stopped by the Prodder cottage on her morning rounds. While she tried to concentrate on making Mary more comfortable and readjusting the splint she wore, Edith stood beside the bed and kept up a constant monologue, going over the old gossip.

" 'Tis a true scandal if you ask me. The whole business. The admiral dying in ladies' drawers! Why, who would 'ave done such a thing to 'im? Something to bring shame down on 'im, it was. On 'im and his missus. Oh yes, she's high-born, they say, but is it a wonder that elder son of hers turned out the way 'e did? Ended up in prison, didn't 'e? And wasn't I the one who said 'e would? 'Tis a shame the things that goes on in that family. I happen to know myself that the admiral tried to make the best of it. For the children's sake, I'm sure. But that Killborn boy, who's not his own, but a stepson, you know, 'e was ungrateful for all the admiral done for 'im. Seen 'im myself speak disrespectful to the admiral. Called 'im a sorry bastard, 'e did. . . ."

Alexandra unwound the long bandage that held Mary's splint in place, trying not to move her leg.

"How is Mrs. Orkwright?" Mary's voice was weak, and Alexandra was surprised to hear her speak at all.

"I'm concerned about her," Alexandra said. "She seems very fragile."

"Did my best for her. I know she's suffered," Mary said. She winced and flailed her arms as Alexandra turned her body. The fever was making her restless.

"Yes," Alexandra said, "grief is suffering of the worst kind, but you mustn't worry about it, Mary."

"*Bastard,* 'e said, in the presence of ladies. I wasn't more than twenty feet away." Edith had hardly paused to breathe and was completely unmindful of Mary's pain. " 'Twas at Nell's shop I heard it when I was buyin' a bit o' mutton for our supper. They was standin' in front of the shop to do their arguing, the admiral and 'is good-for-naught stepson. Nell heard 'em as well, so you can ask her if ye like. The admiral never said a word. A pure gentleman, 'e was. Just suffered the boy to go on ravin' at 'im." She stopped to take a breathe and leaned closer. "They say he killed the admiral, and I tell you it wouldn't surprise me if it's true. Drownded 'im, Nell said. She's sure of it. And dressed 'im in ladies' drawers? Why? I'll tell ye why. ' 'E's a bad seed, 'e is. Why, they say 'is mother, for all 'er fine bloodlines and 'er gentle ways, would o' starved, and John Killborn along with 'er, had not the admiral married 'er. . . ."

Alexandra dampened a cloth in the basin near Mary's bed and bathed her face with it. Mary coughed twice, and Alexandra didn't like the sound of it. It suggested an inflammation of the lungs. "How long did you lie out in the cold before the constable found you, Mary?" she asked.

Mary ignored her. She was still talking about Jane Orkwright. "She's an angel, she is. I did my best for her."

"Of course, Mary. Hush now," Alexandra said when Mary grew agitated again.

"Bloodlines won't put food on the table, now, will they?" Edith continued heedlessly. "We all has to fill our bellies in our own way, don't we? And I guess Mrs. Orkwright found 'er own way, and if ye ask me . . ."

Alexandra bent over Mary with her stethoscope, listening to her lungs. There was a slight whooshing sound just as she expected, judging from the cough. When she examined her further she saw an angry red spot on her backside—the beginning of a bedsore. "Have you been turning Mary frequently and changing the bed linens as I asked you to, Edith?"

" 'Tis a pure shame the way . . . Have I what? Turned 'er? Why, of course. Until it got me down in me back, that is. Can't even lift a spoon now." Edith made her voice sound weaker, and she rubbed at her back. "She's a burden, she is." Edith sank down on Mary's bed, causing Mary to wince with pain again as the mattress shifted. "You mustn't believe her if she tells you I 'aven't cared for her proper. She's gone a bit daft."

" 'Twould help if I could only stand and get out o' bed." Mary's voice was little more than a whisper.

"Yes, but you mustn't," Alexandra said. "You must let the broken bone heal."

"But I grow weaker and weaker with each hour I lie in this bed," Mary said. "Haply I could walk about some with a bit o' 'elp?"

"A bit o' 'elp?" Edith screeched before Alexandra could reply. "And who do ye think could 'elp ye?" She glanced at Alexandra. "She cares not a whit for anyone but 'erself. She can see, plain as day, I'm not a well woman, and yet she wants me to 'elp 'er turn over and to bring 'er a drink o' water. She's nothin' but—"

"Mary needs constant care," Alexandra said, interrupting Edith. "If you are unable to provide it, then we shall have to find another solution."

"If it's hospital yer thinkin', there'll be none o' that." Edith's voice had become a screech. "We can't have people thinkin' we're charity cases."

In truth, Alexandra had been thinking of the hospital in neighboring Bradfordshire where she herself had gone for part of her medical training. It was a charity hospital, of course. Most hospitals were, since the middle and upper classes were treated at home. The Prodders were of neither middle nor upper class, but Edith's pride could keep Mary out of hospital where she would at least receive the care she needed.

"Perhaps you could hire a nurse, then," Alexandra said.

Edith gave her a disdainful look. "Hire a nurse you say? It's not money we're made of, you know."

Alexandra's patience shattered, and she let the shards fly at Edith. "This woman will be removed from this house and taken to hospital. If she is not, she will die, but not soon enough to suit you, I'm afraid. It could be a lingering death that would, I'm sure, be of some inconvenience to you. You may hire a carriage to take her to hospital or I will contact the hospital myself and have the charity carriage convey her there."

Edith gave her a look that was part surprise and part anger. Finally, she spoke. "I'll have her there by morning, and there'll be no charity carriage coming to this house."

Alexandra took the time to readjust Mary's pillows and to give her a bit of laudanum before she left. Edith had left the room in a sullen pout, but she reappeared and volleyed a parting shot just as Alexandra was leaving.

" 'Tis a sad world we live in when a practitioner tries to disgrace a respectable woman such as meself. Yer father would never done it, I can tell you that."

Alexandra, who by now was outside the door, turned around to face her, prepared to refute the unfavorable comparison to her father, but Edith kept talking.

"A sad world, I tells ye. A practitioner what can't cure a mere broken bone, and a constable what's afraid to do 'is duty and arrest a cold-blooded killer. We'll all die in Newton, we will, from the neglect of one or both of ye."

Alexandra was caught by surprise at her statement about the constable. "Constable Snow's afraid?" Alexandra said, in spite of her better judgment.

"You don't believe it?" Edith spat the words at her. " 'Course 'e's afraid. Doesn't want to hurt 'is darling Jane."

Alexandra was too shocked to speak for a moment, but she finally managed to say, "Surely you're not implying—" She was unable to say more before Edith slammed the door.

The remaining house calls went quickly, one a child near the end of her recovery from pneumonia, and Hannibal Talbot, who, though the pain from his bladder stones persisted, refused to allow her in the house. She was home before noon. Nancy's beef and vegetables were still simmering, and she was just dumping the pudding from the boiling cloth when Alexandra arrived. She went straight to her surgery and sat down at her desk. Picking up a pen, she dipped it in the inkwell and tried to catch up on her patient records, but she found it difficult to concentrate. Her thoughts kept returning to Jane and Constable Snow, as they had ever since Edith Prodder made the ugly innuendo.

She didn't know how long Nancy had been standing in the doorway to the surgery when she finally noticed her.

"Nancy! You startled me."

"There's something wrong," Nancy said. "I can always tell when you sit there staring at nothing. What is it? Which one of your patients has worsened?"

"Mary Prodder. I'm having her sent to hospital." Alexandra answered without looking at her.

Nancy said nothing for several seconds, and then said, "Mary Prodder, is it?" before she turned away. Within a few minutes she returned to announce that lunch was ready, and Alexandra followed her to the kitchen for their informal dining. In spite of the fact that most members of the upper middle class took their heavier meal in the evening, Alexandra's father had always insisted it was better for the digestive system to eat as the working class did, with the heavier meal at noon and a light, early supper. She and Nancy still lived by that rule.

Instead of their usual chatter, they each ate their boiled beef in virtual silence. Nancy's only comment was, "Needs a bit a salt, does it not?" To which, Alexandra replied, "What? Oh no, it's quite all right."

Finally, after another long silence, Nancy spoke. " 'Tisn't Mary Prodder, is it? Come now, don't look at me that way. I know 'tisn't Mary. If 'twas a patient troubling you, you'd be talking about the problem. Going over it in your mind. Using me as your sounding board. So what is it now? Something about Mr. Forsythe? Ah, of course 'tis not. Not like you at all to be museful about a gentleman." There was another moment of silence before she spoke again. "Of course!"

She laid her fork and knife aside and leaned toward Alexandra. " 'Tis the admiral! Or else his wife! What have you learned? You want to talk about it, I can see."

Alexandra who had hardly taken a bite of her lunch, stopped toying with the strips of beef on her plate and looked at Nancy. "How is it you read me so well?"

Nancy shrugged. "Your father used to ask the same thing of my mother. They were great friends, the two of them, as you know. Much like the two of us."

Alexandra sighed and looked at Nancy. "All right. I suppose I do want to talk about what's troubling me. It seems Mr. Forsythe may have been correct when he said some are convinced John Killborn murdered his stepfather. And apparently you aren't the only one who suspects the constable is protecting him."

Nancy waited for Alexandra to say more, and when it appeared she would not, she said, "And it troubles you that both Mr. Forsythe and I may be right?"

"Of course not," Alexandra said. "It's just that . . . well, it's what Edith Prodder suggested as a motive."

"Which was . . ."

"She . . . Oh, Nancy, it's nothing but spurious gossip." Alexandra dropped her gaze to her plate, picked up her fork, and stared at the beef.

"Perhaps 'tis no more than gossip," Nancy said. "But 'tis bothering you. A grain of truth in the gossip, perhaps?"

Alexandra lifted her gaze to Nancy and after another pause spoke. "She suggested that the constable may be in love with Jane Orkwright." She shook her head. "I told you. Spurious gossip."

Nancy showed no surprise. "If 'tis spurious, then why does it trouble you so?"

"Well, of course it has to be completely false, doesn't it? Jane Orkwright couldn't possibly be . . ." Alexandra found she couldn't go on.

"Couldn't what?" Nancy leaned forward even more, pressing her. "Couldn't possibly be having an affair? Is that what's troubling you?"

Alexandra kept her eyes down, wanting the conversation

to end. "Of course she couldn't, and of course the suggestion troubles me." She stabbed at the beef.

Nancy appeared to have completely forgotten her food, however. "But you said Edith suggested the constable might be in love with Mrs. Orkwright. She didn't suggest 'twas reciprocal, did she? Perhaps you only read that into it, because you're afraid 'tis true."

Alexandra dropped her fork, and it clattered against her plate. Was Nancy right? Had she somehow suspected a lover all along? But surely not Constable Snow.

Nancy leaned back in her chair and folded her arms. "You must admit, when you think about it, it makes sense."

"Nancy . . ."

"Well, it does, doesn't it? He's been unusually protective all along. Not wanting you to do the autopsy. You have to admit that's a bit odd. If he was afraid you'd find something that would cause trouble for Mrs. Orkwright, something that would point to murder and perhaps to her son, then it begins to make sense, doesn't it?"

Alexandra pushed her chair back, having now completely given up on eating. "That's nothing but speculation based on gossip. It would make just as much sense to say the constable himself killed the admiral. That would certainly give him a motive to squelch evidence, wouldn't it? You could even speculate that Jane killed the admiral because the constable was her lover, and the constable is protecting her. Can't you see how convoluted and ridiculous this can become?"

Nancy had no immediate reply. She wore a thoughtful look and then spoke, as if to herself. "We're forgetting the maid, Annie. If what young Will said is true, and the admiral was cruel to her, then perhaps she had a motive to kill him. And perhaps Constable Snow is in love with Annie, not Mrs. Orkwright. So it could be Annie he's protecting."

Alexandra shook her head. "It's becoming even more tangled."

Nancy stood and began clearing the table. "All right, so maybe 'tis only gossip, but remember you said yourself it often holds a key to the truth."

Alexandra stood as well, knowing it was time to open the

surgery. Patients would be arriving soon. "But where is that key, Nancy? What are we overlooking?"

The technological revolution that was spreading across the United States and seeping into Britain was a curiosity to Nicholas. Anyone with even a modicum of intellect, he assumed, would be curious and excited about the idea of having a conversation with another person twenty miles or more away. A device was held to the ear and another device to the mouth. It was necessary for both parties to have such an instrument, and it was all done with magnetism and electrical currents and some rather curious vibrations and waves of sound. An American named Bell had five years ago, patented the instrument. Although Nicholas had seen the device only a few times, there was some talk that they would soon be commonplace in London.

Another American, Thomas something-or-other, had, only last year, produced an electrical lamp that needed no oil, yet burned for hours.

Nicholas would have dismissed both the speaking device and the lamp as unlikely to become commonplace had it not been for the fact that modern telegraphy, perfected by another American by the name of Morse, had spread so quickly to England from America.

Such amazing technological advances were a worry to Nicholas as well as a curiosity. A worry because it was happening so fast, and he did not completely understand how electricity carried sound, or even codes of dots and dashes nor how or why filament and electricity worked together to produce constant light. He worried that the modern world was leaving him behind, and that a man such as he, with no strong technical bent and who preferred reading the law and the classics, would soon be archaic.

In spite of that fear, he had to live in the current world, so he made occasional use of the bewildering telegraph, and, he supposed, in time, he would use lamps and conversational devices he did not understand.

There was a small telegraph office in Newton-Upon-Sea, and it was there that Nicholas went early in the morning to send one of the coded messages called "telegrams" to his colleague, Lesley Coldwell, in London. The cost of the procedure did not allow one the luxury of refined literacy. Instead, the language had to be curt and primitive.

Find all available information on J. Killborn and family Stop Need immediately Stop

Killborn's actions, along with the mysterious death of his stepfather and the gossip of the townspeople, had aroused Nicholas's curiosity. Perhaps there was some connection to young Killborn's escape and his stepfather's death.

Lesley, a fellow barrister with whom he'd worked on a number of particularly knotty cases, would be delighted to receive the electrically transmitted message. He was something of an aficionado of all things scientific and a dedicated reader of the French author Jules Verne. In fact, Lesley himself was forever scribbling stories about an imagined future in which science and technology had completely changed the world and its people in rather odd ways. He would try the stories out on Nicholas from time to time when Nicholas couldn't avoid it. For that, however, Nicholas calculated that Lesley owed him a favor. He could do his research for him.

Nicholas had returned to his rented room after sending the message on its miraculous journey, prepared to wait several days for a reply. He realized that the search for the information he needed was something that, by rights, he should have done himself when he accepted the case. It was always important to learn as much as possible about one's clients, and a good place to start was certain public records. Lesley would know the procedure. He would know exactly the records to search.

That Nicholas himself had not done the search was owed to the fact he had not been retained as Killborn's barrister until late in the game. As he remembered, that was one of the pitfalls Lesley and his other colleagues had warned him about. It had made them wonder why he'd been so eager to accept the case.

After he had sent the message and returned to his room above the Blue Ram, he'd spent virtually all of his time working at a makeshift desk. In spite of the fact that his official reason for being in Newton-Upon-Sea had literally slipped through his fingers, there was still work to do—an endless number of documents to prepare for the trial, should Killborn be recaptured, as well as research for his defense. Waiting for the answer to his telegram gave him a perfect excuse for staying in town rather than returning to London.

He had in mind to invite Alexandra to dine with him tonight, but he would have to wait until her surgery hours were over before he asked. Eventually, he abandoned his work and turned to fretting about the fact that the tavern was the only place in town to dine, and it was not the sort of place to which one took a lady. He could, of course, have the meal sent up to his room, but it was out of the question to ask her to join him there. Could he take her to the neighboring town of Bradfordshire? Probably not, since it would make their return to Newton far too late to be respectable.

He was still fretting when he heard a knock at his door. Expecting it to be Morton, who was housed in the room next door, coming to inquire about his needs, he called out for him to enter while still seated at his desk. He was surprised to have the door opened by a young man he didn't recognize. The young man was holding something in his hand. When he spoke, his voice had the squeak of an adolescent.

"Telegram for Mr. Nicholas Forsythe, Esquire."

"I am he," Nicholas said, standing and taking the paper from the boy's hand. He was surprised by the quick response from Lesley and once again in awe of the marvels of the modern age in which messages could travel so quickly. He paid the boy and opened the paper, knowing that, since the reply had come so soon, Lesley would likely be telling him he could not spare the time to do his research for him.

He was wrong. Lesley's reply read:

Mother married seven years ago to George E. Orkwright Stop Petitioned Divorce Court for divorce last year Stop Petition withdrawn Stop.

The message left Nicholas with troubling questions. It was a drastic, even scandalous step for a woman of Mrs. Orkwright's class to petition for divorce. Why would she risk the scandal? What would cause a woman who seemed to love her husband as Mrs. Orkwright did to think of divorcing him?

11

Alexandra could hear Hannibal Talbot screaming well be-
fore she reached his front door. His wife, Mildryd, was crying and shivering with cold as she, along with Alexandra,
Nancy, and Zack hurried toward the house. She had come to
fetch Alexandra in the dark of the winter night wearing only
a shawl over her nightgown, and now a fierce and biting
wind had swept in from the north, spitting sleet.

"Oh lord, he's dying, he is!" Mildryd stumbled as she
cried out, and Nancy had to grab her arm to keep her from
falling.

"Now, now, my dear. Wait until Dr. Gladstone has a look
before you pronounce him dead." Nancy spoke in a soothing
tone, but it did little to stop Mildryd's tears. Alexandra had
brought Nancy along knowing she would need her services.
Zack was with them because he saw it as his duty to accompany when either of the two women went out in the dark of
night.

Alexandra opened the unlocked door to the Talbot cottage
and allowed Zack to enter ahead of her. Although he had
been trained to wait outside when Alexandra entered a patient's home, she would not consider leaving him out in the
raw, snarling wind of this night.

"Is it you, woman?" Hannibal called. "Took yer leisure
gettin' here, damn you! Did ye bring the doc . . ." His voice
trailed off into an agonizing groan. As Alexandra entered the

room she saw that his face was pale and damp with sweat. As she watched, his eyes rolled back so that only the whites shown. He seemed about to lose consciousness, which, Alexandra observed, might be of some advantage.

That was not to be, however. Hannibal focused his eyes, and when he saw her, let out a long string of profanities. It was impossible to tell whether they were directed at her or at the pain he was experiencing.

"I drunk the damned water until I near drowned, and I drunk all the bloody tonics you sent. Now I'm worse. Yer damned medicine is going to kill me." His voice was weak, and his lips bloodless.

Alexandra turned to his wife. "Is it true? He's had plenty of water and the infusion of carrot and hare moss?"

Mildryd, who by now was as pale as her husband, nodded. "Made him piss at first, it did, but now he cannot piss more than a drop."

Alexandra nodded and placed her hand on Hannibal's forehead, checking for fever. His head was cold and damp to the touch. At that same moment, he screamed again and clutched his crotch.

"It's me pecker! It hurts like the fires of hell! Aaaargh!"

Each time he groaned or cried out, Zack growled low in this throat.

Alexandra turned to Mildryd. "Clear your table please. Take everything off." Mildryd seemed glad to have something to do, and she set about removing various bowls and platters from the table surface. As soon as she was finished, Nancy spread a large rubber sheet across the table, covering it entirely. Then she and Alexandra moved in practiced unison toward Hannibal, each taking an arm.

"There you go, Mr. T." Nancy spoke in a cheerful voice. "Let us give you a hand to the table."

Hannibal seemed confused. "The table?"

"I must operate, sir," Alexandra said.

"Operate? You? On my private parts?" He seemed about to protest, but he was wracked with pain again and crumbled under the grasps of the two women, almost falling to the floor. They led him, with some difficulty, toward the table. As soon as he was seated on the edge, Nancy pulled a wire apparatus shaped like half a birdcage from the large valise she had brought with her. Several layers of cloth had been packed into the curve of the wire. She quickly doused them with ether and clamped the device over his nose and mouth. Although the use of chloroform had become quite popular with surgeons, especially after the queen had used it for the birth of her last child, Alexandra preferred ether, which she considered less damaging to the body.

"Lie back, Mr. T." Nancy gave him a firm push as she spoke. As soon as he was on his back, she dripped more of the strong smelling liquid into the mask. "Rest now," she crooned. "This will be over soon."

As she washed her hands, Alexandra spoke over her shoulder to a frightened Mildryd. "Perhaps you would like to wait in the other room." Mildryd nodded, but she seemed unable to move. "It's good that you saw to it that your husband drank the water and the tonic. It has helped flushed the inflammation from his body. But if the flow of urine has stopped, inflammation will surely worsen."

Mildryd looked at her uncomprehending. Alexandra glanced at Zack. "Out!" she said, her voice soft. Still looking at Zack, she nodded toward Mildryd. Zack went to the frightened woman immediately and nudged her with his nose, pushing her toward the door. She didn't resist, and when she and Zack were finally clear of the door, Nancy closed it and returned to her duty with the mask.

"Is the inflammation still present?" she asked, dripping a bit more ether into the apparatus.

"I can't be sure, of course, but we have no choice but to operate," Alexandra said. She finished washing her hands and lifted Hannibal Talbot's nightshirt, pushing it above her waist. When she had scrubbed the perineum with carbolic acid, she used a scalpel to make a perpendicular incision between the root of Hannibal's penis and rectum. With her finger she dilated the urethra and the neck of the bladder until she was certain she could insert the forceps and remove the stone, which appeared to be quite large. Once it was out, she dropped it into a basin and repeated the procedure to remove two more smaller stones. Nancy, in the meantime, continued to hold the mask firmly to Hannibal's face and to drip the liquid ether onto the cloth.

Alexandra's stitches to close the wound went quickly. She used catgut, which the body would absorb, for the deep area and a row of linen stitches, which would have to be removed, for the outside.

The operation was completed in less than an hour, and the kitchen as well as the rest of the house was infused with the odor of ether. With the help of Mildryd, Nancy and Alexandra managed to transport a still unconscious Hannibal to his bed. While they waited for him to awaken, Alexandra and Nancy returned the kitchen table to its former state and cleaned their instruments.

By the time they were finished, Hannibal was awake and was vomiting with a violence. Mildryd was alarmed, but Alexandra assured her that vomiting was to be expected after the administration of the anesthesia. She and Nancy waited a little longer until she was certain the paregoric she gave him for pain and nausea had taken effect. Then, with instructions that Hannibal was to be kept quiet until Alexandra came to see him in the morning, they left for home.

Zack lead the way through the darkness and the gnawing wind and sleet, and Alexandra, shivering in spite of her heavy cloak, vowed she would not go another winter without purchasing a carriage. For now, she was looking forward to a cup of warm milk and the comfort of her feather bed. Before they reached the front door, however, and even before Zack's sharp bark, Alexandra knew that something was wrong.

She could make out three figures standing a few feet away from the house, one of them holding a lantern. Two of them were Rob and Artie. But who was the other person? And why were they standing out in the cold wind and sleet?

"Another patient with an emergency?" Nancy asked.

"I don't know," Alexandra said, in spite of the strong feeling she had that this was not a patient. It was more than sixth sense that told her, however. She had, as was her custom, told Rob and Artie where she had gone, and they had been trained to fetch her if a patient came seeking her.

If she had not been convinced before, she was doubly

convinced that the person standing with the boys was no patient when Zack barked again. This time Rob, Artie, and the stranger all three turned toward the sound. The lantern was quickly doused, and the three figures disappeared.

Nancy stopped and took Alexandra's arm in a protective gesture, as if to hold her back. "And what was the meaning of that?" she asked.

"I don't know. Odd, wasn't it?" Alexandra moved toward the house with caution. Zack, however, took no caution. He raced ahead, barking.

"They're up to no good," Nancy said, walking next to Alexandra. The wind whipped their skirts against their legs. "Didn't I tell you there would be trouble if you hired those two? The likes of them can never give up their criminal ways."

"If I remember correctly, my dear Nancy, it was you who hired them." Alexandra had, by now, picked up her pace as much as possible in the wind. "I believe you said they were good boys at heart, and all they needed was a chance for a better life and they would prove to be model citizens."

Nancy's only reply to Alexandra's irrefutable claim was an indignant sniff as she, too, quickened her steps.

By the time they reached the grounds, Zack was in front of the stable barking frantically. There was neither sound nor light coming from the apartment above the stable where the boys lived. Alexandra moved toward the outer stairs that led to the apartment, but Nancy once again caught her arm.

"It could be dangerous!" she whispered.

"Nonsense," Alexandra said, although she felt a moment's hesitancy. She advanced a few steps up the stairway, then called out, "Rob? Artie? Are you all right?"

There was no answer. She called out again, and this time, after a long pause Rob replied. "We's all right, Dr. Gladstone. Just sleeping is all." His voice didn't sound in the least sleepy.

"Who is up there with you?" Alexandra's lips were so numb with cold she could hardly form the words.

There was another pause and a muffled sound of movement and then Rob's voice again. "Nobody, Doc. Just me and Artie."

Zack barked twice, loud and sharp, voicing his disagreement with Rob's claim.

There was another sound of movement and an urgent, incomprehensible murmur from what seemed to be young Artie. Alexandra pulled her skirt up above her shoe tops and hurried up the steps. Behind her Nancy cried out in a frightened voice, warning her not to go any farther. Alexandra ignored her and tried to ignore the fear pounding in her chest. If the boys were in trouble, if someone was up there who could harm them, she had to stop whomever it was. By the time she reached the apartment at the top of the stairs, Nancy was beside her, pounding on the door along with her. Zack was behind them barking his opinion in loud monosyllables.

Finally, the door opened slightly, just wide enough for Rob to wedge his face in the space between the door and the jamb. "What is it? We was sleepin', we was."

"I only wanted to be certain you're both all right." Alexandra spoke in an unnaturally loud voice, then she leaned close to Rob's face and whispered, "I know there's someone in there. I saw him with you in the lantern light."

Rob gave no reply, and it was impossible to see clearly enough in the darkness to judge the expression on his face. Alexandra interpreted his hesitancy as fear. "I'll send Nancy for the constable and I'll stay here nearby. Just try to stay calm."

"No need for the constable!" Rob took a quick, nervous glance over his shoulder. "Nothin's wrong. It's best ye go to the 'ouse, miss. Get out of the cold, what?"

"Rob, I know there's someone in there. Who is it?" Impatience mixed with fear in Alexandra's voice.

Rob seemed about to protest again, but the sound of footsteps behind him distracted him as well as Alexandra. "It's the lady doctor, isn't it?" The voice was that of a male, older than Artie, and Alexandra could make out the form of a young man standing behind Rob, his white shirt reflecting lamplight, giving him an eerie aura. "I want to talk to her." He placed a hand on Rob's shoulder and pulled him out of the way. "Dr. Gladstone?" he said, looking at her.

"Yes, I'm Dr. Gladstone, but who are—"

He glanced at Nancy. "Who is she?"

"This is Nancy," Alexandra said, uneasy.

"Go back to the house, Nancy. Dr. Gladstone will be all right. I promise you. And take the dog with you."

Nancy didn't move. "Do as he says," Alexandra told her.

"But . . ."

"Go, Nancy. Please."

Nancy turned around reluctantly and started down the stairs, the wind making her cloak billow behind her like a sail. Zack was equally reluctant, and Nancy had to pull hard on the scruff of his neck to get him to move. Alexandra was unable to tell whether or not she was successful as the young man took her arm and pulled her into the room, which was warmed by a wood stove designed for cooking.

"I'm John Killborn," the young man said before she could ask again. "Mrs. Jane Orkwright is my mother, and you are her friend, I believe."

"John!" This time it was Alexandra who gave an uneasy glance around. "What are you . . ."

"I must talk to you," he said again, more forcefully this time.

"Perhaps you would like to come into the house. I could have Nancy prepare a hot cup of tea." Alexandra's voice was unsteady. She knew she could be charged with harboring a fugitive if she wasn't careful.

"No, we'll talk here." There was a harsh, commanding edge to his tone.

Alexandra neither moved nor spoke for a moment as she considered the situation. She took a step farther into the apartment. In the opposite end of the room little Artie was trying to light another lamp.

"Over here." John motioned with his head toward the small table and two chairs she had provided for Rob and Artie. She walked with John toward the chairs while the two boys watched her. "Give us some privacy, please." John spoke to the boys without looking at them, and the two of them disappeared immediately into the even smaller adjoining room where their bunks were. Besides the wood-burning stove next to the window and the table and chairs, there were cupboards for dishes and supplies. It was clear, however that the stove was used mostly for heat rather than cooking, and the cupboards were little used as well, since Nancy habitually brought food to the boys when she prepared her own and Alexandra's meals.

When she sat down at the table across from John and saw his face illuminated by the lamp, she was struck by how young he looked. In spite of his size and his mannerisms, he was little more than a boy. Most striking was the terrible sadness in his eyes where she had expected fear.

"What you are doing is very dangerous." Her voice was strained with tension. "You must turn yourself in to the—"

"We are not going to talk about me." A frown creased his otherwise smooth brow. "We are going to talk about my mother." Outside the wind howled and sleet pelted the window.

Alexandra looked at him without speaking. His repeated abruptness had a slightly disorienting effect on her.

"I know you have been a friend to her." He had lost some of his cockiness and seemed a bit uneasy now.

"I have tried to be." Alexandra spoke quietly, waiting to see where he was leading.

John leaned back in his chair, affecting a confident, in-command attitude. "You must tell me how she is holding up." It was clear now that he was making a concerted attempt to cover his uneasiness with bravado.

"Holding up? Why, she's quite distraught. After all, she's lost a husband and in the same week heard of her son's escape from Newgate, which she understands can bring serious repercussions." There was the sting of anger in her voice.

John's fist came down on the table with a hard thud. "I told you we're not here to talk about me!" He stood up, knocking over his chair. He kicked it out of his way. "You don't know my mother, after all. I should have known you'd be like the rest of them. You're no help to me at all."

Rob opened the door a crack and stared at John, a puzzled look on his face. Behind him, Artie was wide-eyed and frightened. John's temper tantrum had obviously surprised both of them.

"If you're hoping not to call attention to your whereabouts,

I suggest you calm yourself." Alexandra, still seated at the table, kept her voice quiet.

John stopped his raging long enough to glance at her. His shoulders drooped, and he looked tired. For a moment she thought he was about to cry. Picking up the chair, he replaced it next to the table and sat down. Alexandra started to reach her hand to cover his, but thought better of it.

John was silent for a moment longer. "I can't stand that they say she did it," he said finally.

"John, you're wrong, no one . . ." Alexandra still kept her voice low, hoping not to disturb him more.

"They'll say it's because of me." He shivered. The wind had whipped up even more, seeping through the window to John's back and defeating the heat emanating from the belly of the stove. "They'll say she was trying to protect me from the bastard."

"Is that true, John? Was she trying to protect you?" Alexandra knew she was risking another outburst.

John surprised her by raising his eyes slowly to look at her. Those eyes glistened with unshed tears. He shook his head slowly. "No."

"So that was not a reason to kill him."

"Of course not," he said, the anger returning to his voice. He seemed agitated again, and Alexandra studied his face, trying to determine whether or not he was lying, but she found it impossible to judge.

"But you didn't get on well with the admiral, did you?" she asked.

"I hated the bastard!"

"Enough to kill him?"

John looked up at her suddenly. His face had gone white. "What are you saying?"

"Did you hate him enough to kill him?"

John stood and leaned toward her across the table. He appeared ready to attack. "I don't like the sound of what you're—"

Rob bounded across the room and had him by the arms before he could say more. "It's all right, bloke. She don't mean nothin' by it," Rob said. At the same time he gave Alexandra a warning look.

"I'm sorry, John. Perhaps I was out of line. You wanted to talk to me about your mother."

He jerked himself free of Rob's grip. "Is she holding up all right? Can you tell me that much at least?"

"She has a lot to bear," Alexandra said, trying to keep any hint of fear or excitement out of her voice. "But she seems to be a strong woman."

"She's not as strong as you think." His anger had not completely dissipated. "But she wouldn't kill the old man. You must understand that."

"I do understand that, of course, but I'm afraid I don't understand your wrath or this particular concern of yours. As I said, I don't think a significant number of people believe your mother killed her husband. More important, the constable doesn't seem to think so."

For a moment John appeared stunned, as if she had given him unexpected news. The sadness returned to his eyes just as quickly, however. He slumped once more into the chair in which he'd been sitting and leaned toward her with the weariness and desperation of an old man. "You must not let your guard down. You must help me protect her."

"Against whom, John? I don't understand."

"Just take my word for it. She is in danger. They will try to make her look guilty."

"Who, John? Who will try to make her look guilty?"

"Everyone. The constable, eventually."

Alexandra, feeling more and more frustrated, shook her head. "But why?"

John hesitated a moment as if he was trying to decide whether or not to give her the answer. Finally, he leaned toward her and spoke. "The reason is simply because she . . ."

There was the sudden mind-shattering sound of a blast and then the tinkle of broken window glass. Almost instantaneously John slumped on the table, which was soon covered with his blood.

12

The door to the boys' sleeping quarters burst open. *"What happened?"* Rob shouted as Alexandra jumped to her feet and hurried around the table to John's side. *"Oh Jesus!"* Rob's face turned a sickly white when he saw John slumped on the table, his upper torso covered with blood. Artie was crying, too frightened to be embarrassed.

"Get back! Stay away from the window!" Alexandra cried. She heard the muffled sound of Zack's bark and was suddenly frightened that he might be outside in harm's way. Whoever shot John could shoot Zack as well.

She tried to block out Zack's frantic barking as she tore John's shirt away to get to the wound, thankful it was his shoulder and not his head. He was conscious still and moaning. It was impossible to see the wound even after his shirt was out of the way. All that was visible was the blood that covered his shoulder and back. Using her fingers to find the wound, she pressed her hand against it to stop the bleeding, but blood seeped through her fingers and within a few seconds her hand was covered.

Her medical bag, which she had taken to the Talbots' house to care for Hannibal, sat on the floor beside the table. As she reached for it, still holding one hand on John's shoulder, she glanced at the window and felt a moment of cold fear that the gunman could still be out there.

"Help me move him away from the window."

The two frightened boys responded immediately to her tension-charged voice. They moved the chair with John still in it to a corner of the room. "He's falling! Hold him in the chair, Rob. And you, Artie! If there's still water in the teapot, bring it to me. And that basin on the cupboard."

She pulled a strip of linen from her bag and folded it to press against the wound in another attempt to stop the bleeding. Artie brought the basin and the water and stepped back, wide-eyed. He had stopped his sniffling and stood like a frightened soldier waiting for his next command.

The bleeding slowed, and she washed the wound clean with the water and another swatch of linen she took from her bag. "Artie! Go to the house and fetch Nancy. Tell her I need . . ."

Before she could say another word, the door burst open, and Nancy and Zack rushed into the room.

"Tannic acid!" Nancy said as soon as she saw the wound. She turned around quickly and left the room.

" 'E's comin' round!" Rob stood behind Alexandra, looking over her shoulder, his voice high-pitched with excitement.

Alexandra, still holding the compress against the wound, saw John's eyes flicker and then open wide, full of both pain and confusion. He moaned, tried to sit up, and at the same time, push her hand away from his shoulder. She had hoped he wouldn't regain consciousness until the wound was cauterized.

"Be still," she said. "You've been wounded."

"Shot." John's voice was low and hoarse.

"Any idea who could have done this?" she asked.

John tried to shrug and winced in pain. "Coppers," he said. "I'm a fugitive." His words were choppy and edged with pain. "You won't . . . Won't turn me in."

"Look! The bullet is stuck in the ceiling," Artie said before she could answer.

"That's because the bloke what shot 'im was aiming up." Rob used his arms, as if holding an imaginary rifle, to illustrate how the shooter might have aimed. " 'E was standing down there, below us." Rob pointed to the area from which the shot had come.

Alexandra paid little attention. She was busy discarding the blood-soaked compress and reaching for another.

"You won't turn me in!" John pleaded again, just as Nancy reappeared holding a glass jar containing the acid, which she quickly opened and poured into a thick bandage.

"This is going to hurt, John. Prepare yourself," Alexandra said. She turned to Rob. "Help me hold him." Rob, still wide-eyed, hesitated, then moved quickly to wrap his arms around John's torso, pinning John's good arm to his side. At the same time she signaled Nancy with a nod of her head.

John watched Nancy approach him, and Alexandra felt his body stiffen and then jerk as the acid-soaked bandage touched him. He cried out, a long piercing sound that made Zack howl in sympathy. Behind her Alexandra heard Artie cough and then gag and run toward the chamber pot. By the time the bleeding stopped, John was pale and had mercifully lost consciousness. Nancy set about helping Alexandra dress the twice-wounded shoulder, removing shards of glass and bits of clothing.

The room was quiet as they worked. Even Zack seemed to hold his breath. Rob, who had backed into a corner and placed his arm around young Artie's shoulder, was the first to speak. "You won't, will you, Doc? Turn 'im in to them coppers what shot 'im?"

Nancy spoke up before Alexandra had a chance to reply. "That wasn't the police out there shooting at him, boy."

"And how can ye be knowin' that?" Rob sounded defiant.

"Because 'tisn't the way they work, now is it? The coppers, I mean." She placed her hands on her hips in an equally defiant gesture. "If 'twas them out looking for him, why, they'd knock on the door in a proper way and ask first. They wouldn't be taking the risk of blowing the heads off innocent people."

"Well now, Nance, ain't you the smart one?" Rob tried to sound mocking, but his eyes gave away his secret. They looked as if he thought Nancy made sense. "But who else would be shooting at 'im?" His mocking tone was gone.

"I think we'd best ask him that when he wakes," Nancy said.

Rob turned to Alexandra. "Even if it weren't the coppers

shooting at 'im, ye won't turn 'im over, will ye?"

"Rob, you must understand—"

"Come along now, boys, you've got to help us get him in the house." Nancy interrupted before Alexandra could make her confession that she was duty bound to turn him over to Constable Snow the next morning. "Dr. Gladstone will want to keep an eye on him tonight."

Nancy motioned for each of them to pick up a foot while she and Alexandra took his arms, bracing him as much as possible to keep from disturbing his wound. The movement made him restless, and he moaned again and opened his eyes.

"A bit of laudanum?" Nancy said, glancing at Alexandra as the four of them, with John in tow, moved toward the door.

Before Alexandra could answer, Rob spoke again, still not willing to give up his demand on Alexandra. "You won't send 'im back to that hellhole at Newgate, will you?"

Alexandra suddenly felt very tired. "Rob, you have to understand that I must do what is right and what is, after all, best for—"

"Now, will you stop it, Robin Foggarty!" It was Nancy again, interrupting. She stopped walking, halting the entire party as she glared at Rob. "Neither of us turned you in to the police to be sent to prison, did we? Although, I might add, you richly deserved it. Roaming with a band of young thugs down on the pier, stealing everything from poor Nell's fresh hams in the butcher shop to the money and jewelry of your betters."

Rob looked a bit chastened. "Well . . ."

Artie, who had been kept busy turning his head first to Nancy and then to Rob and back to Nancy again, finally spoke. "She's right, she is, Rob. She never turned us in to old Snow for what we done."

"Well, then," Nancy said. "You know the kind of people the two of us are, Dr. Gladstone and I, so why will you go around doubting us?"

Rob stared at both of them for a long moment, not speaking. Then he started his backward trek out the door and down the stairs. Nancy had bested him, but he still wore a troubled look. Alexandra was equally troubled. Perhaps Nancy meant well, but she had only succeeded in placing her in a very awkward position. She would have to tell Rob the truth—that she would have to turn John Killborn in to the constable. But she had not the stomach to do it now.

Zack, in the meantime, was acting uncommonly nervous. He started barking as soon as the door was opened, and, in spite of Alexandra's repeated attempts to quiet him, he wouldn't stop.

"Old Zack knows they's someone out there." Little Artie spoke in a frightened whisper. At almost the same moment, Zack cleared the steps in one long, powerful leap and raced toward the wooded area behind the stables.

"Zack!" Alexandra called again, suddenly frightened for all of them, including Zack. Artie was right. Whoever shot John must still be out there. Zack paid no heed, and Alexandra had no choice but to keep moving toward the house.

Rob, however, had a different inclination. "Help them get him inside!" He spoke in a commanding voice as he handed off his part of the burden that was John over to Artie. Then, in less than the length of a breath, he raced away toward the barking Zack.

Both Alexandra and Nancy shouted at once for him to come back, but he disappeared into the darkness. They had no choice but to take John inside. As soon as they placed him in bed, Artie moved toward the door.

"Where are you going?" Alexandra snapped. She had just opened the vial of laudanum Nancy handed her.

Artie stopped and turned around, and she saw the fear in his eyes and in his white face. "I'm going after Rob." His little-boy voice was weak and trembling.

"No! You'll not leave this house without my permission." Alexandra took a step toward him as she spoke, and he cowered in fright.

"But Rob is—"

"Rob has done a foolish thing." Alexandra's voice had softened a little. She knew Rob was the nearest thing to a relative Artie had. He was at once big brother, father, and mother to the little boy. She placed a hand on his shoulder. "We would be quite worried about him if Zack weren't out there with him, wouldn't we? Come along now. You must sleep in the house tonight. Nancy will show you where." She gave him a gentle shove toward Nancy. "And see that you have a proper bath before you get in bed," she called after him.

The suggestion of a bath made Artie grumble in protest as Nancy took him firmly in hand and led him away. As soon as they were out of sight, Alexandra went to the window, searching the darkness for some sign of Zack and Rob. In spite of the reassurance she had given Artie, she felt no such assurance herself. A gunman could fell them both. She saw no sign of either of them, and only the fact that she had not heard another gunshot gave her hope.

She had been at the window searching the night for several minutes when she heard Nancy's voice behind her.

"Do you see them, miss?"

Before Alexandra could answer, she heard Zack's bark and she felt a quickening in her blood.

" 'Tis Zack!" Nancy said. "Lord, I hope the lad is with him."

In the next moment they could hear Zack barking loudly and could see two dark forms moving toward them. Behind them, they heard the sound of rapid footsteps on the stairs and Artie's voice calling, "It's old Zack, ain't it? Is Rob with 'im?" He was so excited he seemed to have forgotten to be embarrassed that he was wearing one of Nancy's nightgowns.

"I'm not sure," Alexandra said. She pulled the child closer to her in an instinctively protective gesture. Artie didn't resist until Rob and Zack came clearly into sight. He pulled away from her and ran to the door, opening it, calling out to Rob.

"Is it you, Rob? You're not kilt, are ye?"

Zack was the only one who answered. He gave a sharp bark and bounded through the open door, almost knocking over Alexandra as he greeted her. Rob stepped inside and edged close to Artie, breathing hard and looking as if he might faint in any minute. He seemed not even to have noticed Artie's unorthodox attire.

"Let me close the door, boy," Nancy said, taking charge and shooing them all into the parlor. "What is it you saw, Rob? You look as if you've seen a ghost."

"Wasn't no ghost," Rob said, "though I thought it was at first."

"You saw someone?" Alexandra guided him toward the kitchen where the stove was still hot and where Nancy could quickly warm a pot of milk.

"A woman," Rob said.

"The witch?" Artie's eyes were wide and frightened.

Rob glanced at him and, for the first time, noticed his clothing. Instead of laughing, though, he seemed to grow more upset. "What in damnation are ye wearin', Artie?"

"Never mind what he's wearing." Nancy spoke over her shoulder as she poured milk into a pot and set it on the stove. "You'll be wearing the same soon enough. Tell us now, what's this about a witch?"

"Wasn't no witch, either," Rob said. "Was only that housekeeper from up at Gull House."

"That's the one!" Artie said. "She's the witch!"

Alexandra glanced from one boy to the other. "Annie? She's the one you're calling a witch?"

"Rob said she was." Artie was suddenly defensive. "Said she was pure witch. Wicked and evil."

"Rob?" Alexandra's tone demanded an explanation.

"Well, she *is* wicked," Rob said. "Never a kind word for no one. Always shouting that if ye don't get out of her way she'll flog ye. But I swear I never called her a witch."

"You'd best stop now, young Rob before you dig yourself a deeper hole." Nancy stirred the milk and gave Rob a warning glance as she spoke.

Alexandra was not inclined to worry about whether or not Rob was lying about having called Annie a witch. She was more concerned with the puzzling fact that the woman had been out so late at night, and apparently in the woods behind her house shooting at people. She glanced at Rob, who was still squirming under Nancy's accusing eye. "Are you certain it was Annie, Rob? It's quite dark out."

"It's dark all right, Doc, but she ran past the stable and the light from our room fell upon her. It was old Annie all right. Not many women what's big as her. Big as a 'orse, she is. Besides, I'd know that nose anywhere. Long as a wit . . . Quite a long nose it is. And anyway, I saw the gun."

"She had a gun?" Alexandra was feeling more and more puzzled.

"Aye," Rob said, eagerly watching Nancy as she poured the milk into four cups.

Alexandra frowned. "But it doesn't make sense. Why would Annie try to kill John Killborn? She's quite loyal to his mother. One would think she wouldn't want to do anything to upset her."

"Unless she thought John could harm Mrs. Orkwright somehow," Nancy said.

Alexandra shook her head. "John is as devoted to his mother as Annie is."

"She done it because she's a witch, maybe," Artie offered, then ducked his head as Rob gave him a warning look.

"Well, we'll not solve the mystery tonight," Nancy said. "So finish your milk now, both of you, and off to bed with you. The morrow will dawn soon enough."

She gave the boys only a brief moment to gulp down their milk. "We'll all be sleeping under the same roof tonight," she said. "The doctor has ordered it, so I want no argument. Shoo! Both of you. Off to bed. I've laid one of the late Dr. Gladstone's nightshirts out for you, Rob. 'Tis a bit large, but 'tis that or another one of my own nightgowns for you. And see that you wash yourself before you crawl between those clean sheets."

Both boys finished their milk and immediately started for the stairs. They had long since learned that it did no good to argue with Nancy. Just as they reached the door, however, Rob turned back to Alexandra. "John is still here, is he? Ye ain't turned him in,'ave ye?"

"He's still here, Rob," Alexandra said before Nancy could answer for her.

Nancy set about clearing the cups and saucers from the table. "You'd best be off to bed yourself, Miss Alex," she said. "We'll not solve this mystery with our minds befuddled from lack of sleep, and besides you have your patients to worry about tomorrow. You've done quite enough for the day, what with an operation and a gunshot wound. No need to worry yet about calling on the constable to tell him about his prisoner, either. It can wait until morning."

"How would I ever survive without you to make all my decisions for me, Nancy?" Alexandra smiled as she stood and made her way to the door and then upstairs to her room. She was certain that, in spite of her weariness, she would not be able to sleep.

She was wrong. She was still sleeping soundly when Nancy brought breakfast to her room the next morning.

"Breakfast? In bed? No, of course not." Alexandra flung the covers back and swung her legs over the edge of the mattress. "Where are the boys?" She grabbed her dressing gown. "And John, is he . . ."

Nancy set the tray down and poured a cup of tea. "John is awake. Just a bit woozy from the laudanum. 'Tis a bad wound he has. He's not likely to have full use of the arm and shoulder again, I'd say." She handed the cup to Alexandra. "The boys are feeding Lucy and getting her saddled and ready for your morning rounds, and yes you will have breakfast, if not in bed, at least in your room, since I've gone to all the trouble to bring it up."

"You are unspeakably impertinent and quite impossible, Nancy," she said as she accepted the tea. "If I had any sense at all I would fire you immediately."

"A bit of jam on your toast, miss?"

Alexandra sighed. "Why don't you decide for me, Nancy? I seem to be quite incapable of doing it myself."

"Now, you know that isn't true," Nancy said, spreading jam on the toast.

After she had eaten and dressed, Alexandra took a quick look at John, lodged in a bedroom upstairs. She was grateful to see that he had fallen asleep again, since she didn't want to have to deal with telling him she would have to notify the constable. She left Nancy with the instructions that John was not to leave the room until she returned from her rounds.

She decided that she would see her patients before she went to the constable's office to tell him about John Killborn. She wasn't sure why she was so reluctant to turn him in, except that she liked him, and Artie and Rob liked him and didn't want him turned over to the authorities. She felt somehow as if she would be betraying all of them. Yet, she told herself, it was ridiculous to let two street urchins and former

petty criminals like Rob and Artie influence her. She would
have to tell the constable about what Rob saw. That would
mean Rob would have to come in for questioning, something
he would be reluctant to do, since he had a street urchin's
distrust of the law.

She had only three patients to see, and Hannibal Talbot
was the last. He was, as she expected, complaining loudly
about the pain he was experiencing and blaming her for all
of the discomfort. He also refused to let her inspect the surgical site.

"I'm not in the habit of showing me privates to just anyone
who comes along," he told her with a self-righteous sniff.

She gave him careful instructions on how to care for the
incision and left, letting him win this time, but knowing he
would have to give in and allow her to remove the stitches
eventually or risk putrification.

Once she was outside, she stood for several minutes in the
street holding Lucy's reins, unwilling to mount her, knowing
that her next stop would have to be Constable Snow's office.
Zack seemed to sense her tension and tried to communicate
with her in his odd syllabic moan. Finally he nudged her
with his cold, wet nose toward Lucy.

She had to ride all the way across town to reach the constable's office on Griffon Street. She was just approaching it
when she saw Nicholas Forsythe emerging from the tavern
across the street where he had lodging.

"Good morning, Mr. Forsythe."

"Dr. Gladstone!" He seemed surprised to see her. "I was
just on my way to your house, hoping I could be there before
you left for your rounds."

"Indeed?"

"I've some information to share with you." He and Zack
exchanged cautious, scrutinizing glances. "I say, I didn't
know you had patients to visit in this part of town." He
approached her, prepared to help her dismount.

"I'm not here to see a patient, Mr. Forsythe." She allowed
him to lift her from the saddle to a standing position. "I've
come to speak with Constable Snow regarding a client of
yours."

"You mean John Killborn, of course, since he's the only

client I have in Newton." He was still holding her waist.

"He is, at the moment, sleeping in my house."

"What?"

"Recovering from a bullet wound."

"I say! What happened? Who shot him? I must see him immediately."

"I'm afraid I don't know with certainty who shot him, and I feel sure Constable Snow will not forbid you to see him, but I—"

"Please, Dr. Gladstone, allow me to handle this. I will, of course, inform Constable Snow, but I must talk to John first."

"But—"

He took her hand and pulled her away from the constable's office. "I've just asked for the carriage to be sent around. We'll tie Lucy to the back, and you—and Zeke—will ride with me. You must tell me everything."

"Zack."

"I beg your pardon?"

"His name is Zack."

"Yes, of course," he said, walking a wide path around Zack as he helped her into the carriage.

Within a few minutes they were on the short drive to Alexandra's house. Zack lay at her feet, his head erect and eyes alert and never for a second leaving Nicholas's face.

13

"A divorce? Jane Orkwright? Are you sure?" Alexandra stared at Nicholas with disbelief after he had given her the news. He was seated across from her in her parlor. "Isn't it possible your friend could have misread the name, or—"

"Possible, but highly unlikely, and yes, I'm quite sure. Lesley Coldwell is one of the most astute barristers I know. Quite familiar with researching court records." Nicholas, uncharacteristically, had not touched the tea Nancy had brought. He'd been more than a little edgy since they arrived because Nancy and Alexandra had both steadfastly refused to allow him to awaken John to question him.

Alexandra saw that Nancy was, as usual, lingering quite unnecessarily over the tea tray. She'd heard everything Nicholas said about the divorce petition and was stalling, hoping to hear more. Nicholas made no attempt to keep her from hearing anything he said.

"I must say, however, I am quite surprised." Alexandra kept her eyes on Nicholas. "That will be all, Nancy, thank you."

Even though she still focused on Nicholas, Alexandra was aware of the annoyed look Nancy gave her just before she turned away, mumbling. It seemed for all the world as if she was addressing Nicholas.

"I beg your pardon?" he said. Apparently he'd gotten the same impression.

"What?" Nancy glanced at him, pretending surprise. "Oh, I was just saying that, unlike Dr. Gladstone, I am not at all surprised at the divorce petition."

"Indeed," Nicholas said, sitting up a bit straighter. "Pray, tell us why."

Alexandra said nothing. She simply rolled her eyes. Nancy had her ways. She would, soon enough, know everything anyone else knew, if not more. Nancy, she was certain, had seen and read the message in the rolling of her eyes but went on with her little act. She even ducked her head demurely.

"Well, of course I'm not as trained as you, a barrister in the Queen's Court, at observing people and their circumstances, but I'm sure you know young John Killborn was not at all fond of his stepfather."

Nicholas appeared disappointed. "That's rather common knowledge. He's made no attempt to hide that fact."

Nancy nodded. "And certainly I'm no expert in the foibles of human behavior or modern psychologism, I believe it's called, but—"

"Nancy, for heaven's sake, what are you getting at?" Alexandra could no longer hide her annoyance.

Unflappable Nancy went on with her charade. "It's only that in my humble way, I have become an observer of humankind, and I've come to believe that it's a mother's natural tendency to protect her children at all costs. Even if it be from her husband."

"Hmmm," Nicholas mused.

"Oh, I know, of course, that many women do end up staying with the husband at the expense of the children. But if they do, they're most often going against their true nature." Nancy had, by now, lost a little of her poor-little-serving-girl expression. "A woman has so much to lose, doesn't she? If things aren't going well at home, that is. Why, she loses either way, I say. Unless she can find another way out."

"Nancy, must you be so tedious?" Alexandra was losing patience, and it seemed Nancy was no longer making sense.

Before Nancy could respond, Nicholas leaned forward in his chair, and with his eyes still on Nancy, said, "I believe she's giving Mrs. Orkwright a motive to murder her husband."

Neither Nancy nor Alexandra spoke nor moved for a moment.

"Oh, come now. You both have to admit once you knew she had at one time considered divorce, that suggested she didn't want him around any longer." There was the slightest hint of defensiveness in Nicholas's tone.

"Not wanting someone around and murdering them are two different matters entirely," Alexandra said.

Nicholas pulled his chin. "But think of what Nancy just said. A woman has so much to lose." He glanced at Nancy. "I say, rather astute of you."

Nancy ducked her head and pretended to be embarrassed.

"You're speaking of a woman's reputation, I suppose," Alexandra said. "A woman of Jane Orkwright's class loses much of her status as well as the respect of her peers if she is divorced. Therefore, she loses if she is forced to live with someone she cannot love or respect or who cannot love or respect her, and she loses as well if she frees herself from him."

"Whereas a divorced man doesn't lose respect," Nancy said, nodding her head with enthusiasm that her point had been taken.

"Ah, but there's more to it than that." Nicholas stood, picked up the teacup and saucer, and paced the floor between the two women. The untouched brew grew colder by the second. "First of all, it's not at all likely a woman could successfully seek a divorce because of some dispute her husband has with one of her children, even if the dispute resulted in physical cruelty. There is, after all, the law of coverture."

"Coverture?" Nancy asked.

"It means simply that a man is allowed a great deal of leeway in chastising his wife and children, since he can be held legally responsible for crimes they commit or for the wife's torts."

"Well, yes, I suppose we all know a man has a legal right to beat his wife and children," Nancy said.

"The courts assume, of course, that sort of thing happens only among the lower classes," Nicholas said. "Not likely in Mrs. Orkwright's situation."

Nancy beamed. "How fortunate for the upper class!"

Nicholas frowned. "You're leading me astray from the subject, Nancy. My point is even if Mrs. Orkwright felt one of her sons needed protection—John, most likely—since he didn't get on with the admiral, divorce is not a likely means of achieving that protection, and I suspect any barrister representing her would tell her so."

Nancy was persistent. "But if she were seeking protection for herself? In the unlikely case of a woman of her class needing it, I mean."

Nicholas shook his head. "Adultery is the only suitable grounds for a woman, and then only if there are aggravating circumstances such as incest or bigamy or bestiality." He turned to Alexandra. "Forgive me for being so blunt." He blushed as he spoke.

Alexandra brushed his apology and his embarrassment aside. "Perhaps that's why she dropped her petition."

"Or perhaps because she could very well lose legal custody of Will," Nicholas said. "The law leans heavily toward granting custody to the father. The mother can, in fact, be forbidden to see her children."

Alexandra was momentarily stunned by this information. "So she would be separated from Will if she were to divorce?"

"Yes, and even on the admiral's death, she might not be given custody of her son," Nicholas said. "And so, as Nancy pointed out, she must find another way."

"But murder?" Alexandra spoke barely above a whisper.

"We have to assume that's a possibility," Nicholas said. "So the question is, is it a probability?"

Alexandra shook her head. "That's very difficult to imagine. In spite of . . ."

"In spite of what?" Nicholas leaned toward her as if she was in a witness box.

Alexandra hesitated a moment. "That John is convinced everyone thinks or eventually will think his mother is guilty."

"He told you that?" Nicholas asked.

"Yes."

"But why?

"He was about to tell me why when he was shot," Alexandra said.

Nicholas's glance moved quickly to the top of the stairs and back to Alexandra again.

"No," she said. "You may not question him yet. Allow him to rest a little longer."

Nicholas's expression was, for a moment, impatient and disgruntled. He seemed about to say something, but hesitated. Then he took a deep breath and spoke. "All right, let's assume for a moment that Mrs. Orkwright did, in fact, kill her husband. How would she carry it out?" He continued to pace the floor.

"She'd drown him!" Nancy was obviously unable to keep quiet any longer.

"That's even more difficult to imagine," Alexandra said.

"Even though his body washed up from the sea? Even though he had a mouth full of seaweed?" Nancy said, challenging her.

"Nancy, I told you there is no way to prove he drowned. The autopsy was not conclusive."

"Of course I know that, Miss Alex, and I, like you, find it hard to believe that Mrs. Orkwright could have drowned her husband. I am simply trying to examine all possibilities." Nancy had discarded her feigned embarrassment and had now grown quite serious.

"How wise you are, Nancy, old girl," Nicholas said. "Let's take it down the path you've started a little further." He turned to Alexandra. "The autopsy was not conclusive in that it did not reveal any certain cause of death, am I correct?"

"Yes," Alexandra said.

"And so," he continued, "we will say that drowning is the cause of death because everything else has been eliminated."

"Probably the cause," Alexandra said.

"Very well. Probably the cause." Nicholas sat down and put his teacup aside, then leaned toward Alexandra. "How did she do it?"

"We keep coming back to that don't we?" Alexandra said. "How could she get him out to sea? She is a small woman and he was a rather large man. She would have a difficult time overcoming him."

"Unless he was unconscious before he was put in the water."

"Even a small person is difficult to handle when he or she is unconscious," Alexandra said. "I find it hard to believe Jane Orkwright could have gotten a man as large as her husband into a boat and out to sea under any circumstance. Especially if he happened to be unconscious."

"What if Annie helped her?" Nancy's words caught the sudden attention of both Alexandra and Nicholas. "Annie could have even acted alone. She's quite a large woman, you know."

"Indeed!" Nicholas said. "And her motive?"

"Loyalty to Mrs. Orkwright," Nancy said. "If Mrs. Orkwright wanted the admiral out of the way for whatever reason, Annie would see to it that it was done. And if she was afraid John knew the truth, she would try to kill him."

Nicholas frowned, then turned to Alexandra. "Would you find it improbable that Annie could commit murder?"

"I find it puzzling," Alexandra said. "If her motive was to protect Jane Orkwright from any form of hurt, then it doesn't make sense that she would try to kill her son."

"I beg your pardon? You and Nancy are both implying Annie tried to kill her son? I thought you said you weren't certain about who—"

"I'm not certain, of course, but there is a suspect," Alexandra said. She told him what the boys claimed they had seen. "So if her interest is in protecting her mistress, it seems it would be rather obvious to her that John's death would be a blow to Jane equally as devastating as anything her husband may have done."

"Perhaps her motive wasn't to protect Mrs. Orkwright after all." Nancy spoke this time with less conviction. She wore a puzzled look.

"Then what?" Nicholas said.

Nancy shrugged. "To hurt her somehow?"

"But why?" Alexandra asked.

"I don't know," Nancy said. "Perhaps because she was in love with the admiral. Perhaps because she killed the admiral herself, and she's threatening to do John harm if Mrs. Orkwright tells what she knows. Perhaps—"

"We're getting nowhere with this," Alexandra said, standing up from her chair. "We're simply making improbably wild guesses, and I must open the surgery. Patients will be arriving soon." She looked at Nicholas. "And we must deal with the problem of turning John over to the constable. And of having Rob tell him what he thinks he saw." She hesitated for a moment, silently wishing there would be a way not to have to do either of those things. She turned toward the stairs. "Young John should be awake by now," she said. "I'll show you to his room."

Nicholas seemed oddly hesitant to follow her at first. "Yes. Yes, of course, he said finally. You must open your surgery, and I must . . ." He moved with some reluctance toward the stairway. He was obviously no more eager to have to turn John in than Rob and Artie were. Yet, Alexandra was sure he was as eager as she to ask him why he thought his mother would look guilty.

When they were upstairs and with Nicholas standing behind her, Alexandra tapped gently on the door to John's room, then opened it when there was no response. John was sitting up in bed, his eyes two dark hollows in a pale, drawn face. He turned his face away as soon as he saw the two of them.

"I might have known you would betray me." His words were angry and clipped.

"And what is that supposed to mean?" Nicholas asked as he stepped in front of Alexandra and walked to the bedside. He had regained his old swagger and confidence. With a hand behind his back, he waved Alexandra away. It was, she assumed, an indication that she was to leave the room, but it was an indication she ignored.

"I should think you would know exactly what it means." John's voice was weak but angry. "She told you I was here, and you've come to take me straight to Newgate."

"It's my responsibility to do what's best for you, John," Nicholas said.

"You make me ill." John looked away again.

"There are several questions I must ask you," Nicholas said. "First, I want you to tell me exactly what score you felt you had to settle that was so urgent you had to escape prison to accomplish it." Nicholas's words had a sharp, authoritative sound.

"It's not your concern, you bastard."

"As I told you before, it is my concern because I am your barrister."

"I don't care if you're the queen's bloody barrister. I don't have to talk to you." John's voice had grown noticeably weaker and his face even more pale. Alexandra could see beads of sweat on his forehead.

"John . . ." she said. Nicholas turned around suddenly as she spoke. It was obvious he hadn't expected her to be there, that he had thought she would disappear when he waved her away. Unsure whether he was angry or merely surprised, she tried to avoid his eyes as she walked toward the bed. "It's true, John, I told Mr. Forsythe about you. I thought it was the right thing to do, the best way to protect you."

"I don't need your protection," John said.

"Obviously you do. Someone shot you." Alexandra said.

"Does this have something to do with the death of your stepfather?" Nicholas asked.

John didn't answer. He only looked at him with his defiant expression.

"And why do you think people will blame your mother for his death?"

Still no answer. John continued to stare the window not speaking.

Nicholas kept pushing. "Does this have something to do with your mother's divorce petition? You'd be much better off if you'd—"

John jerked his head around to face Nicholas. "What divorce petition?"

"The petition your mother made to the Divorce Court," Nicholas said.

John's face grew even more pale. "I don't know what you're talking about. My mother is a lady. She'd never petition for a divorce."

Alexandra touched Nicholas's arm and moved her eyes to indicate that she wanted him to follow her out of the room. He followed reluctantly. "We must let him rest," she said, keeping her voice low. "He's lost quite a lot of blood, and we're getting nowhere with this questioning except to agitate him."

"Do you think the constable or the authorities from Newgate are going to be any easier on him?" Nicholas sounded angry. "He's better off allowing me to question him first so I can prepare a defense."

"Perhaps we could delay turning him in if I can convince the constable young John isn't well enough to—"

Nicholas interrupted. "It is inevitable that one of us will turn him in. No matter how long we postpone it, it's still inevitable." His voice was grave.

Alexandra hesitated, knowing he was right, yet still wishing he weren't. Finally, she gave him a slight nod and turned away toward her surgery. She would put the fate of John Killborn out of her mind. She also must rule herself not to think of Jane Orkwright and her failed divorce petition or of Nancy's last remark about the possibility that Annie may have wanted to hurt her mistress. She would submerge herself in dealing with the usual flood of quinsied throats, nasal catarrh, and rheumatic limbs. Then she would visit Gull House and its occupants one more time.

Zack was reluctant to obey Alexandra's command to stay with Lucy while she knocked at the door at Gull House. She had to send him back to Lucy with a scolding twice. He wanted to wait at the door, as was his custom when she visited a patient. Alexandra, however, knew he was likely to raise the ire of Annie, and she didn't want to give her any excuse for not admitting her.

As she waited for her knock to be answered, she tried to rehearse in her mind what she would say to Jane. Jane would not appreciate anyone prying by asking questions about her motive for petitioning for a divorce, of course, but Alexandra had to admit that prying was precisely what she would be doing. Did it make it any less distasteful that she was doing it because she wanted to help Jane and not for some prurient reason?

When the door opened, she was not surprised to see Annie open it and greet her with her usual angry scowl. She was both surprised and startled, however, when Zack suddenly appeared next to her, barking and snarling with anger equal to the housemaid's. She called his name, scolding him again, telling him to be quiet and go back. He obeyed only so far as to cease his barking, changing his protest to a low, nervous growl. He did not turn around and go back to Lucy.

"What is it you're wanting?" Annie's voice was no more pleasant than her expression, and the sound of it set Zack to barking again. "Get that beast off of this property! Have you no sense but to bring him here to disturb the mistress?"

Alexandra might have given Annie an equally sharp retort had she not seen young Will peering from behind her and clinging to her skirt. His eyes were wide and fixed on Zack. It was difficult to tell whether the child's expression was one of fear or fascination.

Alexandra didn't take time to ponder it, however. She turned around and rebuked Zack sharply. He walked away reluctantly, but turned around before he reached Lucy and stood, his entire body alert, the low growl still rattling nervously in his throat. When she turned back to the door, she ignored Annie and greeted the child, who stood behind her.

"Good afternoon, young Will."

"He's quiet large, isn't he?" Will's eyes were still on Zack. "Does he eat people?"

Alexandra chuckled and was about to respond when Annie interrupted. "Hush, child! Go see to your mother. She needs you."

"Yes, Annie," Will said, lowering his eyes. He turned away and disappeared through a door leading off the hall.

"I've come to call on Mrs. Orkwright." Alexandra's voice was firm. She knew Annie would do her best to turn her away. She had to force herself not to ask the angry woman whether she had indeed taken a shot at John.

"I'm afraid that's not possible, Mrs. Orkwright is not feeling well."

"All the more reason why I should see her." Alexandra maneuvered herself around Annie's large frame.

She found Jane seated in the parlor with her young son standing in front of her. There was a rare smile on her face as the boy described something to her, using broad gestures. She sensed Alexandra's presence and glanced toward her.

"Alexandra! How pleasant to see you again. Please, do

come in. Will was just telling me about your dog. It seems he's quite taken with the animal. Perhaps even a bit afraid of him." She gave Will a loving look.

"I'm not afraid, Mama," the boy insisted. "I'm very brave, just as Papa said I should be."

"Perhaps you are only awed by the dog's size," Alexandra said as she advanced into the room. She had removed her cloak, which Annie had not taken.

"I'm very brave," Will said again.

"Of course you are, darling." Jane caressed his face. "So brave, in fact, that I think you deserve a reward." She glanced toward Annie, who stood grim-faced in the doorway. "See that Master Will has a biscuit. He can take it in the kitchen with you, if he likes."

Annie kept her scowling expression until she shifted her gaze to Will and extended her hand to him. There was a softness in her eyes then, and she smiled at him as she led him away.

"Please, sit here across from me." Jane indicated a chair separated from her own by a small tea table.

"Your housekeeper tells me you're not feeling well," Alexandra said as she took her seat.

"I'm afraid Anne is a bit overly protective," Jane said. In spite of the mild protest, Alexandra noted the dark circles under her eyes and the drawn, tired look of her face. There was something in her eyes as well, a haunting. The ravages of grief did not destroy her beauty, however, but altered it.

"I'm afraid I've a bit of bad news for you, Jane." Alexandra spoke softly, but when she saw the way Jane's face grew deathly pale, she regretted having spoken at all.

"Then tell me." Jane's voice was expressionless and almost inaudible.

It took Alexandra a moment to summon the courage to speak again. "I'm afraid your son has been wounded," she said at length.

"John?" She looked as if she might swoon. "Is he . . ."

"He will live, but he will lose at least part of the use of an arm."

Jane kept her head down. "How was he wounded?"

"He was shot."

She raised her eyes, which were now full of alarm. "Shot? Who . . ."

"We can't be certain, but your housekeeper was seen running away from the scene last night, and—"

"Annie? No! You're mistaken. Who told you this?"

"My stable boys chased her through the woods after—"

"Stable boys? You accept the word of stable boys?"

Alexandra was silent for several seconds, seeing the anger and hurt in Jane's eyes, not certain how to continue. Finally she spoke. "I must tell you John is with a barrister, who will return him to the authorities and intercede for him as much as is possible."

Jane refused to look at her, and there was another long awkward silence between them. Finally Alexandra said, "Your son did not get on well with the admiral, did he?"

Jane glanced at her quickly, anger still seething in her eyes. "No." The word sounded defiant.

"I'm sorry, Jane. Perhaps this is a gross impropriety, but there is something I must discuss with you." When Jane gave her a questioning look, she continued uneasily. "We have both agreed, have we not, that your husband's death seemed a bit . . . unusual. That perhaps he could have been . . ." Alexandra couldn't finish her sentence because of the sudden horrified look she saw on Jane's face.

"Are you suggesting now that John could have murdered my husband? Was it not enough that you accused Annie of harming John?"

"I don't mean to suggest that at all," Alexandra said, feeling both inadequate and embarrassed.

"Then what?" Jane's voice was hard and angry.

Alexandra stood. "I'm sorry, Jane. I am out of bounds. I should never have come here to—"

"Sit down, Alexandra, and tell me what you have been trying to say since you arrived."

Alexandra shook her head. "No, I—"

Jane stood, suddenly confrontational, and Alexandra could see the anger increasing in her eyes. "Tell me, Dr. Gladstone."

"It is none of my business."

"Indeed it is not. But now that you have gone to the trou-

ble of coming here, I insist you tell me what is on your mind.
If it is on your mind, it is no doubt on the mind of others. I
believe I have a right to know."

"Yes," Alexandra said, feeling very small. "Forgive me
for being both prying and cowardly." She kept her eyes level
with Jane's. "I had hoped you could tell me about your . . .
your petition for divorce and whether or not it could have
any bearing on the admiral's death."

There was a slight change in Jane's breathing, but she
recovered quickly. She spoke one word. "No."

Alexandra hesitated. "I'm not certain whether to take your
answer as a refusal to speak of the matter or—"

"I did not choose to kill my husband as a substitute for
divorce." Jane's words embarrassed Alexandra even more.

"Certainly I didn't mean to imply—"

"Of course you did, Dr. Gladstone. Pray tell me why you
would be asking about it for any other reason?"

Alexandra hadn't failed to notice that Jane had dropped
the intimate usage of her Christian name for the more coldly
formal Dr. Gladstone. "Forgive me, Jane. You are too fine
and intelligent a woman for me to attempt so inexpert a de-
ceit." She looked away for a moment and then forced herself
to face Jane again. "I know it sounds lame, but my motive
was truly to protect you."

"Protect me?" There was bitter cynicism in Jane's words.

"Yes, to protect you." Alexandra's voice had regained its
forcefulness. "Don't you know that your son fears you will
be blamed for the admiral's death? Do you not know that
even if no one seeks to blame you now, if knowledge of the
divorce petition becomes common you will—"

"Of course I know what it will mean," Jane said. "There
is nothing I can do about what others think." She paused a
moment, her expression troubled. "You must understand that
my divorce petition was very foolish, and I have come to
regret it. I shall be eternally grateful to my wise and won-
derful late husband for not holding it against me."

Alexandra was growing more and more uncomfortable
with each word Jane uttered. "You need go no further, Jane.
It is quite clear that this is a domestic matter in which I
should have no interest." She slipped her cloak over her

shoulders and started to turn away, but Jane stopped her with sharp words.

"Oh, you have an interest, Dr. Gladstone. You would not be here if you didn't." She waited until she had captured Alexandra's eyes with her own glare that was at once hot with anger and cold with disdain. "I want the gossip to stop, so you must tell everyone who knows of this that my quarrel with my husband was a foolish disagreement over money. I was selfishly demanding more from him. And over certain decisions he had made regarding the management of property that I had before I came into the marriage. I have since come to realize what I was too foolish to know then, that Parliament was wise to leave such matters in the hands of the husband. I, like most women, am ill equipped for such weighty decisions."

Alexandra was well aware of the laws regarding a woman's property, which was one of several reasons she had chosen not to marry. She found it on the tip of her tongue to argue that Jane Orkwright, as well as herself, was equally well equipped as any man to manage property, but she stopped herself. She had already stepped well beyond the bounds of propriety.

"Forgive me, Jane," she said with genuine contriteness. "I shall do my best to see that the gossip goes no further." She saw what she thought was a softening in Jane's expression, and for a moment she thought she was about to speak, but she bit her lip and turned away.

Alexandra took her leave without a word, knowing that anything she said would be unheard. Knowing, too, that she could not have been more foolish than to have come in the first place.

14

Zack didn't greet Alexandra with his usual enthusiasm when she returned to him and Lucy. He was, she supposed, pouting because she'd scolded him and hadn't allowed him to follow her all the way to the house. She gave him an affectionate pat on the head nevertheless and immediately felt something sticky on her hand.

When she looked down at Zack's magnificent back from the saddle, she saw that the black and white hair of his coat was matted and stuck together in spots, and bits of black grass and dry leaves clung to him.

"Zack, what have you gotten into?" she asked, both puzzled and amused. He glanced up at her at the sound of his name. His tail wagged. Obviously he was ready to forgive and forget if the sound of her voice was pleasing rather than scolding. Alexandra laughed. "You're a naughty boy. You have to get in something messy to get even with me for not allowing you to come with me, don't you?"

His answer was a throaty bark and another wag of his tail. He remained happy all the way home, in spite of the biting wind that had come up as the sun sank lower on the horizon.

With her hands on her hips and a scowl on her face, Nancy demanded to know why Zack was so dirty as soon as they entered the house.

"Something he found in the woods, I think." Alexandra sounded distracted as she started up the stairs.

"You're a dirty boy, I'd say," Nancy said to Zack, and then, when she saw the direction Alexandra was headed, spoke to her. "If 'tis John Killborn you're looking for, you won't find him. Mr. Forsythe took him to the constable, just as he said he would."

Alexandra stopped, realizing that she was immensely saddened to know that John was back in custody, in spite of the fact that she'd both encouraged and expected it. Perhaps, she thought, it was Jane's reaction to the news that her son had been wounded that made her feel the way she did.

"Of course," she said absently and turned toward the parlor.

"I'm going to give this animal a bath before I get back to the kitchen." Nancy spoke as she pulled Zack along by the skin on the top of his neck. "You're a messy thing, you are," she said, speaking to Zack and wrinkling her nose.

Zack responded with some of his vowel-like growling that sounded for all the world like a protest.

"Don't bother with the kitchen. I've not much of an appetite for supper. I'll just fix myself a cup of tea," Alexandra said. But Nancy couldn't have heard her as Zack's growling protests grew louder.

Alexandra sat down in the parlor, determined to relax and forget about the death of Admiral Orkwright. She picked up the book she'd been reading aloud to Nancy each evening. The novel was a new one, *The Portrait of a Lady,* by the American writer Henry James. She was captivated by the American woman in the novel, Isabel Archer, and by seeing Europe and Europeans through her eyes. When she tried to read it now, however, Isabel seemed more tiresome than captivating, and she found herself unable to concentrate. She set the book aside, feeling restless. It was not as easy as she had hoped to put aside thoughts of the admiral and of the mystery surrounding his death. Why was John so worried that people would blame his mother for the admiral's death? Why would Annie, or anyone else, try to kill John? Would Constable Snow try to arrest Annie after he'd heard the story from Nicholas and John? He would surely bring Rob in for questioning. It would seem that if Nicholas had, indeed, told him of their suspicion of Annie, that would certainly have given the constable plenty of time to get to Gull House to question the housekeeper by now.

It occurred to her then that she had never had the opportunity to speak with the constable yesterday as she planned. She'd been interrupted and intercepted by Nicholas, who had insisted on driving her home so that he could see John.

Perhaps now would be a good time to speak with Snow. If she hurried, she might be able to reach his office before he left for the day. She took some matches from the mantel and her cloak from the hook in the hall and called out to Nancy that she was leaving for a walk.

There was no response from Nancy, who probably had not heard her over the growls and tremendous splashing noises Zack was wont to make at his bath. That was her own good fortune, Alexandra thought. If Nancy had heard her, she would insist she not go out again, at least not without her.

Alexandra wouldn't take time to have the boys saddle Lucy again, since the hardworking little mare was probably enjoying her oats and settling in for the night. She would walk into the village and have her talk with the constable. If it was terribly late when she finished, she would ask him to escort her home.

The wind was damp and biting as she made her way to the post near the stable where she kept a lantern, but at least there was no sleet this time. It was not quite dark enough to warrant a lantern, but the February light would slip away quickly enough.

She had progressed only a short distance into the edge of the village when she saw the constable astride his gelding. He was several yards away, and apparently headed out of the village, yet far enough to her right that their paths would not cross.

She called to him twice, until he heard his name and turned his head toward her. "Constable Snow, I should like a word with you," she called. Snow stopped his horse and turned to face her, but he made no attempt to advance toward her. It was left to her to walk to him.

"Are you all right, Dr. Gladstone?" he asked when she was closer.

"Quite." She set her lantern on the ground and rubbed her

gloved hands together to try to warm them. "I wanted to inquire about young Killborn. Is he—"

"It was not a mortal wound, as you of course know. He will recover." Snow's interruption left her with the feeling that he wanted to be rid of her. "I've notified Newgate, and he will be transported there within a few days."

"Yes, of course." Alexandra hesitated a moment. "I assume Nicholas instructed you as to the circumstances of his being wounded."

Snow's answer was a curt nod of his head.

"And he told you that my stable boy pursued the one who wounded John and may have, in fact, identified the same." She could see the breath that carried her words evaporate into nothing.

"Dr. Gladstone, please rest assured that I have the matter well in hand."

It was a dismissal, of course, but her curiosity would not allow her to be dismissed so easily. "The boys were quite certain it was Jane Orkwright's housekeeper, Annie, they saw fleeing through the woods. I must say I was surprised."

There was no response from Snow, which left Alexandra feeling nonplussed. She was about to pick up her lantern and resign herself to not learning anything of the progress of his investigation when he surprised her by speaking.

"Thank you, Doctor, for your ministration to the prisoner's wounds and for seeing that he was properly brought back to the gaol."

"No need to thank me, Constable. I was simply doing my duty." Alexandra kept her voice as cool and formal as his.

"The young man, I'm afraid, is in a state of mind to trust no one." Snow's remark sounded as if he were thawing, which surprised Alexandra.

"Quite so." She was cautious, not sure where he was leading her.

Snow seemed nervous and pulled back on the reins unintentionally, making his gelding stomp his feet, reluctant to step back. "I don't suppose he told you anything that would be . . ." He stopped speaking, appearing uncharacteristically unsure of himself.

Alexandra waited a moment before she spoke. "You were

perhaps going to ask if he said anything that would be revealing or pertinent to the death of his stepfather?"

Snow cleared his throat quietly and hesitated briefly before he spoke. "Precisely."

Alexandra was silent again, knowing she appeared to be contemplating it, when in fact she was contemplating Snow. What had John said to him that bothered him so? Was he afraid John had told her something he didn't want her to know? Snow had always been an immensely private man, even in the days when she was a child and he'd been her tutor and the village schoolmaster. But she had never thought of him as the type to have dark secrets as some had suggested. There were rumors that he regularly visited some unknown woman in London. Then there was Edith Podder's speculation that he was in love with Jane Orkwright. Whether or not any of that was true, there was undoubtedly something bothering him now about what John might or might not have said.

Finally she spoke. "He seemed to be inordinately afraid that his mother would be blamed for the admiral's death. He said that you would eventually blame her as well. He seemed to think it was his duty to protect her." She watched Snow's face in the lantern light, but he showed no emotion. There was only a slight tightening of a muscle in his jaw. "What did he mean by that?" she asked.

Snow's glance moved to an undetermined point in the distance. "I have no way of knowing," he said, as if he were speaking not to Alexandra, but to himself.

"Surely you don't still believe there is nothing suspicious about the admiral's death."

Snow brought his cool gaze back to Alexandra, still looking down at her from his horse, as if he were a king looking down on a subject. "My profession demands that I work with concrete facts, and I have had none to make me suspicious."

"Not even the fact that Jane Orkwright believes her husband could have been murdered?" Alexandra was well aware that her question sounded bold and disrespectful.

Snow's eyes narrowed with what she took for anger, suggesting he had taken the question the same way. "Mrs. Orkwright has not told me about any such suspicions," he said. "Perhaps you misunderstood."

"I did not misunderstand, sir. And, to belie your insistence upon concrete facts, you just admitted to me that you thought John might have revealed something to me pertinent to the admiral's death."

"You are a very intelligent woman, Dr. Gladstone. And I very much admire your skill as a physician, but I suggest you leave the dubious practice of mind reading to the charlatans and the intricacies of law enforcement to me." With that he laid the reins against the gelding's neck to turn him away. Before the horse could be completely turned, however, Alexandra spoke again, challenging Snow.

"Do you also choose to ignore what Mr. Forsythe told you? That John said he came here to settle a score?"

Snow stopped the turn and looked down on her again. "Are you suggesting that John Killborn murdered his stepfather?"

"No, I am suggesting that there is more to this than you seem willing to admit. Why would John say that? And why would Annie try to kill him? Doesn't it strike you odd that there is so much dangerous behavior among the family and household of Admiral Orkwright?"

"You are overwrought, Dr. Gladstone. Perhaps it's understandable when one sees so much death and illness and when one's profession keeps one continuously subjected to households where gossip and speculation are rife. I suggest you ask Nancy to prepare one of your formulas for you. Something to soothe you. Perhaps the concoction you gave Miss Hargrove." With that, he turned and rode away from her, headed in the direction of his own cottage.

Alexandra watched him ride away, seething. After complimenting her on her intelligence, he had soundly insulted her by suggesting she was hysterical. It was well known that Lucinda Hargrove, a spinster, was given to hysteria. Alexandra had treated her with a mixture of lobelia, capsicum, and compound spirits of lavender, and the young woman's much talked about hysterical fits had subsided. It was Alexandra's belief as well as the belief of certain others, that her "cure" could well have been because of something other than the formula, however. Approximately the same time she had prescribed the medicine, Lucinda's controlling and tyrannical father died. Lucinda had then taken to receiving a gentleman in her home from time to time, even, it was rumored, into the late hours of the night, and her erratic and histrionic behavior had become an effusive and giggling agreeableness.

It was more than insulting that Constable Snow had suggested that Alexandra, who, at thirty, was also a spinster, might have a similar diagnosis.

Alexandra's anger continued to burn all during the short walk home. She was still angry when she opened the door and was greeted by a damp, but eager and exuberant Zack. His bath, in spite of his protestations, had apparently lifted his spirits, even if it hadn't entirely cleansed his coat of the sticky matter. The bath had done nothing to improve Nancy's mood, however. She stood behind Zack in her soaked apron and with her honey-colored hair pulled loose from its pins so that it hung in damp strands over her unsmiling face where a bit of suds still clung to her chin.

"Never again!" she said to Alexandra by way of a greeting.

"I beg your pardon?" Alexandra said.

Nancy shook her head. "Never again will I attempt to bathe the beast. Not even if he falls into a coal bin. Not even if he falls into a dung heap. Not even if he—"

"No further elaboration is necessary, Nancy. I take your point. You've made it clear before when you've had to bathe him."

"But I mean it this time. Why, you've no idea," Nancy said, shaking her head. "It is easier to bathe an elephant! He argues with me, he does! About getting into the tub. And then there's the tremendous splash when he finally makes up his mind to get in. But that's not the end of it, oh no! He thinks it's great sport to splash more with those enormous paws of his. Big as meat platters, they are. And then there's the shaking, near drowns a body when he sends that water out from all that hair. There's a foot of water on my kitchen floor, and . . ."

Nancy went on for several minutes more about the perils of bathing Zack. She kept on until she was shivering in her damp clothes and grew even more angry when Zack gave another shake to rid himself of the last droplets that clung to his coat, sending the water all over both her and Alexandra.

Alexandra finally sent Nancy upstairs with instructions to change into dry clothes. When Nancy was gone, she went to the kitchen to brew tea and to make a sandwich of cold tongue, then went upstairs to knock on Nancy's door. Nancy opened it wearing a fresh kitchen dress of dark muslin.

"What's this?" she asked, looking at the tray.

"Your supper, Nancy."

"My supper? But where is your own?" Nancy accepted the tray in spite of her protest.

"I've no appetite at the moment." Alexandra moved into the room and, without waiting to be asked, seated herself in one of the chairs near the fireplace.

Nancy sat in the other chair facing Alexandra. "Oh yes, I certainly know what you mean. All that's been happening— the admiral drowned in ladies' underwear, someone shooting at our patients! Why, it's enough to take any decent person's appetite." She took a hearty bite from the sandwich.

"And the constable seems paralyzed, unable or unwilling to act." Alexandra studied the blaze in the fireplace as she spoke. Zack pushed the door open with his nose and came to lie at her feet, warming himself by the fire. For a moment Alexandra let herself be lulled into relaxed contentment until Nancy spoke again.

"There's some who say old Snow has his reasons." She put her sandwich aside for a moment and leaned toward Alexandra. "Do you think it's true? That he's in love with Mrs. Orkwright?"

"I have no way of knowing that." Alexandra's voice was a little too harsh. "It's only gossip, and it does not become either of us to indulge in it."

Nancy studied Alexandra's face for a moment. "Where there's smoke, there's fire, I say. And don't you find it odd that he hasn't called Rob in for questioning? It's as if he wants the whole thing to go away."

"Eat your sandwich, Nancy," Alexandra said with growing impatience. "And tell me, when did you ever bathe an elephant?"

"Humph," Nancy said with a disdainful glance at Zack before she took a bite of her sandwich. Then, still chewing, she touched her napkin to her lips and said, "Annie's the mystery, I say. You figure that one out and you'll understand the whole lot of it."

"Perhaps you're right." Alexandra spoke without much conviction and without moving her eyes from the hypnotizing blaze in the fireplace. Then she glanced at Nancy and, with her weariness evident in her voice, said, "When I saw Annie earlier at Gull House she showed no sign of having been out roaming and shooting at anyone. She was extraordinarily calm and collected."

Nancy shook her head. "She's an odd one, that one."

"And we still haven't come up with a truly good theory for why she would want to kill John," Alexandra said.

Nancy was uncharacteristically silent for a long moment. Finally she spoke. "Now that I think of it, I wonder if he tried to give me a reason. Still . . . it doesn't make sense."

"What do you mean?" Alexandra sounded even more tired.

"After you left for your rounds, and as Mr. Forsythe was trying to get John out of bed and into the carriage, the young man said something. Something odd, now that I think of it."

"Odd?" Nancy had gotten Alexandra's full attention.

"Yes, Mr. Forsythe had asked him, of course, if he knew of any reason why Annie would want to kill him. 'So 'twas Annie did it and not the coppers,' he says. 'I shouldn't be surprised,' he says. 'The old she devil'—his words, mind you, not mine. 'The old she devil has always wanted both of us out of the way.' Now, of course Mr. Forsythe asked him what he meant by that, but he wouldn't say. Then, just as the carriage was leaving, young John stuck his head out the window and said to me, 'It must have been Will.' Said it in a whisper, he did, as if he wanted no one else to hear it. But what did he mean?"

"Why haven't you told me this?" Alexandra demanded.

"I didn't think it was important. He seemed to be a bit out of his head. You've seen patients like that, of course. Especially when they're taking laudanum. But now that I think about it, I wonder . . ."

Alexandra stood, suddenly agitated. "We must talk to him

again. As early as possible tomorrow, before he's sent off to London."

"He didn't mean young Will killed his father, did he?"

Nancy had once again spoken the words Alexandra had not dared speak herself.

15

Neither Alexandra nor Nancy was in the mood for conversation at breakfast the next morning. Then, when Alexandra started her daily rounds to visit homebound patients, her movements seemed slow, labored, and heavy.

Even Zack seemed in a dark mood as he lumbered along beside Lucy as Alexandra rode to the first stop. Zack's head was bowed, and his customary breathy low growls sounded like moans. The substance on his coat that Nancy had failed to remove was sticky and attracted dust along with the black grime from chimney smoke, so that he took on the look of a worn, dirty carpet.

The first stop of the day was the Talbot house. Alexandra knocked at the door and tried to steel herself for Hannibal's ungrateful complaining.

The door opened slightly, and Mildryd Talbot's face, pale and drawn, appeared around the edge. Her wide, perpetually frightened eyes were outlined with dark weariness that threatened to suck an observer in with their neediness.

"It's Dr. Gladstone," she said in a whisper so soft it could not have been meant for anyone to hear. She opened the door and stepped aside, her glance flickering from Alexandra to Hannibal, in his bed by the stove, and back again to Alexandra.

Alexandra stepped inside, and Zack, knowing he'd been

allowed in before, assumed he now had permanent rights and walked in with her.

"Who's there?" Hannibal called from his bed, his voice a weakened bellow.

Mildryd followed Alexandra to the bedside and stayed behind her like a timid child. When she didn't answer her husband's question Alexandra spoke.

"It's Dr. Gladstone. I've come to see how you are progressing." She went to his bed and bent over him, placing the end of the stethoscope on his chest to listen for signs of pneumonia.

"How I progress? What do you expect when you slash me privates?" She removed the stethoscope from her ears where his amplified voice still reverberated.

"There is a great deal of pain, of course, but you'll see improvement in a few days." She placed a hand on his brow, checking for fever. There was none.

"I'm pissin' blood," he growled, and then groaned again.

"The blood will disappear soon."

"Ye've damaged me for good, woman. Ye've made it so I can't diddle me wife the way a man should."

Behind her, Alexandra heard Mildryd gasp.

"The operation will have no effect of that kind," Alexandra said as she touched the blanket that covered him from the waist down. "I must have a look at the incision."

"I told you, you'll not be lookin' at me privates again!" He grabbed the blanket from her and brought it to his chin, clutching it tightly. There was another gasp from Mildryd.

"As you wish." Alexandra stepped away from the bed and picked up her bag, folding the stethoscope inside. Custom was not to examine the body of either sex if he or she was not comfortable with it. "Continue to use the laudanum, but use it sparingly and drink plenty of water. No spirits. If you develop a fever, you must send for me immediately." She closed her bag and glanced at her patient one more time. "Good day, Hannibal." She turned aside, prepared to inquire of Mildryd about her health and to urge her to rest more when Hannibal distracted her with another weakened but angry yell.

"What is it ye've done to the brute? He's filthy as swine,

he is." He looked at Zack with an expression of sympathy for the abuse the two of them had endured at her hands.

"I'm afraid he got into something in the woods. Whatever it is, it defies a washing." Alexandra picked one of the black strands she had thought was grass from Zack's back. It appeared more like threads than grass now, however.

"In the woods, you say?" He still spoke with the same angry tone, and he raised up slightly to have a better look at Zack. "It's pitch mixed with tar. Ye've had 'im in a rowboat, ye'ave. Any oyster man worth 'is salt knows the look and smell of the pitch and tar that stops a leak in a small craft. The brute's too big for a rowboat. Could tip it over, he could, what with the fidgets a big 'un like him gets. If ye had any sense, woman, ye'd not put a brute that size in a rowboat. Could drown ye both."

Alexandra was prepared to defend herself by declaring she'd never had Zack in a rowboat, and that she, in fact, had nothing to do with Zack's dirty coat. But she said nothing. Her thoughts turned to Admiral Orkwright and the ladies' drawers he was wearing. Nancy had identified the sticky substance on that garment as pitch. If it had been used as sealant for a rowboat, did that mean the admiral had been in the rowboat? Had the boat capsized, causing the admiral to drown and then be washed ashore? Had the boat washed ashore and Zack had found it somehow?

"Dr. Gladstone? Are you all right?" It was Mildryd bringing her back to the present.

"What? Of course." She took a moment to reorient herself. "And you, Mildryd, you're not resting well, are you?"

The woman seemed surprised at the question. She wasn't used to having her feelings sought out, but when she finally admitted her fatigue, Alexandra prescribed the daily ingestion of yeast along with an infusion of skullcap. She was about to leave with her soiled four-legged companion when Hannibal called out to her again.

"Gladstone!"

She turned around. He looked at her a moment, apparently reluctant to speak. "The stones," he said finally. "Me wife showed 'em to me. The ones what ye cut out of me."

After another long pause, Alexandra gave him a brief nod

and turned to walk away. His next words stopped her again.

"I thank ye."

The words surprised her, and she turned around slowly, prepared to acknowledge his thanks, but he was staring at the ceiling and refusing to look at her. "The pleasure, Hannibal, was all mine," she said. She saw him flinch at what her statement implied, and she managed to make it out the door before her suppressed laughter erupted.

Her merriment didn't last long. When she glanced at Zack again and saw his soiled coat, her thoughts returned to Admiral Orkwright and the mystery that shrouded his death. Those thoughts were never far from the surface of her consciousness for the remainder of the day, even after she had seen the last of her patients in her surgery. There had been a large number of patients, most of them complaining of catarrh, or "a cold" as it had become fashionable to call it. There was no cure, of course, but she had dispensed several ounces of her usual remedy to control symptoms: a snuff of bloodroot, bayberry bark, and myrrh.

Mrs. Sommer had been in with her usual complaint of gastric uneasiness and flatulence. Since she had steadfastly refused to change her diet, Alexandra had provided a compound tincture of lavender, which she kept in her pharmacy. Along with the lavender, the mixture included oil of anise, cloves, mace, red saunders, brandy, and Jamaica rum. It took some time for the medicine to be prepared, since it had to be macerated for fourteen days and then carefully filtered. She had taken to relying on an apothecary for this and other complicated compounds, a practice that her father had never approved. He preferred to mix everything he administered. She consoled herself for having departed from his teaching by reminding herself that the town had been smaller and life less complicated in his day.

Nancy prepared an early dinner for the two of them. Alexandra occasionally wished she could enjoy a leisurely afternoon tea as other of her status did, but her profession did not allow for that nicety, much less for an elegant, multicourse late dinner when she had to rise so early for her rounds. As they ate, Nancy listened to her account of her day.

"Of course!" she said when Alexandra told her of Hannibal's assessment of where Zack had gotten the sticky substance in his hair. "I should have thought of that myself. And if it's the same substance we found on the admiral's drawers, then he was in a boat when he drowned. The same boat Zack seems to have found at Gull House."

"It does seem likely, doesn't it?" Alexandra carefully cut a small square from the boiled meat Nancy had prepared.

"More than likely, I would say." There was a note of excitement in Nancy's voice. "And that means someone rowed him out to sea and drowned him and then rowed back. Someone at Gull House."

Alexandra moved her head slowly from side to side. "But if it's common for all boats to be sealed with this mixture, then the admiral could have taken one out to sea himself, and the one Zack found, wherever it is, may have no bearing on the case at all. The one the admiral was in could have been dashed against the rocks somewhere and destroyed after he tumbled out."

"Or was pushed out," Nancy said.

"Yes, that's possible."

"You've said all along that he didn't drown himself, that he was murdered," Nancy reminded her.

Alexandra didn't argue with her. She was still rolling it all around in her mind. "The truth is that it doesn't seem likely that he fell out of the boat, and it was then dashed to pieces, does it? If he had been in a boat, it most likely would have washed ashore just as he did. Or if it was dashed to pieces, the admiral's body would have been as well."

"Unless someone pushed him out of the boat and rowed back to shore," Nancy said.

Alexandra laid her fork aside and pushed away from her plate. "In that case it seems unlikely that young Will could have done it, doesn't it? He's not likely to have been strong enough to row out to sea."

"It was ridiculous for us to have considered him in the first place," Nancy said, then added, "I've some turpentine somewhere."

"I beg your pardon?"

"Turpentine. I can use that to clean Zack's hairy back if

it's pitch and tar he got into." Nancy gave the dog a scowling look. "I'll use it tonight, you bad-tempered beast, and there'll be no quarreling on your part."

Zack obliged her with a low mumbling growl that sounded like a grumpy old man.

"I seem to recall your saying you'd never bathe him again," Alexandra said.

"No matter what I said, he'll not sleep in this house looking like that." Nancy's voice was firm and full of authority and contradiction.

Alexandra shook her head, smiling to herself, and argued no further. She went to the parlor prepared to read, but before she could open her book, Nicholas appeared at her door. Once again she was unexpectedly happy to see him.

"What in heaven's name is that noise?" he asked when he had settled himself into one of the chairs next to the fireplace.

"It's only Zack," said Alexandra. "Would you care for some sherry?" He accepted and she poured it for him. She wasn't going to risk distracting Nancy by asking her to serve.

Nicholas took a sip of the sherry. "Did you say it's Zack making all the fuss?"

"He's arguing with Nancy because this is the second bath she's given him in two days."

Nicholas wore a puzzled frown. "Why on earth would she do that?"

Alexandra explained about the pitch and tar used for sealing the seams of rowboats, and explained that Zack must have gotten into one while they were at Gull House. Nicholas offered the same theory she and Nancy had devised, that, since it appeared to be the same substance found on the garment the admiral was wearing, then he could have been in the same boat the admiral had been in.

"We must set out to find it." He was exuberant. "I shall pick you up in the morning before you start your rounds. No need to have Lucy saddled. I shall hire a carriage."

Nicholas had not yet arrived the next morning when Fin Prodder knocked at her door. He had ridden all night from Bradfordshire where he'd been with his mother, Mary, as she

lay in her bed in Bradfordshire Hospital. Since Nancy had
taken breakfast to Artie and Rob, Alexandra opened the door
herself. Fin stood before her shivering in the cold dampness
of a still dark February morning.

"It's me mum, Dr. Gladstone. She's taken a turn for the
worse." His voice was hoarse with weariness, and he
clutched his workingman's cap in both his hands.

"Pneumonia." It was not a question. Mary had spent several hours helpless on the ground in the cold of February.
And if that wasn't enough, experience had taught Alexandra
that an elderly patient, rendered immobile by the splint that
was necessary after a broken hip, more often than not suc-
cumbed to pneumonia.

Fin nodded. "Aye."

"Please come in," she said, stepping aside for him. "And
what do the doctors say of her chances?"

"There is no hope." Fin's voice was choked with emotion.

In spite of the fact that the news was no surprise to Alexandra, she felt the pang of helplessness and the sense of
ineptness she always felt when a patient was dying. At the
same time, she was aware of Fin Podder's pain. "Please, Fin,
come into the parlor. I'll have Nancy—"

Fin shook his head. "I've no time for the niceties of your
parlor, Dr. Gladstone. I've rode since the darkest hour of the
night from Bradfordshire to come here to fetch you."

"To fetch me? I don't understand. The doctors at Bradfordshire Hospital are more experienced at—"

"I got no complaint about the doctors at Bradfordshire."
Fin clutched at his cap again. "It's you she wants. Says she
cannot die in peace until she talks to you."

"Perhaps it's the delirium," Alexandra said. "A pneumonia
patient is often out of her head."

"Out of her head, you say? Sure she is at times. But I
knows me own mum, don't I? She was in her own mind
when she asked for you. Don't you see? It's her last request
I'm trying to grant her. She's entitled to that, ain't she?"

Alexandra sensed a hint of guilt in what he was saying.
He must have known his mother's life was miserable living
with his wife, Edith, and he was now, in some way, trying

to compensate for that. "Have you any idea what is it she wishes to tell me?" She was already reaching for her cloak. "Fin," she said when he didn't answer. She assumed he hadn't heard her, but when she looked at his face, she knew he had, yet he seemed reluctant to speak.

"It's something about the admiral." His voice trembled slightly. "She says it's something you should know. Says she cannot go to her grave until she's sure you understand."

Alexandra felt her heart miss a beat. What could Mary Prodder possibly know about Admiral Orkwright? She'd had no association with him, except that she'd been Jane Orkwright's dressmaker. It was possible, of course, that either Jane or the admiral had confided in her, but about what?

Alexandra took the time to tell Nancy she'd been called away. She was careful not to mention that Mary Prodder wanted to tell her something about the admiral, though. It would take too long to convince a curious and perceptive Nancy that there was no reason for her to come along as well. She left her instructions as to what patients she must see for her during the morning rounds. Nancy was more than competent but would not attempt to minister to patients in a way that was beyond her skill and training. She knew without asking that Nancy would open the surgery for the usual afternoon hours, and she would also not step beyond her rightful bounds, leaving the sickest of the patients for Alexandra when she returned. Alexandra gave her instructions to give her apologies to Mr. Forsythe, who would be arriving soon and to explain that she'd been called to Bradfordshire to see Mary.

It was not until the mention of Mary's name that Nancy became insufferably inquisitive.

"Mary's in hospital, isn't she? Are the physicians there not capable of treating her?"

"Mary is dying, Nancy. I suspect there is nothing any physician can do, neither I nor the ones in Bradfordshire." Alexandra silently chastised herself for even mentioning Bradfordshire or Mary Prodder.

"Then why—?"

Rob, who had delivered a load of coal to the kitchen, was

now enjoying a cup of tea Nancy had given him. He interrupted Nancy before she could complete her question. " 'Tis
a deathbed confession, ain't it? I seen it before. There's many
an old lady or old man I seen dying what wants to unburden
theirselves and tell you the wicked things they done before
they croak. It's like if they give you their secret, God and
the devil won't hold it against 'em."

"Rob!" Alexandra spoke sharply. "You're being disrespectful to the dead and dying. I'll have no more of it." In
spite of her reprimand, Alexandra knew that Rob, as well as
little Artie, as orphaned urchins of the piers before they came
to her, had seen more than their share of death among the
poor.

Nancy, who under most circumstances would have been
the first to scold, was, instead, preoccupied. Finally, she
spoke, as if the truth had just come to her. "Rob tells the
truth, does he not? She wants to tell you something! She
knows something about Mrs. Orkwright and the admiral!"

"So now you are clairvoyant, are you?" Alexandra gave
her a friendly smile. "You know what someone eight miles
away wants to tell me. Perhaps I should save myself the
trouble of the journey and simply listen to you." Alexandra
was trying to hurry out of the kitchen.

"Oh, that's it, all right. I can tell when I've hit upon the
truth when you take that attitude."

Alexandra resisted the temptation to ask Nancy to clarify
what she meant by "that attitude." It didn't matter. Nancy
was about to reveal that bit of truth to her anyway.

"Remember the time when we were children and I guessed
that you were secretly reading that naughty French novel
your father had forbidden you to read?"

"Nancy, I don't believe it's necessary to recall old—"

" 'Oh, Nancy,' you said. 'If you are so clairvoyant you
can tell me what book I'm reading, why not just tell me the
story and save me the trouble of reading it,' you said. And
that's how I knew."

"The doc reads naughty books?" Rob said, then laughed
until he made tea come out his nose.

Nancy, however, didn't laugh, and neither did she scold Rob for his bad manners. She simply looked at Alexandra, holding her gaze for a moment before she spoke. "She knows something. A dressmaker always does."

16

The hospital at Bradfordshire was in what had originally been a middle-class residence. It had undergone a minimum amount of remodeling to create two sizable rooms or wards, one for men and one for women. Other rooms accommodated a few offices and supply rooms, a dining area for staff, and a kitchen that served the entire facility. All the rooms were cold and drafty in winter and sweltering in summer. The blue-cold air that knifed through all the rooms in winter yellowed into a damp and stagnated heaviness in summer.

In spite of its physical disadvantages, and in spite of the fact that it was small, relative to London hospitals, it was, nevertheless, considered a good hospital. One Dr. Agustus Julius Holmes was the senior physician. He was widely respected, and under his leadership Bradfordshire Hospital had flourished.

Dr. Holmes had been Alexandra's mentor while she did part of her training at Bradfordshire. Her late father had arranged that mentorship for her. Her father had been her first and primary teacher, but he insisted that Alexandra have training and tutelage under someone else as well. Agustus Holmes was his choice, and Alexandra was well aware that, had it not been for the fact that he was her father's friend, because of her sex she would not likely have had the opportunity to study with him.

Both he and her father carried the title Physician, while

she was allowed only the title of Surgeon. Physicians were university trained while surgeons served apprenticeships. The classes she'd been forbidden to attend while she was at university had kept her from earning the title of Physician.

When she stepped into the familiar dark and dank environs of the receiving room at Bradfordshire Hospital, she was greeted by Roslind Sullivan, a robust woman of about fifty who was the head of the nursing staff.

"Oh, you're here!" Nurse Sullivan rushed toward Alexandra with open arms and gave her an almost debilitating hug. "You're here to see Mary Prodder."

"Yes, her son came for me. He says she's asking for me."

"It's so good of you to come, although you needn't have really." Nurse Sullivan took Alexandra's cloak and handed it to a boy of about twelve who had been hovering nearby. "See that it's hung up nicely," she said over her shoulder. Then to Alexandra: "Poor Mary's out of her head." She leaned closer to her and whispered, "Lung fever, as you might have guessed. I'm afraid her remaining time is only a few days at best."

"Will she recognize me?" Alexandra walked with the nurse toward the women's ward.

"Not likely," Nurse Sullivan said. "Although one never knows." She picked up one of Alexandra's hands and gave it a gentle pat. "Still, it is so good of you to come. If she does recognize you, it will make her passing more peaceful, I'm certain. The poor woman almost gets to the point of raging when she's asking for you." She shook her head sadly. "Of course she's not in her right mind when she does that. The fever, you know. I dare say she may not even awaken while you're here."

Nurse Sullivan opened the door to the women's ward and stepped aside to allow Alexandra to enter. Little had changed except the faces of the patients since Alexandra had worked and trained there five years ago. The long room, smelling of fever and various bodily excretions, was lined with cots on both sides, and on the cots lay women, primarily of the lower working classes, of varying ages and in varying stages of ill health.

One woman sat up in her bed keening and rocking rhythmically back and forth. A few tried to sleep in spite of the moaning and crying of others. Some wore bandages, and many of them stared at her with empty eyes and pain-racked faces.

Mary Prodder was in a bed near the opposite end of the room. A young nurse bent over her, adjusting the splint on her leg while Mary took in her breath and let it out in a cacophony of rasping, rattling sounds. As Alexandra approached her bed, she saw that Mary was sleeping restlessly.

Nurse Sullivan signaled for the young nurse tending her to leave, and then she herself moved away quietly, leaving Alexandra alone at Mary's bedside. After only a few seconds Mary seemed to sense someone was there and opened her eyes. Alexandra thought she saw a spark of recognition and took her hand, holding it between both of hers. Mary closed her eyes and appeared to be drifting into her restless sleep again. The sleep was interrupted with a rattling cough, and she had to help Mary up to a sitting position to keep her from strangling on the pus-filled phlegm that came from her lungs.

When the coughing fit was over, Mary lay back on the pillows exhausted. Her face was pale and damp with sweat, and her eyes closed. She opened them suddenly and stared at Alexandra. It was impossible to tell whether the wild expression denoted recognition or confusion.

Alexandra, still holding her hand, spoke to her softly. There was no response aside from the wide eyes that watched her still. She placed a hand on the woman's chest and tapped the back of it with the fingers of her other hand, listening for a response. It was as she had expected, dull with no resonation, denoting a congested lung. She got the same result when she tested the other side, and when she placed a hand on Mary's head she felt the heat of a dangerously high fever. With her stethoscope on Mary's chest, she heard a resonating *whoosh, whoosh* from both lungs.

Mary quite unexpectedly whispered her name, "Dr. Gladstone," and the remarkably audible sound heard through the stethoscope confirmed for Alexandra that the lungs were congested and inflamed.

She removed the stethoscope from her ears and replied in a quiet voice, "Yes, it's Dr. Gladstone."

"It was my fault, you know, because . . ." Mary was interrupted by a fit of coughing, a rattling, moist sound that produced nothing. She flailed about restlessly.

Alexandra tried to quiet her. "Hush now, Mary." She stroked her forehead, pushing back a tuft of sweat-dampened gray hair.

"I always hated Papa, and that's the reason I did it. I know it's my fault, but I have scars, see." She tried to raise her gown as if to show her the scars Alexandra had seen before, the same ones Mary had said were caused by a fall from a horse. "You mustn't blame her. 'Twas me told her about his heels." Again Alexandra stroked her head and tried to soothe her, but Mary continued her ranting. "He hated me the most because I was the oldest. We tried to grab Papa's heels, but he was too quick."

"Yes, yes. Now please don't fret about it," Alexandra said, remembering her own conclusion she'd drawn about the scars.

Mary fell into another fit of coughing, and when she finally stopped, she was exhausted. "He's in hell, Papa is," she said in a choked whisper. "I saw him there with my own eyes." Then, after a pause, she added. "You don't believe me."

"Shhh, it's all right. He can't hurt you." Alexandra didn't try to imagine the hell that haunted Mary. She had seen enough of suffering to know that the best one could do was speak platitudes to try to help ease the pain. Mary had said nothing about the admiral as Fin had suggested. Her mind was fever-clouded, and it was likely anything she'd said about the admiral was irrelevant.

"Do you think Mama will be there?" Mary rolled her head violently back and forth on her pillow, still talking nonsense. "I didn't see her there."

"No, of course not. It's all right. You must rest."

Still, Mary refused to heed her. She kept up her ranting. "I will be there, you know. I will be in hell with Papa soon."

"You'll be in heaven, Mary, not hell." Alexandra knew the platitudes all too well.

"It was Annie that helped me put him in there. It wasn't right, you know, for him to be naked."

The mention of Annie suddenly got Alexandra's attention. "Who, Mary? Who are you talking about? You and Annie put someone where?"

Mary lapsed into another seizure of coughing and couldn't answer at first. When she tried to speak, Alexandra leaned close to hear her words, but the cough kept Mary from saying more. Alexandra called for a nurse, and the young woman in the crisp white apron who had been with Mary earlier heard her and came to the bedside.

"Bring her the gelseminum and aconite formula, please," Alexandra said. "For her cough."

The nurse gave her a puzzled look. "Excuse me, but I . . ." She stopped speaking when she saw the stethoscope around Alexandra's neck. "Are you new here? Why aren't you in uniform? All nurses are to wear white smocks or—"

"I am Dr. Gladstone, this patient's doctor from Newton-Upon-Sea."

The young nurse blushed. "I'm sorry, ma'am—I mean doctor. I didn't know. You see, I . . . I've been told to watch Mary's cough and see that she gets . . ."

"The gelseminum and aconite," Alexandra said, finishing the sentence the nurse seemed unable to finish. "Please see that she gets it as soon as possible."

The nurse hurried away to fetch the medicine, and Alexandra turned back to Mary, whose fever-brightened eyes were fixed on her. "I done it." She wheezed and gasped for air. "Not her. I couldn't die with you thinking she done it. Then she helped me get him in the boat."

"Mary, what are you saying? You did what? Tell me, please." Mary's gaze now appeared to be unseeing, in spite of the fact that her eyes had not moved from Alexandra's face. In the next instant the nurse returned with a bottle of medicine and a spoon. Mary immediately reached for Alexandra's hand and went into another coughing spell. The nurse quickly uncurled Mary's fingers from Alexandra's hand, and, giving her a knowing look, she turned to Mary with the bottle and spoon, crooning her own platitudes.

"Excuse me, but I must talk to Mrs. Prodder," Alexandra said.

By now, the nurse had taken full charge. She gave Alexandra an unflinching look of authority and said, "I shall lose my position here if I don't tend my patients as instructed."

Alexandra knew the rules, and she knew the nurse was only doing her duty. She glanced at Mary, who was shaking her head again, trying to refuse the medicine and talking incoherently to someone seen only by her. In the middle of her confused speech, she turned her fever-brightened eyes to Alexandra and said, "It was me what killed the admiral! I will burn in hell for that."

"Hush now," the nurse said before Alexandra could respond. "You're just talking nonsense, my dear. 'Tis the fever makes you talk that way." She glanced at Alexandra. "Poor dear is always talking nonsense about some admiral." She then succeeded in grasping Mary's head and holding it still with one hand long enough to force the spoon full of medicine into her mouth with the other. Mary coughed, expelling most of the medicine, and the nurse had to begin again. By the time the medicine was finally administered, she fell into an exhausted but restless sleep.

Alexandra couldn't move her eyes from Mary's sleeping form, and the words she had just uttered resonated in her mind. Mary had killed the admiral? For what possible reason? It was impossible to believe such a thing. Yet, the night she was found on the ground with a broken hip was the same night the admiral had died. Was that what she'd been doing that night, rather than staying late with a client to fit a dress? Alexandra didn't know how long she had waited at Mary's bedside before Dr. Holmes approached her.

"Alexandra, my dear," he said, walking toward her with a portly dignity that was perhaps a little too theatrical. He did so enjoy his role as master teacher. He took her hand and, bowing over it, brushed it with his lips. "How lovely that you've come to visit us."

"Mrs. Prodder is my patient." Alexandra spoke as she allowed him to lead her away. She soon realized they were going to his office, an inner sanctum reserved for the doctor and his colleagues and to which she was never invited as a student.

He hesitated just before entering, long enough to order tea, then turned back to Alexandra. "Ah yes, Mary. Fractured hip and lung fever."

"Interesting, isn't it? How the two so often go together."

He offered her a chair, then sat down opposite her behind his desk. "If you understand the cause of lung fever, or to speak in medical terms, pneumonia, it isn't at all surprising." Dr. Holmes had slipped into his professorial tone of voice.

"I've been wondering lately if we really do understand the cause," Alexandra said. I've begun to think that the inertia that results from confinement to one's bed affects the lungs by allowing certain fluids to settle there."

Dr. Holmes frowned. "Alexandra, my dear, you are aware, I'm sure, that all the texts say that pneumonia is most often caused by exposure to cold and moisture."

"Of course."

"The relationship you've noticed of inertia to the disease has to do with the bowels, not chest fluids. When a patient is bedfast, proper evacuation may cease due to lack of exercise, and the resultant toxins in the body can result in fevers, such as the lung fever Mary has. You can rest assured, however, that we've given your Mary the proper laxatives and purges."

"Of course, I didn't mean to imply—"

Dr. Holmes waved a hand, a dismissive gesture. "No, no, of course not, and let me add that your observation of the relationship was quite astute of you, but modern science has supplied the answer."

"Perhaps," Alexandra said, still mulling it in her mind. "Nevertheless, I'm quite concerned about Mary. There's congestion in both lungs, and she hallucinates."

"You're quite right to be concerned," Dr. Holmes said, "but again I assure you, she's receiving the best care available. In the final analysis, as with all patients, it remains in the hands of God as to whether or not she recovers." He gave Alexandra a scrutinizing look. "You seem uncommonly concerned, my dear. I'm sure your father warned you, as have I, that there is mental and spiritual danger if one becomes too personally involved."

Alexandra had heard the warning many times from her father, but she had found it difficult not to become personally involved when her patients were neighbors and friends she had known all her life. The only hint her father had ever given her that he experienced the same problem was to confess to her that he had found it necessary to sacrifice something of his soul in order to survive in his profession. He had not discussed the problem beyond that. After several years she had come to understand that it may have been too painful for him to discuss.

It was the utter dependence and unflinching trust placed in her that was so damning and damaging. Mary's words, *I knows ye'll heal me,* still resonated in her soul. And now even Mary knew she was dying. Why else would she feel the need to unburden herself by confessing to murdering the admiral? The thought of that confession once again sent Alexandra's mind reeling. What possible motive could Mary have for that? And who did she mean when she said, "I couldn't bear for you to think it was someone else"? Who was the "someone else"? Did she mean Annie? She'd said something about Annie helping her. Or was she confusing the admiral with her father, whom she obviously hated? And was the "someone else" her mother or another person from her unhappy childhood?

"Alexandra? Are you all right?"

Dr. Holmes's words startled her and brought her out of her troubled musing. "Of course," she said. "I was just thinking of Mary's hallucinations. I say, it was difficult for me to know where the hallucinations ended and reality began."

Dr. Holmes nodded in agreement. "Indeed. She rambles on about her father quite often. Sometimes as if she thinks he's with her."

"Has she ever mentioned a certain Admiral Orkwright in her ramblings?" Alexandra tried not to appear too anxious.

"Can't say. There are so many patients. So many ramblings." He was distracted by the tea tray the nurse had brought. "Cream?" he asked, holding up the pitcher over the cup that had been poured for Alexandra.

During the next few minutes, Dr. Holmes turned the conversation to the telephone exchange recently installed in London. He, like Mr. Forsythe, was fascinated by the science, but speculated that it might prove to be a nuisance to have patients ringing one up at all hours. Alexandra could think of nothing other than Mary's confession. It seemed increasingly bizarre as each minute passed. By the time Dr. Holmes moved on to the recent announcement of a chicken cholera vaccine and the growing popularity for inoculations in the treatment and prevention of disease, Alexandra had lost track of the conversation entirely.

She wanted desperately to get back to Mary. Perhaps after Mary slept awhile and felt more rested she would no longer be incoherent.

Mary was not awake when Alexandra returned to her bedside. She had died peacefully in her sleep.

Nicholas was more than a little dismayed when he arrived at Dr. Gladstone's home, and Nancy told him the doctor had been called away. He had been eager to investigate the mystery of the boat sealant. It was obvious that the admiral had come in contact with the sealant, and it followed that he most likely came in contact with it while in a boat. One could then extrapolate that he had been in the boat when he fell, or was pushed as the case may be, into the sea to drown.

Finding a small craft with fresh sealant on it, as Zack had apparently done, could possibly bring them one step closer to solving the mystery. If the boat was on the admiral's property, as Zack's encounter seemed to suggest, then someone could have placed it there after the admiral died. After he had been taken out to sea and drowned. Who might have done that remained a mystery, and that was precisely the reason he was eager to investigate. He hoped to find something that would help answer the question of who.

"Oh, I know, 'tis a shame, sir. Of course you're disappointed." Nancy had apparently read his mind, or perhaps just his expression. "I know Dr. Gladstone was just as eager as you to get on with the investigation."

"Yes, well, I suppose when duty calls . . ." Nicholas gave

Nancy a faint smile and turned toward the carriage.

"Of course we could still investigate. The two of us, I mean."

Nicholas stopped and turned around slowly. "The two of us?"

"And why not? It's what Dr. Gladstone would want." Nancy wore an enthusiastic look on her face as she stepped out the door, her arms folded around themselves against the cold.

"Indeed. And how do you know that?"

"Well, of course she would," Nancy said, taking a few steps toward him. "She will appreciate whatever we can learn in her absence. She'll see it as saving her time, she will."

Nicholas considered it for a moment. The truth was he had thought of going on to Gull House himself as soon as Nancy told him Alexandra was gone. He would have to take the dog, of course, in the hope that he would lead the way to the boat in question. But he had second thoughts about the animal, who was none too friendly toward him, and who, he suspected, would not be inclined to cooperate. Nancy, on the other hand, got on with Zack as well as Alexandra did.

"Perhaps you're right," he said at length. "Fetch your cloak and gloves. Oh, and bring along something to tie the dog to the carriage so he'll be sure to follow us."

"No need for that," Nancy called to him over her shoulder as she turned back to the door. "He'll follow."

Nancy was right. The dog did follow, his size allowing him to lumber along with the horse without hurrying. As they approached the house, Nancy, with her usual lack of concern for the propriety of the situation, told him where and when to stop.

"Stop the carriage here, sir," she said when they were still several yards away from the steep drive to Gull House at the top of the hill. "I don't think we should go any farther up, lest someone sees us. This will give us a chance to meander in the woods to see if we can spot the boat. We'll let Zack go ahead, of course, since, if I know the old boy as well as I think I do, it's likely he'll go back to the boat that got him into trouble to start with."

Nicholas could see no reason not to do her bidding, so he

secured the horse and carriage to a tree and turned back to help Nancy out of the carriage, only to find she had already alighted. She was standing with her hands on her hips, surveying the woods. The dog sat beside her, his panting breath forming a jagged ghost of a cloud that disappeared quickly into the ether. He showed no sign of wanting to return to the scene of his last crime.

Nancy, who once again appeared to have read his mind, said, "Poor Zack may be afraid I'll scold him. Perhaps we should walk away and leave him to his own devices."

"Perhaps you're right," Nicholas said. "Where do you propose we go?"

"I suggest we take the carriage up to Gull House and leave Zack here, just as Miss Alex did. She told me it peeved him to be left behind, and she thinks that's why he wandered away into the woods."

"Very well." Nicholas stood beside the carriage, ready to help her in, but she was busy now, instructing the dog that he was to stay at the bottom of the hill. The animal actually seemed to be arguing with her with an odd-sounding growl, but in the end, she seemed to think she had succeeded in convincing him and allowed herself to be helped into the carriage and driven away. When Nicholas glanced back at the dog, he didn't appear to be at all malcontent. He wagged his tail a few seconds, then sat down with what someone more sentimental than himself might call a contented look, his breath a puff of white against the gray morning.

Nancy was once again full of advice as Nicholas drove the carriage up the hill. "We will go to the door together, and I shall tell the housekeeper that Dr. Gladstone has instructed me to come to see after Mrs. Orkwright. It won't seem at all strange to her, since I have taken on such duties before in the doctor's absence. As for you, I suppose we can say that the doctor asked you to drive me in your carriage, what with the morning being so cold."

Nicholas had to admit to himself that the old girl was clever, and she was probably as conniving a woman as he'd ever met.

Nancy's artful ruse did at least get them inside, where they were told by the grim, unsmiling woman known as Annie to wait in the parlor. "She's an odd one, that one," Nancy whispered when they were alone. "And dangerous, as you know. Tried to kill young John, if Rob is right. Odd thing, the constable never questioning him, what?"

"I suppose . . ." Nicholas was a bit distracted, "but I'm wondering—"

"Tell you what I think," Nancy interrupted. "I think 'tis because he knows Mrs. Orkwright wouldn't want him asking too many questions. He's fond of her, he is."

"Nancy." Nicholas sounded exasperated. "The important question is why would Annie want to kill John?"

"When a woman kills, she's protecting someone. Sometimes 'tis herself." Nancy whispered without looking at him. Her eyes were still fixed in the direction in which Annie had disappeared.

Nicholas pondered her words. If Annie had indeed taken a shot at John, was she protecting herself? Or Mrs. Orkwright? Or someone else?

He grew restless waiting for Annie to return and found himself walking around the room aimlessly, first staring out the window at the view of the bleak seacoast, then inspecting a rather bad painting of what must have been the admiral's ancestor. Finally, he meandered across the room to the gun cabinet. He was something of a gun aficionado, and his interest was captured by the small but impressive collection he found there. There was a Welby-Green revolver, quite the new thing. It had only been introduced this year. Next to it was a shot gun. The maker was W. J. Jeffery and Company of London, which meant the gun was handmade to suit the owner. Another W. J. Jeffery of a considerable larger caliber was next to it. It was the sort of gun gentlemen used for tiger hunting in India. Nicholas had one himself, also made by Jeffery.

It was the Mauser that astonished him, though. It would have fired the .446-caliber bullet the stable boy had found in the ceiling of the stable. But of even more interest was the fact that there was a smudge of powder at the end of the barrel.

He took a quick glance over his shoulder before he attempted to open the glass door of the cabinet. To his great surprise, it was not locked. Whoever had put the gun back in the cabinet without cleaning it must have been in a hurry and forgot to lock it. He reached for the Mauser, then he held the end of the barrel to his right eye and peered into it. The inside of the barrel was coated with powder residue. It had obviously been fired and not cleaned. It was equally obvious that the remaining guns in the cabinet had been meticulously cleaned, probably by the admiral. It would seem unlikely that he would put one away dirty.

"Sir! What are you doing? Put that away before someone sees you!" Nancy's warning came in an urgent whisper, and when he turned to look at her, he saw that her eyes were wide with alarm.

He said nothing, but he put the rifle away and had just seated himself in the chair he'd occupied before when Annie returned. Nancy still wore her alarmed look, which she quickly masked when she saw Annie.

"Mrs. Orkwright is not yet awake, and I'll not awaken her. She has hardly rested at all since her son was injured and taken back to gaol." Annie's eyes had the cold of the North Sea in them and her large frame menaced the room like a brewing storm.

Nancy stood. "Of course. Dr. Gladstone can see her when she returns." She had accomplished her mission by establishing an excuse for being on the property, so she wasn't going to put up a fuss.

"She's been through too much and needs her rest," Annie said, as if she hadn't heard Nancy and needed to make her point.

"See that she gets it, then." Nancy was already moving toward the door. "And don't bother seeing us out. We can find the way." She turned back to Annie and, with a cheerful smile, said, "Tell Mrs. Orkwright that Dr. Gladstone sends her greeting and will call on her later." Her smile disappeared as they made their way to the carriage. "Did you notice the innocent charade? Pure gall, I'd say. "She spoke in a low voice, as she leaned closer to Nicholas in order for him to hear her.

"If you're referring to the fact that she spoke so casually

about John's injury, then yes, I agree," Nicholas said as he helped Nancy into the carriage.

"Pure gall," Nancy said again.

"Most surprising though, was that she practically flaunted the weapon she used to shoot the boy."

Nancy leaned forward and spoke to him from the back of the carriage. "You found the weapon? Is that what you were doing when you were meddling with the admiral's guns?"

"Meddling?" Nicholas gave the rein a gentle flick across the horse's back.

"Perhaps I overstepped my bounds."

"Of course you did, Nancy. You are perpetually out of bounds." Nicholas threw the words at her from over his shoulder.

There was a long silence that left Nicholas wondering if Nancy actually felt chastened by his words. If she did, it would be quite out of character. Nancy was impertinent, devious, and rather overly confident. The kind of girl who should have been fired long ago. But he had to admit he liked her.

"Excuse me, sir," she said finally, leaning forward again. "You were telling me about the weapon you found."

Nicholas smiled to himself. She was very much in character after all. "The weapon she used to wound John," he said.

"But how can you be sure?"

He told her about the powder residue and how the caliber of bullets fired by the Mauser matched the one found in the ceiling.

"Am I right? Did she try to kill him to protect Mrs. Orkwright?" Nancy said.

"We don't know, do we? As you said, if we could solve the puzzle that is Annie, we could get to the bottom of this." Nicholas stopped the carriage at the bottom of hill where they had left Zack, but Zack was nowhere in sight. They got out of the carriage and called his name. Within a few minutes Zack came bounding dutifully out of the woods.

Nancy put her hands to her face. "Just look at him! He's covered with that sticky pitch and tar again."

"And that is precisely what we'd hoped for." Nicholas

took a cautious step toward Zack. "Come on, boy, show us where you've been." Zack ignored him and lay down at Nancy's feet.

Nicholas knew he was going to have to learn to get along with the beast, but for now, he was determined to find the boat, so he walked into the woods himself. It was not until Nancy ventured into the woods that Zack followed, however. But follow was all he was in the mood to do. He showed no inclination at all of leading them to the spot where he'd encountered the sealant.

Almost half an hour elapsed before Nicholas saw the pile of dead branches and leaves near an area of dense brush. As he drew closer he saw that the branches covered the prow of a small wooden craft. The rest of the boat had been pushed, stern first, into the brush where it rested upside down. Pitch and tar oozed from the seams on the bottom of the boat.

Nicholas turned around and signaled for Nancy, who was searching several yards away. "Look," he said when she drew closer. "Someone has gone to a bit of trouble to hide this."

Nancy frowned. "But why would anyone want it hidden?"

"If the admiral was supposed to have rowed himself out to sea, then fell out of his boat and drowned, the boat should still be out there, or else washed up to shore, battered and broken."

"Of course!" Nancy said. "But whoever rowed him out to sea to drown him had to use the boat to come back."

"Precisely."

"But who?"

"Who indeed." Nicholas was struggling with the boat, trying to right it. "Help me turn this boat over, Nancy. Perhaps something to answer that perplexing question will reveal itself.

When the craft was finally righted, there was nothing to see except the interior of the boat and a bit of leaves, dry grass, and twigs and other debris on the floor that had been caught by the sticky sealant.

*   *   *

By the time Mary's body had been prepared by the nurses and removed from the ward and Alexandra had spent some time comforting Fin, it was too late to start the long drive home. She and Fin were each given rooms in the dormitories for the night, and Fin drove her home in grieving silence the next day.

It was half past noon when they arrived. Lucy was saddled and waiting for her in the stable yard. The boys had obviously expected her back early enough to do her rounds. Only one carriage was waiting in the front. Perhaps that meant there were only a few patients waiting to see her. She could assume one or two had walked from the village. It would be fortunate for her if the patient load was small. She was tired, both physically and emotionally, because of the long ride, because of the ordeal of Mary's death, and most of all because of Mary's strange confession. She'd been mulling over all of it during the drive home.

She bid Fin good-bye and walked to the door with her key ready, but before she could insert the key, Nancy opened the door and greeted her with, "We have news!"

Zack immediately forced himself in front of Nancy in order to greet Alexandra with a happy bark and a nudge of her thigh with his nose that was almost enough to unbalance her. That left her with no choice but to greet him with a hug and a scratch under his neck. She was dismayed to find that her hands and the front of her dress were covered with the same sticky substance Nancy had cleaned from Zack's coat earlier.

"What sort of news?" she asked, peering around Zack's head.

Nicholas then surprised her by stepping into the hall from the parlor.

"Mr. Forsythe!"

"Good morning, Alexandra."

At the same time, Nancy said, "We found the boat."

Alexandra stood and glanced from Nancy back to Nicholas. "You found—"

"Near Gull House," Nicholas said. "Someone had attempted to hide it."

"So that means the murderer is someone at Gull House!" Nancy sounded excited.

"Not necessarily." Alexandra walked to the parlor, removing her cloak and gloves.

Nancy hurried to receive them. "Oh, I know it's not absolute proof, but with all the other evidence we have—"

"Someone else has confessed to the murder. Someone not at Gull House."

Nancy stopped on her way to hang Alexandra's cloak and turned to face her. "Someone . . . Who?"

At the same time, Nicholas said, "Confessed? To the constable?"

Alexandra sat down in her favorite chair next to the fire. "Not to the constable, sir, to me."

Nicholas sat down across from her. "But—"

"Mary Prodder told me she killed the admiral herself."

Nancy, for once, was speechless. She simply stared at her. Nicholas gave her an incredulous look. "The same Mary Prodder who is confined to her bed with a broken leg?" he asked.

"Yes, the same. Her last words to me before she died were a confession."

Nancy gasped and whispered, "She died? Oh no. I am so sorry, miss." She was well aware of the effect a patient's death had on Alexandra.

"I don't understand," Nicholas said. "How could she have possibly killed him when she couldn't walk?"

Alexandra shook her head. "Her injury occurred on the same night the admiral apparently died. She could have fallen on her way home after killing him." Alexandra felt very tired as well as depressed. It was a welcome feeling to have Zack nuzzling her ankles now, in spite of the fact that he was covered with that sticky substance, along with dirt and bits of the same odd black grass he'd attracted before. She found herself absently pulling the grass from his back and twisting it with her fingers. It was then that she realized it wasn't grass at all. If Nancy and Nicholas were speaking to her, she didn't know it for some time as she shifted and sorted through everything she knew about the admiral's death. Zack continued to nuzzle her, and she heard Nancy say something about his needing another bath.

"It's not an easy feat to get that animal into the tub," Nancy said.

It was the mention of the tub that started Alexandra to thinking of the admiral in his tub when he was drunk and of all that Mary had said. She looked at Nancy and then at Nicholas. "I must go to Gull House," she said.

He gave her a surprised look. "Shall I take you in my hired carriage?"

"I must go alone."

"Alone?" Nancy blurted. "Of course not, we must all go."

Alexandra reached for the cloak and gloves Nancy still held. "I think I know who killed the admiral, and you're right, Nancy, the killer is at Gull House."

"If you know, then you can't go without us!" Nancy called to her as she walked out the door.

Alexandra turned back to her and saw Nicholas standing behind her. "I'm sorry," she said. "Too many people will upset all of them."

"All of them?" Nancy called, but Alexandra made no reply as she hurried to the stables.

As soon as she reached the stable yard, both Artie and Rob materialized from somewhere to help her mount Lucy. They were talkative as usual.

"Did the old lady make her confession?" Rob asked.

"Yes," she said.

"Did she die?" Artie asked.

"I'm afraid she did."

"Was it something grand and awful? The confession, I mean." Rob asked.

"Don't be impertinent, Rob."

"You're late making your rounds, miss," Artie added.

"I am, indeed," she said, taking the reins from Rob and nudging Lucy to a quick trot so she wouldn't have to answer any more questions.

Just as she expected, Annie was reluctant to allow her in the house. "Mrs. Orkwright is resting," she said, "and she doesn't need your services anyway. I told that troublesome maid of yours the same. She should have relayed it to you."

"I'm not here to offer my services. I'm here on an urgent personal matter."

Annie hesitated a moment, and something changed in her eyes. "It's John, isn't it? What are you going to tell her?"

Alexandra took a step into the hall. If Annie chose, she could easily stop her, since she was heavier by three stone. But Annie didn't stop her. She moved away, her expression grim and defeated as Alexandra entered.

Neither did Annie walk ahead of Alexandra to announce her arrival, as was her duty. Instead, she followed as Alexandra made her way to the parlor where she assumed Jane would be. She was right. Jane sat alone in the cold room, lighted only by the smoky coal fire in the fireplace. She stared out the window at the bleak afternoon while she twisted a handkerchief in her hands. She looked as if she'd been crying. Sensing a presence in the room, she turned her face toward Alexandra and Annie.

Annie spoke to her from behind Alexandra. "Dr. Gladstone is here to see you, madam. She says it's urgent."

Jane stiffened. "Is it John? Is something wrong?"

Alexandra hesitated, then said, "I must speak to you in private, Jane."

"No," Jane said, shaking her head. "Annie will remain with me. I know what you are about to say. Annie has told me everything."

"Everything?" Alexandra felt uncertain.

"I know that she wounded John, but I also know that it was an accident."

"It is hardly an accident when the firearm is aimed directly at a person and then discharged," Alexandra said.

"But I didn't aim it at him!" Annie spoke in a voice far more plaintive than Alexandra ever imagined she could. "I only meant to frighten him. I meant for the bullet to go through the room. I never meant to hit the boy, I swear."

Alexandra felt a flare of anger. "Surely you know how dangerous it is to fire into a room full of people. You could have killed any one of us. You certainly frightened us all. But why? Why did you want to do that to John?"

Alexandra saw that Annie was now near tears. The woman glanced quickly at Jane and then back to Alexandra, then she tried to speak. "I . . ."

"Perhaps it's best you leave us after all," Jane said before Annie could say more.

Annie said nothing, but she was reluctant to leave. Finally, though, she put both hands to her face and left the room sobbing. Jane stood and went to a table and lit a lamp before she turned back to Alexandra.

"Sit down, please," she said, indicating a chair. When Alexandra was seated, Jane sat down across from her. "What Annie did was foolish, perhaps even a little insane, but she told me everything. She was afraid of what John would say."

"I see."

"Annie did not kill my husband." Jane's voice shook slightly.

"I know."

There was a long silence while Jane's gaze held Alexandra. "How long have you known?"

"An hour. Less, perhaps."

Jane nodded. She sat very straight in her chair with her hands folded casually in her lap. Her eyes were two luminous dark orbs in her pale face. She seemed unable to speak at first, and then she said, "I suppose I should ask how you knew."

"Just before she died, Mary Prodder told me she killed the admiral."

"Mary? Dead?" The word sounded almost like a gasp as Jane brought one of her hands up to cover her mouth.

"Yes. I'm sorry. I know how fond of you she was, and you of her." Alexandra's voice shook as she continued. "I never believed her, of course. She made the confession in the hopes that no one would find out the truth. She wasn't lucid all of the time before she died, but she said something while she was rambling. She said, 'You mustn't blame her. 'Twas me told her about the heels. She kept going on. She said, 'We tried to grab Papa's heels, but he was too quick.' She'd told me about her father, how brutal he was, how he beat her. I thought it was just the agony of her past flooding her mind. That happens when one is dying. But then I kept thinking about grabbing someone by the heels. I couldn't think what she meant by that until my maid made mention of a bathtub, and that got me thinking about the fact that you said the admiral had a bath the night he died. If he was drunk enough not to resist, a person could take him by the heels and pull his head under."

Jane stood and walked to the window, pulling her dark, shawl closer around her as Alexandra had seen her do before. "He was drunk, I told you that much," she said, her back to Alexandra as she stared out the window again.

"And Mary told you how to do it," Alexandra said.

There was no response from Jane. She kept her back to Alexandra and continued to stare out the window.

"And she must have helped you get him in the boat. You could not have done it alone," Alexandra said after a long silence.

Jane turned suddenly to face her. "How did you know about the boat?"

"There was sealant on the . . . the garment the admiral was wearing, and there were fibers from your black shawl in the boat."

Jane's eyes were bright, almost feverish. "But how did you find the boat? It was supposed to be . . ." Jane turned away again. "It doesn't matter now."

"Did Mary and Annie both help you, Jane? You're too small to have done it alone."

"No one helped, I did it myself."

"No she didn't." The voice startled Alexandra and she turned to see Annie entering the room. She had obviously been listening at the door. "We both helped her. Mary and I, and I hid the boat."

"Don't try to take the blame," Jane said.

Annie ignored her and turned to Alexandra. "He was brutal to her. You see how she rubs her shoulder. Pulled it from her socket, he did, but she was too ashamed to seek your help. I forced her shoulder back into its socket myself, as best I could. And that's not all. He hit her once so hard she—"

"Annie!" Jane took a step toward her as if to warn her, but Annie continued.

"So hard she lost consciousness. He deserved to die. So when I saw him in the tub—"

"Don't try to take the blame, Annie," Jane said. "She

knows the truth." She turned back to Alexandra. "I didn't plan anything, you know. It just . . . happened." She put her hand to her shoulder and massaged it as Alexandra had seen her do before. "Thank God John ran away before he could hurt him. But Will . . . One day he . . ." She looked down at her hands. "I couldn't let him hurt Will again. I could put up with his brutality because I had to. I tried to divorce him, just as you guessed. But the barrister I hired told me that if the divorce was granted my husband would have custody of Will." She put her head in her hands again for a few seconds, then looked at Alexandra again, shaking her head. "I couldn't divorce him and lose Will. But when he hit Will, I knew I couldn't . . . I couldn't let it go on. . . ."

Alexandra saw the desperation in Jane's face as she tried to continue, and she remembered Nancy's words that a mother will sacrifice anything for her children.

"Will's broken arm?" Alexandra asked.

Jane looked at her. "It wasn't a fall. I lied to you about that. Will would never tell you the truth, either, because his father told him not to. Will was afraid of him. Not just for what he'd done to him, but because of the way he treated Annie as well, although, thank God, I don't think Will ever knew that he . . . that he hurt me. Annie is right. He was brutal."

"Jane, I—"

"No," Jane said, interrupting her. "I must tell you what happened. I have to tell someone. He asked Annie to prepare a bath for him in his room. I could hear him in there, splashing the water and singing in his awful drunken voice. I started thinking about what Mary had told me just a little while earlier while she was fitting my dress. She was here when George came home drunk, and she had long ago guessed the truth about my husband and what he had done to me. She had told me before about her father, how he hit her. But this time, with my husband up in his room bathing, she told me how she and her mother tried pulling her father's heels while he bathed. It would have worked, she said, if he'd been drunk or unconscious. Dearest Mary. I knew the reason she was telling me about her father was to help me."

Annie went to Jane and put an arm around her shoulder,

but Jane winced and moved away from her, agitated.

"I opened the door to his room, slowly. He didn't know I was there, but when I saw him there in the tub, it was as if Mary was standing next to me encouraging me, telling me it was wrong to have to live that way." She stopped, twisting her handkerchief around her fingers.

"I dressed him then," she continued. "In the undergarment. I ran back to my room and it was lying on my bed because Annie had just laundered it. It was all I could find in my haste. I know it sounds silly, but I wanted the body out of the house and it seemed so indecent, so . . . improper to take him naked through the garden to the boat."

"You had planned ahead about the boat, then," Alexandra said.

Jane shook her head. "No, no, I . . ." She stopped, looked at Annie, confused, and tried to go on, but Annie interrupted her.

"She came downstairs and Mary and I could see on her face that something was wrong," Annie said. "She couldn't speak, but we went upstairs, and we found him. I knew we had to do something, so I told her I'd take him out to sea. She couldn't do it by herself, don't you see? We had to help, Mary and I. We tied a rope under his arms and dragged him outside."

"Alexandra, please understand, I knew what I had done was wrong." Jane's voice shook. "But it was too late, and all I could do was worry what would happen to Will if anyone found out." For the first time tears escaped her eyes and ran down her face. "The storm was already making the waves high. I wouldn't let Annie and Mary take the boat. I knew I had to be the one to . . . It was difficult for me to row back after I pushed him into the water, but I didn't think it would wash his body . . . Oh my God! What have I done to Will? What will happen to him now?"

Alexandra could not speak for a moment, knowing the agony Jane was experiencing. "All those times you refused to allow me to examine your own body was not due to modesty, but because you didn't want me to see what he had done to you." Alexandra's voice was soft, filled with horror.

Jane didn't answer. She collapsed into her chair, old tears

drying on her face, too weary and demoralized to cry more.

"It was what he did to Will, though, that drove you to it," Alexandra said. "That must have been what John meant when he said it must have been Will. He meant it was what happened to Will that made you do it."

Jane shook her head sadly. "My poor John, he ran away and became a criminal out of defiance. I see that now. I saw him once after he escaped, you know. He came here to see me. I couldn't keep anything from John. He knew how brutal his stepfather was, knew how he beat me. He came back to kill him, but I had already . . . I told him what I had done, and he was terrified that I would be found out and hanged or sent to prison. I tried to assure him that people would only think he'd drowned. That was why I gave you permission to do the autopsy. I thought you would prove he had drowned, and no one would talk." She looked away again, lost in her own thoughts for a moment before she continued.

"It was what I dressed the admiral in, of course, that made people talk. I should have thought, should have taken the time to . . ." She shook her head slowly. "It all happened so quickly, I . . ." She looked at Alexandra, her face pale. "Don't blame Annie for what she did. It's true, she was only trying to frighten John into leaving. She was afraid he would talk. We were all so upset, we all did foolish things. I only hope that Will can forgive me one day."

"Don't let them take her!" Annie's voice was desperate. "It was me that killed him."

"Sit down." Alexandra spoke quietly, but with a firmness that startled Annie. She sat in the chair Alexandra had occupied, trembling. "Everyone loves you, Jane. They're all trying to take the blame for you."

"But they mustn't," Jane said. "I killed my husband. I must take the consequences."

Alexandra ignored her. She paced the floor for a few seconds more, thinking. She turned to Annie. "You must know there are several in Newton who suspect her. You must help her leave here. All three of you must leave." Alexandra heard her own voice trembling. "Nancy and I will help you. We will say you've gone to London because it was too painful for you to stay here, but you won't go to London, of course.

You'll go to Edinburgh, and you will change your name. There is a friend of my father's there who will help you."

Jane seemed unable to speak for a moment. Finally, she said, "Why are you doing this?" Her face was still pale, but there was a light in her eyes that hadn't been there before.

Alexandra held her gaze for a moment before she spoke. "I should think, Jane, that you wouldn't have to ask."

It was three days before Alexandra and Nancy could complete all the arrangements to send Jane, her son, and her housemaid away secretly. Alexandra found it impossible to tell even Nicholas the truth or ask him to help her. She feared it would compromise his position as a member of the bar. She thought it a stroke of luck that duty called him to London before the arrangements were complete and he realized what she was doing. He felt it necessary to accompany Constable Snow, who was returning John Killborn to prison.

Nicholas was preoccupied before he left and hardly had time to speak to Alexandra. He knew, and she knew as well, that the court was not likely to be lenient for John because of his two escapes. Alexandra had found it difficult to tell Jane the truth—that John would most likely hang. But it seemed the best thing to do.

Because Nicholas and Constable Snow were to have left that morning, Alexandra was startled when, as she was out for a walk with Zack, she saw the constable riding his gelding toward his cottage.

He seemed disconcerted to see Alexandra at first, but he quickly put aside his discomfort and spoke to her cordially.

"Good evening, Dr. Gladstone."

"Good evening, Constable. I must say I'm surprised to see you. Did you send Mr. Forsythe to London alone with the prisoner?"

"I'm afraid there was no prisoner to return to London," Snow said. "Mr. Forsythe has returned to London alone."

"No prisoner? I don't understand."

"I regret to say he has escaped again."

"Then you must search for him, of course." There was dread in Alexandra's voice.

"Both Mr. Forsythe and I agree that, unfortunately, that won't be possible. Mr. Forsythe seems to think there's some evidence he has gone to Scotland. That's out of my territory, I'm afraid."

Alexandra found she could not speak.

The constable tipped his hat and was about to ride away again, when he turned back to her. "I almost forgot. Forsythe said to tell you he's having a telephone device installed and he invites you to come to London to see it at your earliest convenience."

He turned away once again, and she called after him. "You knew! Why didn't you tell me? You knew!" The cold February wind caught her words and scattered them across the dale.

COMING IN PAPERBACK MARCH 2003

THE TRUE CRIME FILES OF SIR ARTHUR CONAN DOYLE

SIR ARTHUR CONAN DOYLE,
Rediscovered by Stephen Hines with an
introduction by Steven Womack

__0-425-18900-7

BERKLEY PRIME CRIME